The Window-Shade Job

In This Series

The Window-Shade Job

The Window-Shade Job

George Bixley

DAGMAR MIURA

LOS ANGELES

Published by Dagmar Miura
Los Angeles
www.dagmarmiura.com

The Window-Shade Job

First published 2020

ISBN: 978-1-951130-16-9

ONE

"I punched the wrong guy," Slater said, and flashed his palms at his sides. He was sitting in a circle of folding chairs with a dozen other men who also had no choice about being here. The coordinator, Miguel, a nebbishy guy with a thin mustache, had just addressed him directly: "What about you, Slater—why are you here?"

The group was called "Men Keeping It Cool," but that was just a euphemism for what it really was, a court-ordered anger-management class. Slater had picked this one because it was close to his office, but it was also right on Skid Row, and from the looks of them, some of these losers could be homeless.

"You mean that it's wrong to assault people," the coordinator said. Despite his Hispanic name, Miguel looked pretty Anglo. Slater was the opposite—he had his father's dark Latin coloring and black hair, but he didn't speak any Spanish beyond ordering tacos.

"That's not true." Slater held his gaze. "I usually only rough up people who can't call the cops because they're lowlifes and running a scam. But I miscalculated."

Miguel stifled a sigh. "Let's call that a starting point. Later on, we're going to explore how we feel when we're being violent."

Watching him, Slater recognized that glassy look, the evasive language. Miguel sounded like the parade of shrinks Doris had sent him to in his youth. This was a similar waste of time. But he had no choice.

"Ivan," Miguel said, checking the notes in his lap and then eyeing a guy across the circle. "Why are you here?"

Ivan had his head shaved, and sat with his arms folded, wearing a tank top that exposed the intricate tattoos around his biceps.

"I shouted at my boss," he said, and sat up. "I was really upset. He didn't deserve that—he's actually a decent guy. After I calmed down, I just had this crushing, crippling feeling of guilt."

"You're here voluntarily?" Slater demanded.

"There's no cross-talk here," Miguel said.

"I'm not cross. But that's the stupidest thing I've ever heard."

"'No cross-talk' means we don't comment on other people's shares," Miguel said.

Slater waved his arm. "So you just let other people continue to be stupid."

"We all know that you know what cross-talk means," Ivan said.

Meeting his gaze, Slater jutted his chin. "Let's you and I have a talk after."

Ivan's brow furrowed, and he shifted uncomfortably in his chair.

Miguel raised his voice. "Slater—stop talking."

Avoiding his gaze, Slater folded his arms and clenched his teeth. He was just going to have to put up with this.

An hour later, when the session ended, the participants waited for Miguel to sign their attendance slips, one by one, except Ivan, who didn't even need it. He hustled out ahead of the others.

As Miguel signed Slater's sheet, he asked, "Did you ever do any twelve-step?"

"I don't need that stuff. I don't really need this either."

"Right." He handed him the paper and met his eye. "See you next week."

Stepping out onto Los Angeles Street, superfluously named after the city, and the county, and the region, Slater felt a blast of hot air and squinted in the bright midday sun. He'd already paid for the afternoon at the little surface parking lot up the street, and Andy's place was only a couple of blocks. He'd walk.

The heat of the day felt good as he strode through the bustling neighborhood, and he didn't bother to cross to the shaded side. Andy lived in an old warehouse building that had been converted to lofts, and Slater strode into the lobby and up to his floor to rap on his door. Sometimes it took a while for him to get there. When Andy eventually pulled it open, he was clad in boxers and a tank top, revealing his sinewy musculature. His mousy brown hair was a perfectly tousled mess.

Slater followed him inside, pushing the door closed. Apart from the bathroom, the loft had no interior walls, so his bed and desk and everything else were in the same room. Big industrial windows at the back of the space looked out on Pershing Square.

Andy dropped into his computer chair and swiveled toward him. "How was it?"

"A bunch of men with emotional problems. It felt like group therapy."

"That sounds like a … good thing. With the momentum, maybe we could … go to an AA meeting."

"I've got that under control."

Andy raised his eyebrows, his head gently undulating with his random muscle twitches. "So no blackouts or … hangovers in the last month or so?"

"You want me to fill my downtime with meetings. I'm not going to do it."

"Right now your downtime is boozing and mindless sex. Meetings might be … an improvement."

Slater put his hands on his hips. "You're kind of being a hard-ass."

"And you love it." Andy gestured vaguely. "I should tell you that Doris asked me what I knew about it."

4

"Why are you talking to her?" Slater demanded, raising his voice.

"I can talk to whoever I want. Don't get … pissed at me."

"It's none of her business."

"I'm just giving you a head's up. She asked me what I knew because you … didn't call her back."

"She's acting like you're my boyfriend," Slater said, eyeing him. "You're not my boyfriend."

"I've heard that tune in every key."

"What does that mean?"

"You've made that abundantly clear." Andy frowned. "Talk to her and she won't have to … go through me."

"How did she even know about my legal troubles?"

"Ask her yourself." His rhythmic random muscle movements intensified.

"Now I've got you all steamed," Slater said, his tone softening.

"I think you … enjoy that too." Andy rose and gestured toward his bed. "You want to help me de-stress?"

Slater went over and stretched out beside him, and pushed his fingers into the tangle of Andy's hair, and met his eager mouth. As he explored the warm intensity, he felt his dick swelling in his jeans, and ran a hand under Andy's shirt. Slater helped him pull it off, then slid his boxers down and grabbed his rock-hard cock.

Sitting up, Slater pulled off his own shirt and untied his boots, then pushed off his jeans. When he turned back to Andy, he swung his knee over his legs and pressed his cock into his belly. Andy reached for his neck and pulled him closer, locking their mouths together.

Slater shifted onto his side, then rolled onto his back and lifted Andy until he was straddling him, running his hands over his thighs and his torso. Andy's CP made his metabolism run hot, and right now the heat felt great. He'd learned how to work with the random twitching, how to lean into it, when to resist it, when to move with it.

Reaching for the bedside drawer, Slater grabbed the lube and filled his hand, then took hold of Andy. Their mouths together, Andy squirmed and thrust against him, and soon came, then pulled away, his whole body spasming. Sliding onto his side, he shifted position and grabbed Slater's cock. Slater buried his nose in Andy's hair, a hand firmly on his butt, and thrust until he came too.

As he caught his breath, he wrapped an arm around Andy's chest, and they lay together for a while, warm and sweaty and content. Eventually Slater got up and grabbed a hand towel from the bathroom. Once they'd cleaned up, he started to get dressed.

"Are you working today?" Andy said.

"I'm supposed to help Max on a job." He leaned over to tie his boots, then turned back to Andy, who was lying there with his head propped on his arm, watching him. "Bye, beautiful."

Andy kept his place cold because his body ran hot, but once Slater was outside on the street, the sweaty summer heat enveloped him again as he walked toward the lot where he'd left his car.

Seeing Andy always put him in a good mood. It wasn't very often that Slater wanted to sleep with anyone more than once, but Andy was a twelve-stepper, and part of working the steps was learning not to put demands on people, and that made him easy to be around.

The lot was configured for stack parking, but Slater's classic black Thunderbird was at the front of the line, so the attendant hadn't taken his keys. Climbing in behind the wheel, he started the engine and pulled into the traffic, driving the few blocks to the surface lot across the street from the building where he and his business partner had an office.

It was a century-old high-rise in the Fashion District, originally built as office space but today filled with clothing factories. The location amid the blue-collar industry made their little suite feel inconspicuous, and the rent was a lot cheaper than in the newer part of Downtown LA, where the financiers and the law firms and the accountants worked.

The day laborers who hung around the lobby early in the day, waiting for gigs sewing or cutting or transporting garments, were gone by the time Slater walked in. He rode up to the ninth floor and went around behind the elevator shaft, admiring the sign on the office door as he paused to twist his key in the lock:

SLATER IBÁÑEZ

MAXIMILLIAN CONROY

INVESTIGATIONS

Inside was a small room with a receptionist's desk, and at either side, an office for each of them. No one used the front desk, and the only thing in the outer office besides it and the coatrack was a small statue on the desktop, a plaster skeleton wearing a crown and holding a scythe. It was an image of Rey Pascual, a gift from the woman Slater sometimes bought *pupusas* from. His business partner, Max, obviously wasn't sick of looking at it yet because it was still sitting here.

The woman who'd rented them the furniture when they moved in said that the front office would look weird without a desk, so they'd let her bring one, along with the coatrack. It still looked empty—they'd tried a potted plant, but without consistent light it had withered. Rey Pascual fulfilled the same purpose, drawing attention from a space that looked stark and uninhabited. There was no risk of him shriveling up like the pothos had—he was already dead.

Slater stepped in the doorway to Max's office. Sitting behind his desk, Max was dressed for a meeting, in a charcoal suit with a red necktie. These days he wore his drab brown hair in a trendy cut, and with the suit the overall look was sharp, but it didn't disguise who he was—with his thick neck, his gut spilling over his belt, and the sidearm bulging in the holster under his jacket, Max was clearly the heavy. They had a good rapport, him and Max, and Slater didn't want to punch him in the face very often. More important was that Max had a PI license, which meant he had access to resources that Slater didn't.

"How was anger management?" Max said, looking up from his computer screen and sitting back.

Slater dropped into one of the chairs facing his desk. "Infuriating."

He chuckled. "So—thanks for taking on this gig."

"I don't mind doing some legwork." He knew Max was double-booked, and even though Slater hated window-shade jobs, he couldn't say no to the work—things had been slow. "What have we got?"

"The pigeon is a man named Hayk."

"Like 'take a hike'?"

"It sounds like that," Max said, and spelled it. "He thinks his wife is cheating on him."

"They usually are, if they decide to come to us."

"This guy likes structure, so I'm going to introduce you as an operative under my direction. Don't take it the wrong way, like I'm pulling rank, or trying to be the boss."

Slater threw up his hands. "You can introduce me as your personal seamstress if it helps get the gig."

"I'm pretty sure we've already got it. He's coming here to iron out the details."

"It's fine with me if I don't have to handle the guy. You're better with people. What's his story?"

Max sat forward, arms on his desk. "When he called, Hayk said some lawyer recommended me."

"Have you had a face-to-face?"

"Once—I went to meet him at a driving range in Glendale."

"You play golf?" Slater said, and frowned.

"Some of my clients do, so I do. A driving range isn't really golf. You just stand around and hit balls. Anyway, Hayk feels shady to me. He's in the construction business, but I don't get the sense that he's a gangster."

"If he were, he wouldn't need us to do his dirty work."

"Probably not. So while we're there, swinging golf clubs, he takes a phone call. I'm assuming it was from an employee. I could only hear his side of the conversation. He said, 'Tell her it was neighborhood kids with firecrackers, or a car backfiring.'"

"He was trying to explain away gunshots," Slater said.

"That's what I thought too."

"An engine backfiring is a bit of a stretch. Cars haven't done that in fifty years."

Max raised an eyebrow. "Yours might."

Before Slater could retort, there was a sharp knock at the door.

"That'll be Hayk," Max said, and got up, stepping out to the front office. Slater followed, hanging back as Max opened the door.

Hayk greeted him and stepped inside. Built burly like Max, he had hooded eyes, thick lips, and dark hair that was thinning on top. Why did no one ever tell straight guys that they had to wear their hair shorter once they started losing it? There was confidence in the way he carried himself, Slater saw—not swagger, just the bearing of someone who was usually in charge.

Once he'd introduced them, Max stepped into his office and waved Hayk to one of the chairs in front of his desk. Slater followed, taking the one closest to the door. As he sat down, Hayk sighed, and rubbed his eyes. Slater eyed him sidelong. The guy looked weary.

"Slater is going to do some of the work on the ground," Max said, as he pulled a yellow legal pad from his desk drawer.

"I just want to know the truth," Hayk said, eyeing them in turn. "It's a simple yes or no. Is my wife sleeping with somebody else?"

"We'll get to the bottom of it," Max said.

"Maybe you can also find out who's the guy," Hayk said. "A name and address. So I can take care of him."

Max nodded thoughtfully, his brow furrowing in concern. "What is it specifically that makes you think your wife is up to something?"

"I told you that last night," he said, and frowned.

"I want my operative to hear it firsthand."

Hayk eyed Slater. "She disappears in the evening when I'm out working. The security cameras at the house show that she leaves ten minutes after I do."

"What's her name?" Slater said.

"Bella," Hayk said flatly.

Max scribbled on the notepad. "What does she drive?"

"Usually the Bentley. It's blue."

Glancing up, Max said, "I think the way to start is that I'll get Slater to tail her to see where she goes."

"Do you have a photo of her?" Slater said.

Hayk turned to meet his gaze. "Probably. But why don't you come over and meet her? I told her I was going out tonight, so I know she made plans too. When she leaves, you can follow her."

"It's not optimal to have an operative meet the target," Max said, absently waggling his pen between his thick fingers. "She might recognize him later."

"You don't have other operatives?" Hayk demanded, raising his voice. "You should see how this woman treats me."

"I can come to your place," Slater said. "It'll make it easier to run the tail. Where do you live?"

Hayk recited his address, and Slater pulled out his phone to thumb-type it.

"Come over after dinner," Hayk said, and then turned to Max. "Do you need some money now?"

"Just a deposit," Max said.

Slater rose and went into his own office. He left the door open so he could listen to the transaction, then leaned back in his chair and lifted his feet onto the desk. He heard the chair scrape on the concrete as Hayk rose to leave, and once he was gone, Slater got up and went out to the front.

"Have you started your other job yet?"

"I'm doing a stakeout on the Westside tonight," Max said, and flipped the bolt on the door. "It's another window-shade job. I'm envious of yours— you get to see where Hayk lives."

"You think he has money?"

"I know he does. He just paid me in cash, and he peeled a bunch of C-notes off a bankroll that thick." He held his finger and thumb wide apart.

"That's old-school," Slater said. "Like a riverboat gambler."

"Or a gangster."

"Is it weird that he wants me to meet the wife?"

Max pursed his lips for a moment. "He wants an ally, right—someone to see what he sees, to validate his experience with her. He needs someone to tell him he's not crazy. That he's not imagining things."

"That sounds like emotional support. Maybe he needs to go to the pound and adopt a dog."

"Just listening to these people helps them," Max said. "It makes us a full-service agency." He stepped into his office. "You'll need a camera."

From his bottom desk drawer he lifted out a chunky SLR with a heavy long lens.

"Please tell me I'm not shooting film," Slater said, eyeing it from the doorway.

"It's digital. You can take out the memory card." He flipped the camera over and pointed out the slot. "Otherwise just focus and shoot. The exposure and everything else is automatic."

Slater took hold of it and looked through the eyepiece, aiming the lens out the little window behind Max's desk at the wall of the building next door. He twisted the focusing ring and snapped a couple of test shots. It wasn't totally digital, as it had a mechanical shutter that clicked softly with each press of the button.

"I think I can handle it," he said finally, and slung the strap over his shoulder, the lens hanging down his back. "Good luck at the window shades tonight."

"Back at you, buddy."

Locking the door as he left, Slater went down to the street and trotted across in a break in the traffic, the heavy lens slapping the small of his back. His apartment was just west of Downtown in gritty Westlake, and a few minutes later he nosed the Thunderbird into the alley behind his building, waiting for the heavy steel door to roll up. This private garage was the main reason he lived here—it was an extremely rare find in a crowded central neighborhood.

He killed the engine and waited for the door to roll down, then went out the back door, into the hall, and trotted up two flights to his grungy apartment. It should have been renovated decades ago, with the kitchen sink and ancient appliances at one end of the main room, and the bedroom and bathroom off to one side. It didn't feel cramped because he didn't have much furniture—a basic thrift-store sofa and a recliner that fit in with the timeworn stained carpet.

He eyed the half-full fifth of bourbon on the kitchen counter, its amber glow warm and enticing in the low light, waiting patiently for him. Not yet, he reminded himself. Pulling off his boots, he dropped onto the sofa and set an alarm for later—he knew he'd fall asleep as soon as he stretched out.

TWO

When the alarm sounded, Slater scrabbled for his phone on the carpet beside him and slapped it off, then sat up and rubbed his eyes. He found the note with Hayk's address and put it into the navigation app. Even in the evening traffic it said it would only take twenty minutes to get there.

Once he was fully awake, he locked his door and trotted down the two flights to his garage, then backed the Thunderbird into the alley, waiting for the steel door to roll down. The app directed him through Echo Park and onto the 2, into the Glendale hills. It made sense—Hayk looked kind of Armenian, and Glendale was full of Armenians.

Dusk was encroaching, and when he got to the bottom of the exit ramp he flicked on his headlights. The app had him climb into the hills on winding roads that became narrower higher up.

When he got to the address, he found a tall hedge with a gate that had been left open, revealing the driveway leading up. Slater cruised past and pulled into the next driveway to turn around, then parked across the street and killed the engine. Before he climbed out he surveyed the street in the fading light. All he could see from the road were hedges and fences and widely spaced gates. There wasn't any traffic, and not a pedestrian in sight—it was dead quiet up here.

Walking up Hayk's driveway, he found a black Bimmer and a metallic-blue Bentley parked in the wide gravel courtyard. That was Bella's car. It had a vanity plate, in the 1970s style, yellow lettering on cobalt blue. Slater made a mental note of the word it spelled out: ARKAYA21. A garage sat to one side, with all four doors down, and behind the cars was the house. It was a riff on a plantation mansion, with a neoclassical facade and white columns. The construction was recent—that walkway, the windows, the front door—nothing looked more than a few years old.

Slater rang the bell, and a moment later a woman pulled it open, frowning at the sight of him. This had to be Bella. Her salon-lightened hair was expensively styled to tumble on her shoulders, and she wore bright-red lipstick that matched her manicure. A Breton top and linen trousers highlighted her curves. Glam and good-looking, she was younger than Hayk—the archetypal trophy wife.

"You can just leave it on the step," she said. "People don't steal packages up here."

Slater suppressed an angry retort. "I'm here to meet Hayk."

Bella scowled and gave him the once-over, then turned to shout into the house. "Hayk!"

The man appeared on the curving staircase, ambling down and flashing a smile, his demeanor shifted from a few hours ago—he seemed relaxed now, at ease in his own realm.

"Slater, this is my lovely wife, Bella."

Slater dug deep to affect a civil tone. "Ma'am."

"OK," she said evenly.

"Slater is a business associate," Hayk said. "We're going to do some work tonight."

"I thought you were going out," she said sharply.

"I am going out." Hayk threw up his hands. "I said I was going out, so I'm going out."

Bella stalked off toward the back of the house, past the staircase and out of view. Glancing at Slater, Hayk went after her, leaving him in the foyer, the front door still hanging open.

Stepping inside, Slater looked around at the space, and the yawning living room through the archway at the side. There was shiny marble everywhere, on the floors, the tabletops, the decorative columns flanking the windows. It felt cold and lifeless. A mausoleum.

Bella hadn't gone far, and Slater could hear her and Hayk both, their voices undistorted. They had to be standing in the next room, and hadn't bothered to close the door.

"Why do you bring these people into our home?" she demanded. "He looks like one of your hoods. If you're going out, what is he doing here?"

"You don't get to trash-talk my business. It's what pays for all your clothes, and your jewelry, and that new nose."

"Why did you leave him alone? Does he steal?"

Hayk scoffed audibly, and a moment later reappeared in the foyer.

"Let's go," he said grimly, and led the way out.

Slater followed, closing the door behind them.

"So that's my princess," Hayk said. Glancing around, he added quietly, "Where's your ride?"

"It's on the street. I didn't want Bella to see it."

"Smart." Hayk gestured to the black Bimmer. "In case she's watching, get in."

Slater climbed in the passenger's side, and Hayk rolled through the gate, gravel crunching under the tires, and paused at the bottom of the drive to press a button on the visor. In the side mirror Slater watched the gate roll closed, obscuring the view of the house. He popped his door open.

"She won't be long," Hayk said, watching him climb out.

He walked over to the Thunderbird and got in behind the wheel. Once Hayk's Bimmer disappeared around the next bend, the street was dark, with the daylight almost gone, the sky pink at the horizon. As he waited, it gradually faded to indigo, and then to black.

The vanity plate, he remembered: *arkaya*. He pulled out his phone and searched for the word, and soon found what it meant—"princess" in Armenian.

The gate rolled open, and Bella's sleek car appeared, looking black and aqueous in the darkness. It was a nice set of wheels, befitting a New World princess. Slater slouched lower in the driver's seat as the Bentley paused to wait for the gate to close. It was too dark to get a look at the driver, but it had to be her. Once her taillights had disappeared around the curve in the road ahead, he started the engine and flicked on his lights, shifting into gear, and headed after her.

Bella drove fast on the winding hillside roads, confident on the familiar streets of her neighborhood, and Slater had to concentrate to keep up. She led him out of the hills, but not the same way he'd come up here. They'd gone east, he realized, eyeing the street signs, as he followed her across the Arroyo. Slater accelerated to keep pace with the Bentley's taillights as Bella merged onto the 210.

The evening traffic was thinning out, and Slater stayed back, letting a few vehicles fill the space between them. The classic Thunderbird was so distinctive that it wasn't optimal for a tail job, and he didn't want her to catch sight of it and get suspicious.

In Pasadena, Bella suddenly merged rapidly across half a dozen lanes, not bothering to signal. Was she trying to ditch him, or was she just that kind of driver? Slater had to work fast to make it over to the exit she took, flooring it to squeeze between two rigs in the truck lane, then decelerating rapidly onto the ramp. The Bentley turned right and cruised down the boulevard. Bella hadn't made him, Slater decided, as she wasn't acting evasive.

Rolling into South Pasadena, her taillights abruptly turned left onto a side street, with Slater not far behind. As he made the turn he saw her pull into a driveway, and by the time he got there, she'd doused the lights. It didn't matter now—he'd seen where she'd stopped, recognized that license plate.

As Slater cruised past he saw that the driveway had a gate across it, just beyond the nose of the Bentley. He parked farther up the block, killing the engine and eyeing his mirror. The street was a dense collection of houses on narrow lots, most of them with well-established foliage. He could see the back half of the Bentley, but not Bella. The house next to the driveway was dark. If she was headed inside, those lights would go on.

Then Bella appeared, strolling aimlessly down to the sidewalk, her phone held to her ear. Slater instinctively slouched in his seat, adjusting the rearview to keep an eye on her, and rolled down his window. There wasn't any traffic on the narrow street, and the residential neighborhood was quiet, so he could hear her side of the call.

"It's me," she said. "I'm at the rental. I need the lock-box code."

A moment later she lowered the phone and flipped her hair back, marching up the driveway and out of view.

From the backseat Slater grabbed his blue ball cap and pulled it low over his brow, then slung Max's camera over his shoulder as he climbed out. Bella had made it inside, he saw, as the lights were on now, glowing warm yellow around the edges of the heavy drapes in the front window. In the dim street lighting he studied the house as he approached, scanning for security cameras. Turning into the driveway, he walked past the Bentley to the gate. No camera at the front door, where Bella must have gone in, and none on the eaves. That wasn't too surprising—it was a quiet neighborhood, and at a short-term rental, guest privacy would outweigh the security concerns.

The gate across the driveway came to chest height, but the rail along the top was smooth. Slater grasped it and heaved himself up, swinging one boot over to briefly straddle it, then the other, dropping to the ground as noiselessly as he could. The camera lens thumped him in the back as he landed. A floodlight over the side door came on, and Slater dipped his chin, blocking the glare with the bill of his cap, and hustled past the house into the back-yard. It was likely just a motion-activated fixture, but he wasn't going to hang around to find out.

The space behind the house was a few yards of turf with a row of tall *Podocarpus* lining the wooden fence at the back of the lot. They were planted in wooden boxes, he saw as he got closer. Why would anyone do that? If you put them in the earth they'd grow into a hedge that would hide the neighbors completely. The boxes were just stunting their growth. But for the task at hand they were actually useful, in that Slater could step between the boxes, in among the cool feathery leaves, and stand out of sight in the shadows.

He couldn't see the side door from here, but no one was in the yard, and no one was looking out the big glass sliding doors, which meant no one had noticed the floodlight go on. A moment later it switched itself off, leaving the yard in darkness.

The sliders looked into a kitchen, and with the lights on inside he had a great view of that room. Planting his feet comfortably apart, he pulled the camera around and aimed it at the glass doors, then the window farther along the wall, where the curtains were drawn. This thing had a great zoom, but it was too heavy to hold up for very long, and he lowered it to keep watch.

A minute later Bella appeared in the kitchen. She'd changed clothes before she left home, now clad in a low-cut red party dress with a short skirt. Slater watched her without bothering to peer through the lens. She paced around the room, pulling open drawers and closing them again, finally retrieving something from one of them. A corkscrew, he realized, as she went to work on a wine bottle that sat on the counter. Despite her long manicured nails she quickly had the cork out. Next she opened and closed cabinet doors until she found long-stemmed glasses, pulling out two and pouring into them from the bottle.

For a while she disappeared, and Slater gazed at the pair of wineglasses waiting on the counter. She was definitely meeting someone who hadn't shown up yet. Raising the camera, he snapped a close-up of the glasses and the bottle. At maximum zoom he could read the label: SAINT-ÉMILION, GRAND VIN

DE BOURDEAUX. That sounded suitably bougie.

There was movement again as Bella walked into view, a smile on her face, and flicked her hair with the back of her hand in that coquettish way. Following her now was another person—a man, about her height, and darker than her, dressed for an office job in black pants and a collared shirt. Raising the camera again, he focused on him as Bella handed him a wineglass. He was hot, Slater decided, with a prominent chin and natty black hair. He snapped several photos of his face, zooming out a little to include his pleasing pecs in his gray satin dress shirt.

They were talking, but the sliders were closed, and Slater couldn't hear the conversation. Setting the glass down, the guy stepped closer to Bella, grabbing her waist and shifting her back against the counter. She put a hand on his shoulder, running the other through his black hair, and leaned in to kiss him. Slater took a series of photos of them in that embrace. They were positioned at an angle from his perspective, so her features were evident: that hairstyle, a blingy diamond earring, and at times, most of her face. The guy was facing away from him, but he wasn't the one who mattered.

The floodlight at the side of the house went on, and Slater stepped back, deeper into the podocarps, closer to the wooden fence. A lanky guy wearing a loose Hawaiian shirt wandered into the back-yard. He was swarthy and had jet-black hair, but he wasn't Latin; maybe Filipino. Cargo shorts and white gym socks under tan huaraches completed the outfit, and as he got closer, Slater saw he had a dark mustache.

In his hand dangled an SLR camera, like Max's but with a shorter lens. Treading across the lawn, he froze when Bella and her paramour came into view through the glass sliders. He slowly retreated a few paces, as if that would make him less visible in the middle of the backyard. With his back to Slater, he waited a moment, then raised the camera, aiming it at the glass. It was dark out, and the kitchen was well lit, so the pair inside were oblivious to his ham-fisted antics.

Who the hell was this guy? If Hayk had hired two agencies, it was a waste of his resources. More likely, someone else had hired this guy—someone who wanted evidence of the cheating. Maybe the spouse of Bella's hot boyfriend. Slater sighed. He hated window-shade jobs.

He quietly shifted position and took a couple of shots of the watcher in the Hawaiian shirt. The kitchen was empty now, and the guy stood staring at the glass, as if willing them to return. The lights went on in the nearby window, and the watcher started, dropping his camera to the grass with a thud. He sank to his knees to retrieve it.

The window had been slid half open, but the curtains were drawn, so no one was going to be peeping into that room. Maybe the watcher couldn't see that from his vantage point, with the sill just above his head. He rose and stepped below the window, holding his camera as high as he could reach, aiming it at the glass, presumably snapping photos.

When he lowered the camera, he stepped away and studied the little screen on the back. Slater lifted his own camera and zoomed in on his features, illuminated by the blue glow, and took a couple of shots. The guy was only a few yards away—he should have heard the sound of the shutter, but he was oblivious. He definitely wasn't experienced at running surveillance.

Through the curtains came a woman's voice, moaning with pleasure. The watcher in the Hawaiian shirt heard it too, and he cocked his head and looked up at the window. It was Bella, and her voice grew louder, culminating a few minutes later in a shriek. The guy with her was moaning now too, and verbally, at least, they climaxed at the same time. No way did that really happen. But it was predictable—Bella looked like that type.

The performance over, the watcher strolled toward the driveway. Slater stepped out of the podocarps and treaded quietly across the lawn, watching from a distance as the guy activated the floodlight and then awkwardly climbed over the gate. The bright fixture effectively blinded him to Slater, standing just beyond the pool of light in the darkness. Lifting the camera, Slater photographed the guy hugging the top of the gate, then zoomed in on his face for a close-up. The Hawaiian shirt disappeared as he dropped to the ground on the other side, landing with a grunt.

Slater waited a few seconds before he followed, vaulting over the gate with the camera slapping his back. Striding past the Bentley, he scanned the street, and caught sight of the Hawaiian shirt in front of the next house, walking away. Hustling to catch up to him, he waited to speak until the guy heard him approaching, and turned to look back, concern in his eyes.

"Who hired you?" Slater demanded, stepping up to him.

He recoiled but stood his ground, his face contorting into a grimace. "The fuck are you?"

Slater stepped closer and slapped his face, left and then right, a rapid kovac. The guy yelped and hopped backward, batting Slater away.

"Why are you photographing people through the windows?"

"I could get you thrown in jail," he growled, massaging his cheek. But he didn't reach for his phone—he didn't really want to deal with the police. The fact that he didn't make a run for it either meant that his curiosity overpowered his anger at being manhandled.

"Sing, brother," Slater said, "or I'll flatten you." He stepped closer and slapped him again.

"Stop it," he shouted, and pushed Slater away.

"Who are you working for?"

"The woman," he hissed. "I'm working for the woman in that house."

Slater frowned. "I'm supposed to believe that Bella hired you to document her own cheating? Bullshit."

"You know Bella?" he said, eyeing him warily. "How do you know she's cheating?"

"I'm the one asking the questions."

The guy stood up straighter and jutted his chin. "I'm not afraid of you."

"But I bet you're afraid of the cops. You were creeping around someone else's backyard with a camera. Maybe I'll give them a call, and tell them to send a prowl car, and I'll detain you until they get here. You know I can handle you."

Slater could see the wheels turning, and concern furrowed his brow as he thought it through. This guy clearly wasn't very bright. Slater was also carrying a camera, and from what he'd already said, it would be easy to surmise that Slater's words were just bluster—he'd been in that backyard too, so he'd never call the police.

"What is your game?" Slater said.

He ran a hand through his hair and took a breath. "Bella is kind of a revenue stream for me."

"You're blackmailing her?"

"That's an ugly word. She pays me to keep her secrets. Look, she has money—you don't need to call the cops. You and I can come to an arrangement."

Slater put his hands on his hips. "What kind of an arrangement?"

"First, tell me why you're here, and how you know Bella."

"You don't have any leverage, chump. I'm holding all the cards. What exactly are you proposing?"

The guy looked him over. "Is that a camera? I wish you'd tell me who you're working for."

"Maybe I'm working for myself."

"See, that's the kind of thing I'm talking about. There's no need to horn in here, or double-bill the woman. It's already my gig. I'll cut you in."

"How much are you making from her?" Slater said.

"We can talk about that, *vato*, but not here. I just overheard the happy ending—she'll be leaving soon."

"Show me your phone, and unlock it."

He frowned. "No way."

"Then I'll use my own to get the law out here, and we can all of us have a friendly chat."

The guy huffed but pulled his phone out of his cargo shorts and handed it over. Slater took it and sent a text to himself, thumb-typing his own name in the message field.

"What are you doing?" the guy said.

Ignoring him, he found the owner's details, then pulled out his own phone and photographed the screen.

"You're Tato?" Slater said.

"It's *tah*-to, not *tay*-to."

"This address is near here—is it where you live?"

"It's my office."

Slater handed him the device and watched him tuck it into a pocket.

"So now you know who I am," Tato said. "I would have told you. Call me next week and we'll set up a meeting."

"That's not how it's going to work. If I don't hear from Tato tomorrow, Bella will be hearing from me."

Tato scowled. "I don't even have your number."

"I just texted myself from your phone. My

name is there too. Look in your messages." Slater glanced back toward the house where Bella's car was parked. "Go on, then—get out of here, if you're going."

Tato eyed him for a moment, then turned and continued up the sidewalk. Past the next driveway he stepped into the street and climbed up behind the wheel of a mustard-yellow Humvee. Slater folded his arms and watched him pull out. It seemed odd that he was driving that extremely unsubtle behemoth when he'd come here to creep around that backyard, theoretically trying to be inconspicuous.

Once Tato was gone, he went to the Thunderbird and got in, resting the camera in his lap. It was still warm out, and he rolled down the window to get some air, keeping an eye on the Bentley in the rearview mirror. Like Tato had said, Bella wouldn't be staying the night.

It might be interesting to see where Tato's profit-sharing offer would lead. It was something extra to put in his report to Hayk—that Bella was being squeezed by a third party.

Not long after, the woman appeared, standing beside the Bentley to adjust her hair and find her keys before she climbed in. Soon the car backed into the street and drove off, toward the boulevard, in the direction she'd come. Slater watched the taillights disappear at the corner, then turned his attention to the driveway. It was a rental, likely just for the hookup, so the boyfriend wouldn't be staying long either.

Sure enough, the guy appeared in the driveway, and strolled leisurely up the street. Slater slouched down as he passed by on the opposite sidewalk, but the guy didn't even glance his way. Great butt, Slater saw, watching him walk away. This guy was totally fuckable.

He toyed with the idea of a foot tail, but before Slater could move to climb out, the guy stepped into the street in front of a light-gray Ranger. The parking lights flashed as he unlocked it and climbed in. Slater lifted the camera and zoomed in on his front plate, snapping a grainy photo. He checked the little screen to make sure it was legible, then watched as the Ranger's headlights came on and it pulled into the street.

He could follow him, but it was much easier to spot a tail in light evening traffic, especially with a car like Slater's. It would be easy enough to track him down later with the plate number.

Slater watched the Ranger roll by, then scrolled through the photos on the camera's screen. He hadn't got a shot of the pair of them having sex, but the make-out images were clear evidence of infidelity. One shot of Bella, when she'd been in the kitchen, showed her adjusting her hair, a distant look in her eye. It could be an image from a cosmetics ad. She really was beautiful.

When he got to the last photo, the boyfriend's plate, he copied the number into his phone, then set the camera aside and texted Max:

Still on the Westside?

His reply came a moment later:

I'm back at the office. Where you at?

Slater thumb-typed a quick response:

Be there in a few minutes.

THREE

Sitting up, Slater started the engine and headed for the freeway. The drive downtown was quick at this hour, and the lot across from their building was practically empty. When he got into the office, the lights were on, and Max was behind his desk, still wearing his charcoal suit but with his necktie now loose at his collar.

"You're done with your stakeout already?" Slater said, dropping into the chair across from him and setting the camera on the desktop.

Max waved a hand. "I followed the target and the girlfriend to LAX. I'm waiting for a callback to find out where they're going. If they're gone for more than a day or two, I'll have to contract with an agency wherever they are to get eyes on them."

Slater told him about his evening and what he'd seen.

"So Hayk was right," Max said.

"I guess he knows her better than anyone."

"You got good photos?"

He pushed the camera toward him. "The blinds were down in the bedroom, so I didn't get images of the carnal act, but I got plenty of the foreplay."

Max scrolled through the images, a smile spreading across his face. "These are great. There's no denying what they're doing."

"I can try again for sex photos. If they rent the same house, maybe I can get in first and plant a video camera."

"This is all we need," Max said, setting the camera down. "For most of these clients, the sex is secondary. It's about the lies and the emotional betrayal."

"That'll be evident from what I got."

"The guy in the Hawaiian shirt is an unexpected twist. It would be good to know how and why he's chiseling Bella."

"His name is Tato," Slater said. "I've got his number. Give me a day or two to figure it out. I also want to look into the boyfriend—can that repo friend of yours run an LPR search, maybe find out where the guy lives?"

"Let's call him," Max said, and reached inside his jacket for his phone.

Auto repossession people were much more enthusiastic even than the police about using automated license-plate readers to build databases of cars and their movements. The cops were usually more interested in who the driver was, but to repossess a vehicle, repo companies only needed to find the car itself.

"I know you're not supposed to," Max was saying into the phone, waving a hand in the air. "I'll make it worth your while."

Slater winced. This was going to be expensive.

"Yeah, I guess I can pay you that much. … I have the plate number right here." He eyed Slater, who pulled up the number on his phone and handed it across the desk. Max recited it and waited.

"Excellent," he said finally. "Can you email me that? … I'll give you the money when I see you. … I'll see you when I see you, man. You know where to find me." He ended the call and turned to his computer. "He's sending it now."

"He got a hit in the database?"

"A lot of hits, he said." Max peered at the screen, clicking his mouse. "Here it is. … Last seen eleven minutes ago on the 710."

"Impressive," Slater said, and leaned on the desk as Max twisted the screen so they could both look at it.

"They have those plate readers on every tow truck now, and some of the cab companies have outfitted their entire fleets. Even ride-share drivers install them to make extra cash."

"Who would have thought Big Brother would have nothing to do with the government?"

"Here's where he lives," Max said, pointing to a label on the map, POSSIBLE RESIDENCE. "He spends a lot of time here too." It was labeled POSSIBLE WORK LOCATION.

"How does the software determine things like that?" Slater said, peering at the screen.

"If the car is spotted in the same place every night, in a residential zone, that's probably where he lives. The work location is in a commercial zone, see? Tweedy Boulevard. His wheels are regularly there during the day." Max zoomed out on the map. "He also spends time in Pasadena and the OC."

"Give me the mouse," Slater said.

As he moved around on the map, he saw that there were dots all over the metropolis, and the software had drawn circles around a few places where the plate had been spotted multiple times. The potential home and work locations didn't identify a specific address but rather an estimated location, a circle that covered about half a block.

"None of the hits are near that rental house in South Pas," Slater said.

"Maybe they use different rentals each time for their hookups. I would. Was it the kind of street where tow trucks and repo guys would be cruising past?"

"Not at all—it's narrow and out of the way." He sat back. "Can you forward me all that?"

"Done," Max said, pulling the screen back toward him and tapping at his keyboard.

"So how much do we owe the repo guy?"

"He wants eighty."

"Dollars?" Slater demanded. "Are you kidding me? I thought he'd want ten times that much, and that you'd talk him down to three or four hundred."

Max laughed. "Repo is a dangerous job, and the

profit margins are low. This guy doesn't have big numbers like that in his head. Querying the database cost him twenty bucks, so to him, asking for eighty is a significant markup."

"Tell this guy I have a crush on him now."

"I'm not going to do that, because his prices will go up. You wouldn't be into him anyway. His teeth are all messed up." Max stifled a yawn. "I'll pay him out of petty cash."

"It's great information, but it still doesn't give us the boyfriend's name."

"What do you want for eighty bucks? I can query the DMV, but it'll cost more than that."

"Don't bother," Slater said. "I'll make Conrad do it for free."

On the desktop, Max's phone buzzed, and he picked it up to look at the screen.

"This is my airline contact," Max said.

"We'll talk tomorrow," Slater said, and got up, taking the camera. In his own office he squatted in front of the old-school safe that was bolted to the floor behind his desk, twisting the dial to enter the combination. Once he had it open, he put the camera inside, on top of the cash box and the messy stack of paper, then locked it again. He'd deal with copying the photos later.

As he was leaving, he heard Max on the phone. His words made him grin.

"Aspen?" he demanded. "Who the hell goes to a ski resort in freaking August?"

When he got down to his car, before he started the engine, Slater checked the tracking app on his phone to see where Conrad, his idiot ex-boyfriend, was at. When they'd been together, Slater had managed to install a hidden tracker on his phone. It wasn't really stalking, he reasoned, as he needed to know where the guy was sometimes—Conrad was a cop, and he had access to some useful resources. Besides, it was his own damn fault for letting Slater see the code to unlock it.

The moron's phone, at least, was at his place, out in the Valley. He dialed and listened to it ring.

"I'm surprised you picked up," Slater said when he answered. "I thought you'd be fucking some sweaty twinkie."

"A pleasant good-evening to you too," Conrad said flatly. "What do you want, Slater?"

"I need you to run a plate for me."

"That's illegal."

"Not if it's part of some investigation you're doing. I want to know whether this guy is going to mess with me. I'm not sure how dangerous he is."

Those were persuasive words, Slater knew. He'd figured out that Conrad helped him when he thought Slater might be in danger, in a bumbling effort to protect him. All he had to do was frame it like he was at risk and Conrad would usually agree to the ask.

Conrad sighed. "I'll see what I can do tomorrow," he said finally. "I'm going in at eleven. Text me the tag."

"And make it snappy," Slater said. "I've got work to do."

He ended the call before Conrad could reply,

then texted him the plate number, adding:

It's a gray Ranger.

Firing up the Thunderbird's throaty engine, Slater pulled onto the dark street and drove to his apartment. The fifth of bourbon was still there on the counter, rich and golden and beautiful. Under his booze rules, guys came first, then the sauce. He thought about it as he locked the door, eyeing the fifth. That stakeout had wiped him out, plus he'd messed around with Andy earlier. He could take a night off from hooking up.

One of the recently amended booze rules was restricted quantities, and he poured out half an inch of the heady liquid into a tumbler. He hated that this paltry dribble was all he was allowed to have. Maybe he could supplement it a little. He wasn't seeing anyone tonight, and he'd been working late—he deserved it. It didn't fit with the rules, but it was only a little more. He filled the glass and took a satisfying slurp, then killed the room lights and sat in his recliner, cranking up the footrest.

Conrad had better come through with that tag. Freaking Conrad. So beautiful, so hot, but such a mess. Pushing the thought away, he slurped at his bourbon, relishing the burn in his throat, then set it on the carpet and put on the radio. This was the time of night when the music got good.

Grabbing his glass, he tried to pace himself, to sip it slowly. Ideally the warmth of it would help him crash before he wanted to get up and pour another.

FOUR

When he woke, Slater was in his own bed. He couldn't remember exactly how he'd gotten here, but he was alone, and it didn't look like anyone else had been with him. His mouth was dry, though he didn't feel hung over. Scrabbling for his phone, he checked his call history, relieved to see that he hadn't dialed anyone overnight.

Setting it down again, he dozed off, soon to be startled awake by the phone ringing, with an obnoxious ring tone that made his heart pound: *"No wire hangers—ever! I buy you three-hundred-dollar dresses, and you treat them like they were some dishrag!"*

Slater picked up and demanded, "Why are you bugging Andy, woman?"

"Because you wouldn't talk to me," Doris said. "Why wouldn't you tell your own mother you were going up in front of a judge?"

"It was no big deal. A misdemeanor. How do you know about it?"

"Court proceedings are public record."

"Bullshit."

She hesitated. "Conrad may have mentioned it."

"Why are you talking to that idiot? Is he stalking me now?"

"I don't think that's how he found out," Doris said. "I want you to tell me what happened."

"There's nothing to tell."

"I'll be downtown tomorrow. Do you have time for lunch?"

He rubbed his eyes. "Fine, Doris—I'll eat with you, if that's what you want."

"That's exactly what I want," she said, and they talked about where to meet.

After he ended the call, Slater sat up in bed and checked on Conrad's location. The dick-smack was at his station. Why hadn't he called back? It was time to nudge him. Before he could dial, a text flashed on the screen. It was from Conrad:

I have that thing for you. I'm at the station today.

Slater had to grin. The drooling idiot was smart enough, at least, to know not to put in writing what they were up to. He thumb-typed a response:

Finally. I'll be there soon.

Pushing himself out of bed, he washed up and went to look in the icebox. There was a jar of pickles, and he fished one out and munched on it. The only other edibles inside were left over from a bygone take-out meal: a couple of dried-out tortillas wrapped in foil. The first bite was chewy and slow going, like damp cardboard. He ran them under the kitchen tap and threw them in the microwave for a few seconds, which made them a little more palatable.

Once he was dressed he went down to his garage, where he opened the cabinet that sat just past the nose of the Thunderbird. It looked like a standard storage box, the kind made of flimsy sheet metal that office-supply stores sold, but in reality it was heavily armored, a safe that didn't look like a safe, concealed in plain sight.

Inside he kept all the illicit tech that he bought from the Russians in Glendale. He still had a couple of vehicle trackers, and he disconnected one from its charger. It was an unmarked black plastic box, about the size of a phone but twice as thick, with magnetic ribs covering one side. Locking the cabinet again, he put the tracker in the trunk of his car, tucking it in a corner under the carpet.

When the garage door rolled up, he backed the Thunderbird into the alley and waited for it to descend again. Conrad's station was close to his neighborhood, just a few minutes' drive. Once he'd parked on the street out front, Slater texted him:

Zip up your fly and come outside.

It was already sweaty hot out, he found when he climbed out of the car, and he stood there for a second to stretch. Walking past, headed toward the station's front entrance, a cop in uniform glanced toward Slater, then stopped and let out a wolf whistle.

It was about the Thunderbird, he knew, not about Slater. Despite the dumb cop haircut, the guy was fuckable, he decided, eyeing the pleasing contours of his uniform.

"A fellow traveler on the road to Sunland," he said.

Slater frowned. "What does that mean?"

"It's where all those auto wreckers are. I go out there all the time for parts."

"Right. I don't maintain it myself."

"You're smart not to overdo the polish on the chrome," he said, stepping closer and looking over the car. "It's better to leave it alone. What year is it?"

"It's a '78. What do you drive that needs old parts?"

He jabbed his thumb toward the station. "It's around back. A 1980 SR5."

"That's the four-by-four?"

"It's got the clearance for off-roading, but I'd never do that. It might get damaged. In the garage I'm restoring a '63 T-bird."

"That's definitely the pinnacle year for the series."

Conrad strode out the station door, also in uniform today. He stepped up and greeted his colleague, who clapped him on the shoulder.

"See you on the road to Sunland," the guy said to Slater, and walked away.

Conrad flashed that easy smile. His jawline, the jet-black hair, the barrel chest—everything about him was infuriating. Even worse was how affable he was. He'd smiled when he caught sight of Slater, as soon as he'd stepped outside, even though Slater treated him so badly.

"Are you hitting on my colleagues now?" Conrad said.

Slater jutted his chin. "What's it to you?"

"That guy is not your type. He started doing yoga so that he could meet women."

"Ten minutes in a dark room and I'd change his mind."

Conrad laughed. "Always the swagger with you."

"What did you find out?"

"I got the vehicle owner's name for you. His name is Ram, even though he's driving a Ford." Conrad glanced toward the building, but no one was in sight. From his shirt pocket he produced a yellow sticky note and handed it over. "He's got no record. Just a few parking tickets."

"Everybody gets parking tickets," Slater said, palming the note.

"Why are you interested in this guy?"

"It's a window-shade case."

"That makes sense. It doesn't seem like he's a knucklehead." Conrad put his hands on his hips. "People can act nuts when it comes to their love lives. Just watch your step."

"So why are you gossiping about me with Doris?"

"I saw that you had a court date, and I knew that you'd never tell her."

"My legal problems are none of your damn business," Slater said. "How did you even see that? Have you got my name flagged?"

"I happened to notice it in the course of my duties."

"That sounds like a line out of some cop handbook. Are you stalking me? Do you have a tracker on my car?"

"Why would I do that?" Conrad demanded. "We agreed to split up, and move on."

"Actually, you agreed with yourself to split me up. I remember your boot on my backside as I landed in the gutter."

"Nobody got dumped in the gutter." His brow furrowed. "Doris said you were moving on, with this Andy guy."

"That's not serious. He's just a friend."

"Is that because you don't want to get too involved with someone who has a disability?"

"You know me better than that," Slater snapped. "And he's not really disabled. Not where it matters—his personality and his mind. Unlike you, with your cold black heart and your breathtakingly low IQ."

Conrad grinned. "It can't be that low. They let me wear a badge."

Slater hated that about Conrad, how he kept his cool, how he never reacted. His ego was secure and serene no matter how many potshots Slater took at it. It probably made him good at his job, but right now he wanted to slap that grin off his face.

"Quit snooping into my legal problems," Slater

growled, jabbing a finger at him. "And quit bugging me."

As he turned to walk back to the Thunderbird, Conrad called after him, "You're welcome, by the way."

Climbing in behind the wheel, he started the engine to get the air-conditioning blowing, his gaze on Conrad's broad shoulders as he walked back into the station. He took a breath and looked away.

On his phone Slater pulled up the plate-reader data Max had sent last night. Comparing it to the sticky note Conrad had just given him, the address where this Ram guy had registered the Ranger was on the same block where the LPR software said it was often parked at night.

When he did a web search with the guy's full name, it came up with a business on Tweedy Boulevard, also right where the database said Ram's vehicle was regularly sighted. It was called Tax and Immigration Service. That made it sound like he was a lawyer.

The street-view images of the address showed a shabby little storefront in a crowded row of shops, with the business name plastered in the front window in big red letters. No lawyer would go that far down-market. Ram had to be running some other kind of business.

Slater put the address into his navigation app and shifted into gear. The software sent him on the 101 and the 710, exiting onto the boulevard in South Gate. Slowing down as he cruised by the storefront, the Ranger was nowhere in sight.

It made sense that it wouldn't be out front, as this stretch was all short-term metered parking. The shutter on the shop was up and the lights were on—Ram's business was open.

He turned onto the side street and parked at a meter, then retrieved the vehicle tracker from his trunk, tucking it into his belt in the small of his back. Rather than heading for the boulevard, he walked into the alley behind the strip of businesses. Sure enough, there was the Ranger, pulled up behind Ram's office.

Why would a white-collar guy need a pickup? And why would tow trucks be in this alley often enough to get multiple hits on Ram's plate? He stopped to look over the vehicle and survey the gritty roadway, the dumpsters, the fortified back doors of the businesses. Farther up the block was a spiked metal fence with coils of razor wire looping along the top, a dozen cars parked tightly together inside. A repair shop, or a body shop. That explained the tow trucks. This alley was fairly wide—if he was driving a heavy vehicle, he'd probably use it as a shortcut too.

Scanning the buildings, there was a camera a few doors down from where Ram's car was parked, but it was pointed the other way. He couldn't see one on Ram's office, or one that might have a view of his back door. Glancing up and down the alley to make sure he was alone, Slater stepped to the driver's side of the Ranger, then retrieved the tracker from his belt, pausing to find its tiny recessed power switch and sliding it on with a fingernail.

With his handkerchief he wiped the case to remove his prints, then held it in the cloth and crouched at the rear tire, reaching up into the wheel well. The vehicle had lots of clearance around the tire, and in a moment he felt the magnetic ribs connect to a steel component with a satisfying tug. Rising again, he wiped his brow and then stuffed his hankie into his jeans, scanning the alley to make sure he hadn't been observed.

The Russians he dealt with, Svetlana and her brother, Igor, had engineered the tracker to sniff out Wi-Fi signals and calculate its position based on the public databases of access points. Because it didn't use GPS, it didn't need a view of the sky, and even though the location it came up with was far less accurate, it was usually enough. It didn't work at all where there wasn't any Wi-Fi, like out in the countryside, but it also used a lot less battery power than a GPS receiver, usually reporting for four or five days before it died.

Striding back to the side street, he walked past his car to the boulevard and approached Ram's business, unmistakable by the red lettering shouting from the front window.

A bell at the top of the door tinkled as he stepped in. It was a lone room with a couple of desks and some file cabinets, lit by old fluorescent ceiling panels, the floor covered with timeworn commercial carpeting. At the back was a closed door, but it wasn't far enough from the street to be the one that opened onto the alley. There had to be a back room.

The only person here was Ram. He rose and stepped from behind his desk when Slater came in. Wearing dress pants and a collared shirt, like he had been last night, he called out a greeting in Spanish.

"*No comprendo,*" Slater said, making the vowels sound as drawn-out and English as he could.

Ram looked him over, a wry grin on his face. His gaze lingered on Slater's crotch, just long enough for him to notice.

"I thought you were here about an immigration issue," Ram said.

Slater put his hands on his hips. "You think because I look Latino that I must have immigration problems."

His brow furrowed. "Actually, it's because you look like a *cholo.*"

Stepping up to him, Slater slapped him hard, left and then right, a firm kovac. "I am not a *cholo,*" he said through his teeth.

Ram shoved him away and took a step back, anger flashing in his eyes.

"Get the fuck out of my office."

Slater went at him again, easily pushing aside Ram's arms when he tried to block him, tried to protect his face.

"Why do you make me do this to you?" he demanded, and landed another open-handed blow.

Ram twisted away and scuttled behind his desk chair, wheeling it around between them.

"I have to take classes because of lowlifes like you," Slater shouted. "Eight fricking weeks to learn how not to do this."

"I'm calling the cops," Ram said, both hands on the back of the chair, ready to shove it at him, eyeing Slater warily.

"You can do that, but I wish you'd listen to me for half a second instead of running your mouth. I'm working for Bella's husband."

Ram straightened up, his expression shifting. "How did you find me?"

"You don't get to ask questions."

"So you've come to chase me off, is that it? Or is it just to rough me up?"

"If I wanted to rough you up," Slater said, "you'd be unconscious right now. The kovac was just to get you to pay attention."

"Slapping me around doesn't seem like a great way to make me listen."

"Technically, I didn't really put my hands on you."

Ram smirked. "I could think of worse things."

"Are you seriously flirting with me right now?" Slater demanded.

Ram flashed his palms at his sides. "Not if that's problematic. Or if it makes you hit me again."

"I didn't hit you," Slater said flatly. "Why would you flirt with me when you're fucking that blond?"

"That's not serious," he said, holding his gaze. "But you—you're seriously hot."

Slater moved closer, sidestepping the chair. Ram arched his back and stood up straighter, concern in his eyes, but he didn't flinch as Slater grabbed his biceps and shoved him back against the file cabinet. Leaning into him, Slater massaged his arms and got close enough to smell his hair, redolent of soap and sweat.

"Oh, man," Ram said, breathing hard.

Slater met his mouth and pressed his body against him. He could feel the guy's wood swelling in his pants. Ram reached for his hair and pushed his fingers into it as Slater focused on his insistent mouth.

After a moment Slater pulled back, panting, and sat on the edge of the desk. "Aren't you a ball of fire."

"You're a really good kisser." Ram absently adjusted his crotch. "Are you going to tell Hayk about me?"

"He already knows there's someone. That's why he hired me. The real question is, what are you doing with Bella?"

"It's just a fling, like I said. It's not serious for either of us."

"If that's true," Slater said, "why pick someone who's married? There are a million single women in this town."

Ram gestured helplessly.

"Do you know anything about Hayk?"

"Bella sort of implied that he's a scary fellow."

"Good, because he is. He already said that he'd come for you."

"So you want me to pay you not to tell him who I am, is that it?"

"I'm not a penny-ante chiseler," Slater snapped. "I don't want your money."

"So why are you here?"

"To tell you to break it off. It took me less than a day to find you. Hayk might send someone else, and you'll end up in a shallow grave out in the Mojave."

"If Hayk is paying you to find out who I am," Ram said, "why wouldn't you just tell him? It makes no sense that you'd come here if it's not a grift."

"He's paying me to find out what Bella is doing. You're not the target."

"OK, but why are you being so soft about it?"

Slater's eyes narrowed. "It's almost like you want me to punch you."

Ram dropped his chin, a smile playing on his lips. "Oh, I can think of much more rewarding things you could do to me."

"Dude—focus. I don't care what you do about Bella. Just consider this visit a head's up."

"You don't seem like a guy with misty-eyed notions about protecting the innocent."

"In no way are you innocent. You knew she was married to a guy like Hayk, and you're sleeping with her anyway." Slater waved an arm. "I don't really care about you, and whether you live or die. It's about me—I don't want to be complicit in a civilian getting iced when it's so easily avoidable."

"Or," Ram said intently, "you think I'm hot. The thought of this pretty face getting messed up is just too painful."

Slater sighed. "That would be unfortunate."

"You like me," he said intently.

"I don't know you, and I know next to nothing about you. Except that you're not very smart. But yeah, you are fuckable."

Ram threw up his hands. "There it is."

"It's not going to work." Slater shook his head. "I don't do straight guys."

"I'm not a straight guy."

"Despite the glaring evidence at your short-term rental in South Pas."

His brow furrowed. "Were you peeping on us?"

"I didn't have to. You're not very discreet."

"So you didn't actually see anything. But you want to. I know you want a piece of this." He gestured up and down his torso. "And I'd really like to see you naked."

Slater furrowed his brow. What was with this guy?

"I guess I could fuck you in the back room," Slater said finally.

"I'd like to take more time with it. What are you doing later?"

Slater stood up and fished a business card out of his jeans, handing it over. "I'm around."

"Insurance investigator?" Ram said, studying the card.

"Don't worry about that. It's my day job. But that's my number."

With that, he went out to the street and walked around to his car, lost in thought. Was Ram really that clueless, or was he just pretending to be? It could be a calculated performance to throw Slater off. He started the engine and got the air blowing. Before he could pull out, his phone rang.

Glancing at the screen, he saw it was Tato. It

hadn't been long enough since he'd left Ram's office for the two of them to have had much of a conversation, and the idea that they were colluding didn't feel quite right. Still, it was suspicious that he'd just been to see one of the other men in Bella's life.

"We need to talk," Tato said when he picked up. He sounded gruff, like he'd had a chance to think it through, and he wasn't intimidated anymore.

"I'll come to your office," Slater said.

"That's where I'm at now. It's in South Pasadena."

"I know where it is," Slater said, and ended the call.

In reality he only had a vague idea of where it was, so he pulled up the photo he'd taken of Tato's phone screen, then punched the address into his navigation app.

FIVE

Half an hour later Slater pulled into an angle-parking space in front of a short row of shops at the base of a shrubby slope. That had to be Raymond Hill, he decided, leaning over the steering wheel and gazing up at it. The brick building at its base predated the strip-mall era, fronting the sidewalk with street parking instead of a dedicated asphalt lot. It wasn't clear which business was Tato's, although he knew this was the right place, as his obnoxious yellow Humvee was parked here, a couple of stalls away. Why hadn't he thought to bring another vehicle tracker? But it would be hard to put it on the Humvee anyway. It was too exposed here—someone would see him doing it.

At the left end of the building was a box-and-ship place, next to a smoke shop, and next to that a place with a bunch of dishes in the window and a sign that said IMPORTS. The business at the far end had its mesh shutter down, but there was an old-fashioned lamp in the window, so maybe it was an antiques store. Finally he spotted some street numbers, in the shadows above the entrance to the shipping store. Those matched Tato's.

Climbing out of his car, Slater walked behind the Humvee, holding his phone low and pausing to surreptitiously photograph the rear license plate. When he stepped inside the shipping store, behind the long counter he found a twenty-something woman with unkempt frizzy blond hair. Her skin was beaded with sweat, probably from the midday heat, although junkies looked like that too when they went into withdrawal. She eyed him as he came in, her expression dour and disinterested.

"Can I help you?"

"I'm here to see Tato."

"I'll tell him." She stepped over to the door into the back, pulling it open and calling out, "You have a guest."

Slater couldn't place her accent, but it sounded like the Russians he knew. Looking around, he saw the shop was stocked with utilitarian shipping products—corrugated boxes and bubble wrap and rolls of packing tape. Oddly, there were no cameras inside.

Tato appeared in the doorway, wearing a dark-blue work shirt, and scowled at the sight of him.

"Come on back," he said, beckoning as he turned away.

The woman stepped aside as Slater walked past the floor scale and into the back room. It was much

58

larger than the space with the retail counter, with a worktable against one wall and two desks with big computer monitors. The only windows were long and shallow, overhead on the side wall, meant to provide lighting alone, as they were too high up to see anything outside except the sky.

Tato stepped behind him and closed the door, flipping the bolt.

"Are you worried that someone will walk in on us?" Slater said.

Tato scoffed and went over to sit behind one of the desks.

There was no surveillance in here either, Slater saw, looking around at the ceiling.

"There are no cameras anywhere."

"You're very observant," Tato said, raising an eyebrow.

"Why?" Slater demanded. "Retailers always have cameras, to watch the till and the entrance."

"Not everything I do is about the shipping business, as you well know. I don't need to create a video record of that." He waved to the chair facing his desk. "Do you want to sit down?"

Tato pulled out his bottom drawer and started digging through a row of file folders. Slater looked around the space as he sat. The walls were painted clean white, but the bricks were uneven, which meant it was old. On the side wall, next to the fire door, there was a loading dock with the metal shutter rolled down, painted white to match the rest of the interior. It must be an artifact from one of the building's earlier incarnations, as now one of the desks was positioned in front of it.

Behind Tato, on the back wall, there was another disused door, built of wide wooden planks and hanging from a rail on big rollers. Almost concealing it was a set of wire storage shelves, laden with boxes and stacks of paper and plastic tubs, but the door was still visible through the clutter. It was painted white too, except for the metal wheels at the top and the rail they rolled on.

Tato finally pulled out a manila folder and set it on his desktop.

"So how much are you getting from Bella?" Slater said.

"I'm not going to tell you that." He pushed the folder a few inches to the side and folded his hands on the desktop. "I'm willing to offer you a monthly cut of one hundred dollars."

Slater eyed the folder. It was just for show—Tato hadn't looked in it, hadn't needed to check anything. He'd already planned what he was going to say. If his offer represented ten or twenty percent of what he was getting from Bella, it meant he wasn't bleeding her dry. He must be in it for the long haul, a parasite rather than a predator, billing her just a few hundred a month. To a woman with Bella's resources, that would be a minor outlay, like a car payment.

"No thanks," Slater said, and held Tato's gaze.

"I can't go any higher. I have expenses."

"That's not enough scratch to interest me."

Tato leaned back in his chair and absently stroked his mustache. "Not many people would turn up their noses at easy cash."

"It's chump change, brother. Not enough to make it worth getting into business with a guy like you."

"So what are you going to do?"

Slater frowned. "About what?"

"Are you going to interfere with my revenue stream?"

"I don't care about your small-time stuff—selling cardboard boxes, chiseling rich women."

"I'm not a small-timer," Tato said intently.

"Whatever you say." Slater rose and walked to the door. He could feel Tato's eyes on him.

"Are you going after Bela?" he demanded.

"You mean to blackmail her?" Slater said, turning back. He spread his palms. "I'm not a lowlife."

"I know you're a PI. I found a listing with your phone number."

"You got that one wrong too. You're trash, Tato. Leave me out of it."

"Fuck you," he snapped.

Ignoring that, Slater unlocked the door and stepped into the front office. The clerk with the ratty blond hair was talking to a guy across the counter. He glanced at Slater, but from his indifferent expression, they hadn't overheard his conversation with Tato. She had a small cardboard package in hand, and set it on the scale between them.

"It'll take longer," she said, pressing buttons on the readout, "but it's only twelve dollars."

As he walked out, Slater eyed the alarm panel beside the front door. That particular model was overkill for this place—it was the kind of system that could manage dozens of doors and windows and motion detectors. That kind of security, at least, Tato wasn't averse to.

As he climbed into his car and cranked up the air, something nagged at the edge of his mind. He stared at the storefront for a minute before he backed out and rolled a few feet down the street, craning to get a look at the side of the building. He could see the outside of Tato's high office windows, and the fire door, and the erstwhile loading dock. In front of it was an ancient patch of crumbling asphalt, just wide enough to back a freight truck into. No one had done that for a long time, though, as the space was surrounded by a low chain-link fence in front, a stretch of thick laurel hedge shielding it from the boulevard, and the slope of Raymond Hill behind.

Then it clicked—the thing that didn't make sense. The loading dock faced the disused side yard, but the big rolling door was on the back wall of Tato's office, and that wall abutted the steep hillside. Why would there be a door there? Inching the car forward, Slater could see that behind the building was a concrete retaining wall, so stained with grime that it had to be as old as the structure was. It went up about twenty feet. Covering the narrow gap between the back of the building and the hillside was another short length of chain-link fence, topped by a spool of razor wire.

Behind him another driver tapped the horn. Pulling his attention back to the street, Slater drove the few yards to the corner, then turned onto the boulevard that ran along the base of the hill. Cruising in the curb lane for a minute, he eyed the hill and its extensive retaining wall. He'd driven past this a thousand times and never noticed what it looked like, or the ancient concrete, or how it had been constructed. Finally he pulled into the left lane to make a U-turn and headed for the 110.

The eighty-year-old freeway was the first to be built in the metropolis, and the ramps were extremely short, with stop signs to enter the travel lanes rather than a merge zone. When it was Slater's turn, he watched for a break in the oncoming vehicles and then gunned it. The Thunderbird was happy to oblige, its engine roaring loud but true, quickly reaching the speed of the traffic.

Driving the length of the Arroyo, he mulled his visit to Tato's shop. It wasn't just about small-time extortion. Something else was going on. A retail business with no cameras, and a huge rolling door than opened onto an ancient retaining wall. What was Tato up to? By the time he got downtown and pulled into the lot across from his building, he knew that he couldn't let it go. He wanted to find out what was going on with that guy.

A few of the day laborers were still hanging around the lobby, waiting for gigs in the building's garment factories. Upstairs the office was dark. Slater flicked on the lights and poked his head into Max's office before he went to his own, where he dropped into his chair and heaved his boots up on the desk. Pulling the keyboard onto his lap, he woke the computer and searched for information about the neighborhood around Tato's shop.

Today Raymond Hill was covered with low-rise postwar apartment buildings, he knew, but he soon found an article that outlined its earlier history. In the nineteenth century the hilltop had been the grounds of a sprawling hotel for wealthy Easterners who came to spend the winter in the comparatively warm surroundings. The resort was convenient to a train station, the article explained, so it was possible for well-heeled guests to cross the country by rail and disembark practically at the hotel's doorstep.

There was still a rail right-of-way near there, he remembered, just across the boulevard from Tato's side street. Light-rail metro trains were using it now. Whatever station had been there for the hotel was long gone, along with the hotel—it had burned down in 1895.

Keys rattled in the lock, pulling his attention away, and he heard the door swing open. Slater got up and stepped into the front office. Max was wearing his gray suit again, but without a necktie.

"Did you find the boyfriend?" Max said.

"I met him this morning." Slater followed him into his office and sat across his desk, then told him what he'd learned about Ram and about Tato.

"Excellent work," Max said finally. "It's enough—we can report to the client."

"When he gets this news, is Hayk going to whack his wife?"

"I didn't get that vibe. He'll be angry, but only an idiot would do that when he knows that you and I know all the details."

"What about the boyfriend? Do we give him Ram's name?"

"That's a whole other question. Can Ram take care of himself?"

Slater shook his head. "His storefront feels like bunco, but I'm pretty sure he's a civilian. From talking to him I know he's an idiot."

"I'm not sure what Hayk would do about him."

"Yesterday when we talked to Hayk, he didn't specifically ask us to get a name. We can just tell him that there's a guy, identity unknown. The photos of them pawing each other don't show his face."

Max nodded. "That works. What about the blackmailer?"

"That'll take care of itself. Once Bella knows that Hayk knows, she'll stop paying Tato."

"I guess there's no reason to give Hayk someone else to go after."

"So what's involved in the report?"

Max sat up and leaned on his desk. "It has to be on paper. First, you'll have to write up a simple timeline, and print it out."

"It sounds like that damn anger-management class. I have to do written homework."

"Except this isn't court ordered," Max said, "and you're getting paid. You'll want to print out some of the photos. I use that print shop on Maple. Do them in eight-by-ten size. That's always more impactful. They can do a thin white border around the edges. Mentally I think that contains the image to the past, so it's not bleeding off the page into the here and now. Get them to pull up the warm tones, the reds and yellows, and deemphasize the blues. Don't crop out the window frame or the drapes— it's important to show context. And get them made with a glossy finish, not matte."

"You really have this down to a science."

"When we first met, you taught me about *sang froid.* Maybe I can teach you about window-shade cases."

"You already had *sang froid,*" Slater said. "You just needed a way to conceptualize it."

"I needed to stop working for crooks, more like."

"Are we both going to meet with Hayk?"

"I'm happy to do the talking, but you'll have to be there to answer questions."

Slater stood up. "I'll get everything together by morning."

In his own office, he squatted in front of the safe in the corner and spent a minute getting it open, then took out Max's camera. At his desk, he pried out the little black memory card and plugged it into his computer, then copied the photos to his online storage. Pocketing the card, he called good-bye to Max and headed down to the street.

The print shop Max had mentioned was just a few blocks away, so he walked, enjoying the heat of the midafternoon sun on his face. When he pushed open the door, an electronic chime sounded. The clerk appeared from the back as he stepped into the tiny space. In her thirties, maybe, she wore glasses and had her dark hair bundled on top of her head.

"I need to make some eight-by-tens from some

of these photos," Slater said, setting the memory card on the counter.

"Let's see what you've got." She slid the card into the computer and studied the screen, then twisted it so that Slater could see.

"That one," he said, pointing it out, "and that one … you don't need to crop any of them. Glossy finish, thin white border. And shift the color balance so they're warmer."

"She looks like a natural blond," the clerk said, zooming in on one of the images of Bella.

"How can you tell?"

"Her roots are blond. Although maybe it's just a really good dye job." She clicked on the next photo, Bella and Ram embracing, and next a close-up of Ram in profile.

"I don't need either of those," Slater said.

"I'm thinking that's not her husband."

"I'm not paying you to think."

"The hot ones always go for that type. Blond, I mean." She eyed Slater, a wry grin on her face. "I don't suppose you'd know anything about that."

"I only go for men," Slater said flatly. "I don't care whether they're blond or not."

"That's the other thing all the decent guys do. It's either blonds or other guys."

"I don't actually fit in that category. Decent, I mean. When should I come back for the prints?"

"I'll do it now," she said. "Go get a coffee."

Slater stepped out to the street. He didn't need coffee, but his stomach was grumbling. It was a little early in the day for street food, but he walked to

the next corner anyway and scanned the neighborhood for a cart or a food truck. Sure enough, there
was a taco cart already set up at the end of the next
block.

Approaching the vendor, he ordered a couple
of tacos. It always elicited astonishment and mirth
that he didn't want the *carne* in them, just the beans
and the onions and the salsa. They thought he
was stupid to miss out on it, that they were taking
advantage of him by charging him full price. Once
he had the food in hand, he went to the curb and
ate it over the gutter.

Walking back to the print shop, Slater stepped
inside. The clerk approached the counter, and rec-
ognizing him, turned back to grab the photos. She
lifted her glasses up onto her head and set a manila
envelope on the countertop, then slid the prints out
of it. Max was right: the images were lurid when
they were blown up like this.

"These are perfect," he said. "What do I owe
you?"

After he'd paid her, he walked back to the office.
Max was gone. At his own desk, he started to type
up his timeline.

> 20:10. Tailed Bella from Glendale in the blue
>   Bentley, tag no. ARKAYA21.
> 20:42. Bella enters a short-term rental property at—

Pausing, he pulled out his phone to find the
address. After he typed it, he added a few more
lines, then stared absently at the screen, thinking
about what he'd seen in the kitchen, what he'd

heard through the open window. He wasn't going to add the part about Tato, obviously.

What was Tato doing in that shipping store? When he'd asked him about the absence of security cameras, the guy had implied that he was up to something. It had to be more than just blackmailing bored rich people. Cameras wouldn't matter for that. He took a deep breath, thinking it through. If he was going to get into Tato's shop, he'd need to disarm that alarm system.

The timeline wasn't finished yet, but he got up and locked the computer anyway, then went down to his car, and drove to his apartment. Once he'd pulled into his garage, he climbed out and waited for the door to roll down, then went to look through the gardening equipment that hung on the back wall and lined the workbench.

Propped in the corner were a half-dozen stray metal stakes that might work. They were painted green, and sharp at one end, to be driven into the earth. The top end had a hard flat cap to pound on with a mallet. They were used to hold up saplings, three stakes arrayed in a triangle around the immature trunk to provide support until the tree was strong enough to stand on its own. Slater had trained in horticulture at community college, and at one time he'd done a lot of gardening, but not so much since he'd been investigating insurance fraud and tangling with lowlifes.

Gathering the stakes in a bundle, he set the tips on the floor. They came up to chest height—that might be just about right.

Once he'd loaded them into the trunk of the Thunderbird, he backed into the alley and drove to South Pas. He'd need a story to spin to Tato about why he'd returned, and spent most of the drive concocting one. It didn't have to be that convincing—the guy wasn't very bright.

When he pulled up in front of Tato's shipping store, the sign in the window still said OPEN, but the Humvee was gone. That might make things easier. He pulled the stakes out of the trunk and walked inside, eyeing the frizzy blond clerk.

"No Tato?" he asked her.

"He'll be back later," she said, eyeing the bundle in his hand.

"I'm sure you can help me. I need a box to ship these in."

She furrowed her brow but picked up a measuring tape and walked around the end of the counter, spooling it out and crouching for a moment to measure the stakes up from the floor.

"Fifty-six inches," she said. "I think we have a sixty-inch box for shipping artworks."

As she went behind the counter and opened the door to the back room, Slater stepped over to the alarm panel beside the front door. Hopefully this would work—the Russians he knew were savvy about deception, so they weren't easy to fool.

Resting the points of the stakes on the floor, he waited until she was out of view, then punched the 5 button several times on the alarm's keypad, and then the ARM button. The panel started beeping wildly in protest. Slater set the tops of the stakes against the keypad and stepped back.

The woman hustled back into the room and shot him a look.

"I just put the stakes down, and it started beeping," he said, putting his hands on top of his head and raising his voice over the electronic racket. "Did I break something?"

She grabbed the stakes and hurriedly thrust them at him, clearly frazzled by the noise and the threat that the alarm was about to go off. As she turned back to the panel, Slater positioned himself to look over her shoulder as she punched in the code to disarm it: 2-0-1-2, then the OFF button. The machine emitted one last lengthy beep and fell silent.

That was easy—he didn't even have to work to commit the sequence of numbers to memory. The last year of the Mayan calendar was 2012.

"Is that the burglar alarm?" Slater said, making a point of losing his grip on a few of the stakes and then fumbling with them. "I wasn't looking where I put them."

"It's OK," she said, pushing her hair back. "Nothing's broken. Just lay them on the floor or something."

As she went into the back room again, Slater had to grin. It had worked perfectly—she'd pegged him as stupid and careless rather than deceptive, and now he knew the alarm code.

The year 2012 was supposed to be the New Age apocalypse, predicated on the assumption that the ancient Mayan calendar designers had some foreknowledge about the end of the world, but it had never happened. At the time, Doris had said, "I have a calendar that ends too. Every year on December 31st."

When the clerk came back, she had a long flat box in hand, and set it on the counter. "Are you shipping those today?"

"I'll take the box and pack it myself. I have a few more of these to put in."

She nodded and stepped over to the register. "What are they, anyway?"

"They're for gardening," he said, meeting her eye. "They hold up trees. Some of them are defective, so I have to send them back to the manufacturer."

"Fifteen thirty-two," she said, tapping at the keypad.

He pulled his wad of cash out of his jeans and handed her a twenty. "I guess cardboard isn't cheap."

She didn't respond to that as she popped open the cash drawer and handed him his change.

He thanked her and walked out to his car, ditching the box and the stakes in the trunk before he climbed in behind the wheel.

SIX

The late-afternoon traffic was sluggish, and it took a while to get downtown. Once he was back behind his desk, Slater woke his computer and looked at what he'd already done with the timeline, then rubbed his eyes. Why was this so difficult?

He pulled up the photos he'd taken with Max's camera to refresh his memory, then checked the metadata of a few of them to get the time stamp before he continued typing.

20:48. Bella embraces unknown male in the kitchen of the rental property. See attached photo.

Eventually he had it all spelled out. The last entry he made was for when Bella drove away from the rental in the blue Bentley. It didn't seem like a lot of writing for the amount of work it had taken; the whole thing fit on a single page. After he printed it, he reread the list. Satisfied, he put the sheet in his desk drawer with the manila envelope that contained the glossy photos.

The memory card, he remembered. He found the card in his pocket, then picked up Max's heavy camera and slid it into its slot. Walking over to the other office, he set it in Max's bottom desk drawer. As he went back to his own desk, his phone rang. The caller ID read TAX AND IMMIG. He knew who that was.

"I'm in for the night," Ram said when he picked up. "Do you want to come over?"

"Where's 'over'?"

Ram recited his address, but Slater didn't need to write it down—it was the one Conrad had given him, the same place the LPR database had linked to the gray Ranger.

"Give me half an hour," Slater said, and ended the call.

On his phone he checked his tracking software. The tracker on Ram's car was working, and showed that it was in Downey. The estimated green circle on the map covered parts of different blocks, but it overlapped with the address Ram had just given him. Everything lined up—Ram wasn't messing with him.

Eyeing the statue of Rey Pascual on the way out, Slater flicked off the lights and locked the door. Downey wasn't that far away, and the navigation app sent him on the 710.

Once he was off the freeway, in the fading daylight he could see that the neighborhood was mid-century bungalows on wide lots with neat yards. Fifty years ago it would have been a middle-income area, but today it had a distinct working-class vibe. That explained why the repo guys with the plate readers were sniffing around: people who lived closer to the edge were more likely to default on their car payments.

The house number was painted on the curb in front of Ram's place, but Slater didn't need to check the address, as the gray Ranger was parked in the driveway. When he knocked on the front door, Ram soon pulled it open. He was wearing a bathrobe and a big smile.

"Did you just get out of the shower?" Slater said.

"I was waiting for you."

The moment the door closed, Ram was on him, his hands on his chest, then his shoulders, pawing his back, unbuttoning his shirt. Slater went with it, even though it felt like being pulled into a whirlwind, his tongue in his mouth for a brief moment before Ram moved on to his neck, and his ear, and his chest.

Ram knelt in front of him and started to unbuckle his belt.

"Are we going to do this right here?" Slater said.

"We don't have to." Ram rose and pulled the end of his belt, leading him deeper into the house.

Glancing at the living room as they walked through, he saw a sofa and chair set in matching plaid, and a blue shag carpet. Was it an intentionally retro look, or was this a time capsule that had just never been renovated?

As they entered the bedroom, Ram dropped his bathrobe. He was already hard. Pushing Slater's shirt off, he stepped closer, and met his mouth as he shoved his jeans down.

Slater put a hand on his chest to slow him down. "Let me get my boots off."

Once he'd stepped out of them and slid off his jeans, Ram pushed him backward onto the bed, then climbed up to straddle him.

"You are really into this," Slater said.

Leaning in, Ram kissed him again as he squeezed his cock, grinding his own against Slater's thigh. The guy was moving fast, like he was hyperactive. It wasn't meth, Slater decided; he was just ecstatic about sex. But it was distracting.

Sitting up, Slater grabbed his shoulders and flipped him onto the bed, face-down, then climbed on top of him.

"What just happened?" Ram said, breathing hard. "How did you do that?"

"Middle-school wrestling." Slater leaned on his shoulders with his palms and pressed his thighs onto Ram's hips.

"What are you going to do?"

"That's a great question. What do you want me to do?"

"You should fuck me."

"If you have a condom."

"Under that side," he said, and flapped his arm.

Slater moved to the edge of the bed and found a condom, then rolled it on. He grabbed a bottle of lube and turned back to Ram, straddling him again.

Starting slowly, he worked his way into him, gently at first, and tried to tune out Ram's verbalizations.

"Yes," Ram intoned. "Do it—yes."

Pounding him now, Slater leaned closer, his mouth next to his ear, and whispered "Sh-h-h."

"Oh, man," Ram cried. "Come on, do it. Do it!"

Slater put his nose in Ram's hair, smelling his sweat, and strained into him as he came. Shifting onto his side, he pulled away to catch his breath.

"That didn't take you very long," Ram said. "I thought we'd spend some time on this."

"I couldn't help myself. It's because you're so beautiful."

Ram's eyes narrowed, considering that. "What are we going to do about me?" he said, and stroked his cock.

Slater shifted position and took him into his mouth, using one hand to dampen his enthusiastic hip thrusts, and massaged his chest with the other. Despite his exhortation to take his time, in less than a minute Ram shuddered and came, yowling and arching his back.

He rolled onto his side, and Ram shifted closer again, kissing him intently. Slater went with it for a while, then broke away and wrapped his arm over his eyes, taking a deep breath.

"That sounded heavy," Ram said.

"What did?"

"That breath. It sounded like the weight of the world. Existential angst."

"Are you a shrink?" Slater said.

"I'm an accountant. But you sounded stressed

out, for a man who just released all that tension."

Slater lifted his arm to look. Ram was gazing at him, his head propped on his arm, his expression still energized.

"I shouldn't be doing this," Slater muttered.

"Because I sleep with women?" Ram said. "Does that gross you out? Is it because when you saw me with Bella, you couldn't figure out which one of us was the man, and which one was the other man?"

"I don't care who you sleep with. And I didn't see you with Bella."

"Is it because of Jesus?"

Slater scoffed. "I'm Jewish. I don't have a sex hang-up—it's because you're part of a job. It was a bad idea to get into your bed."

"Because Hayk hired you to spy on Bella."

"Something like that. I need to keep my dick out of my cases."

"That's total jive, man. Sex is sex."

"You said you're an accountant," Slater said. "Not a lawyer? The sign on your office implies that you provide legal services."

"I'm a notary. That's a legal service. I help people fill out immigration forms, but I don't represent them at hearings."

"Do they know you're not a lawyer when they walk in?"

"I'm up-front about it."

"OK," Slater said evenly, studying his face. "Ram is a Sikh name."

"It could be, but I'm not Sikh." He frowned. "How do you know about Sikhs?"

"I knew a guy. He was a bad-ass."

"They're known for that," Ram said, and shifted onto his back. "They chased the Japanese out of Burma in World War II."

"So where did you meet Bella? She doesn't seem like the kind of woman who'd spend much time on Tweedy Boulevard."

"I thought you weren't going to rat me out to Hayk."

"I won't."

"So don't ask me about her. Like you said, that's part of a job. This isn't the time for work."

Slater covered his eyes again and stifled a sigh.

Thankfully Ram was quiet for a while, and he started to drift toward sleep.

Sometime later, he woke to a hand massaging his chest.

"I think I could go again," Ram said.

"You're a better man than me." Slater sat up. "I have to go."

He swung his feet to the floor and snatched up his shirt, then found his jeans and his boots. Ram watched him as he got dressed, but Slater avoided his gaze—the guy was casually stroking himself, the invitation tacit, but Slater didn't want to get drawn into that again.

"Is the front door bolted?" Slater said, rising after tying his boots.

"Buzz kill," Ram said, but then got up. "I'll let you out."

He followed Slater and pulled the door wide, even though he was totally naked and sporting a woody. Slater stepped out and walked down the driveway.

"Call me," Ram called after him, before he closed the door.

It was finally cooling off a little, and a few stars were visible overhead as Slater climbed into his car.

He glanced at the dashboard clock as he drove toward his apartment. It was later than he'd thought—late enough to check out Tato's business. Once he'd pulled into his garage, and killed the engine, and the door rolled all the way down, he opened the armored cabinet. He grabbed the lock reader—a small key-size probe with a wire attached—and wound it around his hand, then stuffed it into his hip pocket. The heavy binder full of keys he loaded into the trunk of the Thunderbird. There hadn't been an opportunity to check the lock on that fire door at Tato's business, but with any luck it was a standard hardware-store model, meaning he'd probably be able to open it.

Backing the car into the alley again, he headed for South Pas, driving fast on the freeway in the light late-night traffic. The mesh shutter was down on Tato's shop, and on all the others in the row. Eyeing the building as he cruised past, he turned the corner onto the boulevard, and parked along the sidewalk at the base of the hill, next to the retaining wall. A couple of other vehicles were here, but it was too far a walk from the residential streets for people to leave their cars overnight. Before he climbed out he pulled a pair of black latex gloves from the box on the floor in the backseat and wriggled his hands into them, then donned his blue ball cap.

Walking back around the corner to the shops, he scanned for cameras again, in case one of the adjacent businesses had different ideas about security than Tato. Finding none, he stepped into the yard beside the building and approached the back entrance to Tato's place.

He went over to the short length of fence between the building and the concreted hillside. It was too dark back there to see much, but it looked like the retaining wall came close to the building. Stepping back to the fire door, a smile spread across his face when he saw that it had a standard lock on it.

Glancing over his shoulder, he pulled the lock reader out of his jeans and connected its short cable to the port on his phone. It launched one of Svetlana's apps, showing a black screen with the word "готов" on it. He squatted and slid the end of the probe, the size and shape of a key, into the lock. Svetlana had once explained how it worked, by measuring the electrical resistance of the pins inside the mechanism to predict the length of each. It wasn't foolproof, and once in a while he couldn't get an accurate reading, but this time the screen flashed green and provided a number: 347. Tucking the probe away, he walked back to the Thunderbird and opened the trunk, pausing and looking sidelong at the boulevard as a car went by. A white sedan—not Tato, and not the cops. It was just regular traffic. No one was interested in what he was doing.

Slater flipped open the thick binder of keys and

found the sheet with number 347, pulling it out of its little pouch. Slamming the trunk, he strolled back toward Tato's shop.

Eyeing the street again to make sure he wasn't being observed, he tried the ghost key in the lock. It twisted freely—thank you, Svetlana. He pulled open the door and stepped inside, then closed it behind him.

The alarm started beeping, as he'd anticipated it would, but there was no alarm panel inside this door. He hustled through the dark room to the doorway into the shop and pushed it open. The lights were off but the shop was illuminated by the dim streetlamps outside. The metal security shutter cast a shadowy grid on the floor, and past the counter he could see the alarm panel, lit in green.

On the keypad he punched 2-0-1-2 and the OFF button. It stopped beeping, and Slater took a deep breath. No Mayan apocalypse, no alarm company armed response. It was still risky to spend much time here, as Tato might have the system set up to alert him whenever someone entered the business. The guy might show up himself to see who it was coming in at this hour. He might even send the cops. But most people didn't bother with that level of micromanagement, and only bothered to check if something unexpected happened.

Walking into the back room again, he closed the door to the shop. His vision was already adjusting to the ambient light from the high windows, so he didn't bother to turn on the room lights.

At Tato's desk, he sat down and tugged on the

bottom drawer, the one Tato had dug through to produce the file folder that he never opened. It wasn't locked, and he pulled out the stack of file folders, plopping them on the desk. For this he'd need light. He adjusted the hood of Tato's desk lamp so it was aimed at the files, hovering just above them, and winced at the glare when he clicked it on.

The first folder was paperwork related to the shipping business, mostly purchase orders for things like cardboard boxes and bulk envelopes and other supplies. The latex gloves made it easy to quickly riffle through the pages. The next folder was more of the same, and the next. None of them had anything to do with Bella or the blackmail scheme. It would be foolish of him to document it; at least Tato understood that much. The file folder he'd pulled out today really had been just a prop.

Slater tucked the folders back in the drawer and killed the lamp, manipulating it into the position he'd found it in. Sitting back, he glanced around the room, waiting for his eyes to readjust to the low light. That hinky rolling door on the back wall, partly hidden behind the wire shelving unit, came into focus, and he got up and walked over to it. Slater double-checked his reckoning, but based on where the fire door and the disused loading dock were, he was right—behind the rolling door should be the concrete retaining wall that held up Raymond Hill. Up close it was huge—at least eight feet across. When he looked up at the wheels and the rail they ran on, there was no trace of rust.

The wire storage rack in front of it looked heavy,

laden with boxes and plastic tubs and stacks of padded envelopes, but it was on wheels. Even in the low light he could make out the path they made on the concrete floor, a gentle curve arcing away from the wall. Grabbing the post at the end of the rack, he pulled on it, but it didn't budge. He crouched to study the little rubber wheels. They had brakes on them, he saw, and rose again, using his boot to release the brake on one wheel, then the other. This time when he pulled on the post, the shelves rolled smoothly away from the wall, the wheels following the arc on the floor.

Now there was enough space to step in front of the big rolling door. It didn't have a handle on it, but the wheels above were at the end of their track, so it could only move in one direction, to the left. Slater grasped the thick wooden end of it with his latex-clad fingers and pushed. The door moved surprisingly easily, rolling silently along its rail.

Behind it was a void of inky blackness, the feeble light of the room illuminating only a few feet of concrete wall in a space almost as wide as the door. The air inside was cooler than in Tato's office. He stood there for a moment and peered in, listening, but there was only silence. He could smell earth.

Stepping inside, he turned on his phone's flashlight and held it high. Three wooden pallets were stacked against the wall at the far side, and beyond that sat a couple of sets of flat cardboard boxes, shrink-wrapped in green-tinted plastic. On the opposite side were a couple of huge wooden crates, big enough to hold a kitchen appliance. They were empty, the wooden lids resting inside, ready to be nailed on. Beyond them, leaning on the wall, was a small array of chunks of two-by-four and laths of varying lengths.

It was just a storage space for Tato's business—except the space had no back wall. Holding his light higher and aiming it farther inside, where the hillside should be, he could see the concrete walls and ceiling and gritty floor continue for a few yards, stretching into blackness. He stood and peered into the void. What the hell was Tato up to?

The first rule of being stealthy was to leave things the way you found them. Turning back toward the shop, Slater pulled on the wire shelving unit, rolling it back into place, then got a grip on the big door and rolled it closed. If Tato or the cops did show up, at least it wouldn't be obvious that he was in here.

Slater turned back to the void and held his phone at his waist, the lamp facing forward, and started walking. Once he was past the initial jumble of storage, the space was empty, the concrete walls unvarying as he went farther. This wasn't just an extended storage space—he couldn't believe how far the tunnel went, the walls ahead of him still fading to nothingness in the feeble light. What was this place?

After what felt like a long time, trudging along with the gritty concrete crunching under his boots, he saw the glint of a structure ahead in the distance. As he approached, it resolved into a set of steel posts, then a larger room, and then a flight of stairs leading upward between the posts. The steps were wide and heavy, and made of steel, like the stairwell in the building where his office was.

As he came to the foot of the staircase he saw there was an ancient freight elevator next to it. He'd seen them in old industrial buildings, and they were wide enough to carry a lot of stuff, but the mechanism was little more than a platform with a motor attached. This one was about six feet square and had no cabin, no walls or roof, just a low wooden gate at the front of the platform. Slater stepped close to the gate and cast his light around. An electric box was mounted at one side with the controls: three big buttons marked UP, DOWN, and STOP. The metal platform had some dust on it, but not much—this lift was still in use.

The tunnel was the only way in, Slater saw, looking around. It ended here at the stairs and the elevator, and the only way out, besides the way he'd come, was up. Tracing the steel posts upward with his light, he couldn't see the top, but just above his head the four concrete walls formed a shaft, with only enough room for the elevator and the stairs. Listening for a moment, there was only overwhelming silence. When he cast his light back along the tunnel, it looked the same as when he'd walked here, concrete walls fading into the void.

The stairs were solid, he found, treading on the bottom one, and he climbed to the first landing. It was about six feet up, he estimated, looking back down, and the next flight was the same length. The second landing faced the black void of the elevator shaft, with a steel mesh panel that ran between the newel posts, separating the stairwell from the shaft. In the wan light he studied the fixtures and their ancient flat-green paint. Definitely from another era, he knew, but he couldn't guess how old they were.

Walking up the zigzagging staircase, he was amazed again at how far it was—he counted ten half-flights to reach the top. It had to be over sixty feet from the bottom.

The top of the stairs were fronted by a few yards of concrete landing. At the other end, a low wooden gate stretched across the yawning blackness of the elevator shaft. In the wall between them was a lone door, painted flat gray, the color of the surrounding concrete. It wasn't very wide, about like Tato's fire door, but it looked heavy, likely made of steel. It had a pull handle but no latch or lock. Slater decided against heaving on it, and instead stood close to it and listened, but there was only dead silence.

Beside the doorway was a wall switch, he saw, positioned closer to the elevator shaft. The conduit from it ran overhead to a bulb protected by a wire cage, then continued beyond into the shaft. There were likely similar bulbs below to illuminate the stairs. The switch and the wiring looked a lot newer than the stairwell and the elevator equipment, but what really didn't make sense was the size of the door at the top. Nothing very large would fit through it, and that made the big freight capacity of the elevator useless. The only explanation was that the elevator predated the door, and there had once been something else up here—at the very least, a wider exit, like the loading dock in Tato's office.

Slater cast his light around for a last look, then trotted down the stairwell. At the bottom he looked at the elevator platform again, then stepped around under the stairs. In the anemic beam of his flashlight sat a dusty steamer trunk, made of some battered tan material and held together by tarnished brass fittings. The round hasp on the front was closed, with no key in the lock. When he tried it, it wasn't locked, and with a little force it came up, with a metallic shriek of protest.

When he lifted the trunk's lid, it was almost empty, save for a dusty bundle of fabric at the bottom. Glad that he was wearing gloves, he reached in and picked up the material. It was gray in this light, with a pattern of tiny brown leaves and flowers. It looked old. Setting his phone on the ground, he held out the fabric. It wasn't a garment, just a swatch of cloth. Under it was another, and he took it out too. It had torn edges and an irregular shape.

Under them, on the wooden bottom of the trunk, was a small scrap of paper, and he reached in to retrieve it, studying it in the light of his phone. Torn along the edge, one side was blank but the other bore an engraved image of a child, wearing a white tunic, holding up a garland, his face turned to the sky. The image was printed in a fine spidery pattern of green ink, meant to be hard to duplicate, like a banknote or an old stock certificate. At the bottom was printed LOS ANGELES, CALIFORNIA, and below that, TUNNEL 4, ROW 18, SEAT 6. It was an old-timey ticket to something. The name of the event must have been on the part that was torn off.

The only other thing in the trunk was a flat plastic box, about the size of his palm. It had been crushed, the case broken, exposing a green circuit board inside. A lone wire dangled from it. It was nowhere nearly as old as the trunk or the ticket stub, but still it looked ancient.

Setting the ticket stub on the ground, he aimed his phone at it, squeezing his eyes shut as he took the photo so that the flash wouldn't mess up his low-light vision. He checked the screen to make sure it was a clear image, then draped the two swatches of fabric on the trunk and photographed them too. He put the ticket stub back where he'd found it, then dropped the fabric on top and closed the trunk. He screwed his eyes shut and took a photo of it with the lid open, and then one with it closed, the hasp in place. The electronic device, whatever the hell it was, was coming with him, and he tucked it into his belt in the small of his back.

He aimed his light down the long tunnel and started walking. After a minute he switched it off and walked in the pitch blackness. The only sensory input was the sound of his boots crunching on the gritty concrete. Once in a while he'd stray off course, and his arm would brush the tunnel wall, and he'd correct his trajectory. He wasn't even sure if the tunnel was straight. It was strange to walk with no reference points, no vision. It felt like floating.

He almost walked into the big door at the end, stopping short as he caught sight of the faint light leaking in along the top. Pressing on it with his fingertips, he pushed it outward an inch or so, until he could see through the gap into the office, and stood for a moment, listening for activity. The only sound was the low hum of a machine somewhere, maybe the compressor in a refrigerator or the fan in a PC.

Rolling the door open, the room looked the same as when he'd left it, although the light from the high windows looked bright after his time in the darkness. He pushed the shelving unit far enough away from the opening to step out, then rolled the door closed, pushed the shelves back, and set the brakes on the wheels.

He'd been here long enough. Striding over to the door into the shop, he cracked it open. The room was still quiet, illuminated from the street. Pulling the door wide, he went to the alarm and rearmed it, then went out through the back room, closing the door to the shop and then locking the fire door with his key as he left. On the walk back to his car, he peeled off the black gloves and stuffed them into his hip pocket.

As he approached the corner, a car pulled up behind him and slowed, making his heart pound. The old-timey electronic device would be visible in the back of his pants, but there was nothing he could do about it now, and he kept walking. The car sped up again to make a right onto the boulevard. Just someone out late. It wasn't about him.

Slater glanced back at Tato's shop as he rounded the corner, to make sure no one was around, then strode to his car and climbed in. The broken device jabbed him in the spine as he sat, and he cursed and arched his back to retrieve it and toss it onto the floor on the passenger's side. Starting the engine, he flicked on his headlights and dropped it into gear, making a quick U-turn and heading back to the city.

What the hell was that tunnel for, and what was behind the door at the top of the stairs? Tato had more going on than the retail business and the penny-ante grifting.

Hustling up the stairs to his apartment, he set the broken device on the kitchen counter, examining it briefly for a logo or a part number, but found nothing. In the better light he saw that the housing was made of blue plastic with an opaque panel on one side. He was too exhausted to think clearly about it anymore, and dropped it, then grabbed a tumbler, pouring out his paltry ration of bourbon. As he slammed it he relished the burn, coughing as the heady vapor hit his nose. Leaving the empty tumbler in the kitchen, he went to the sofa, and kicked off his boots, and stretched out.

SEVEN

Sunlight streamed through the grimy windows when Slater woke. It was hot, and he was in his own bed, with all the sheets shoved to one side. He didn't remember coming to bed, but it didn't matter, as he was clear-headed today, without the stink of hangover in the air. Stretching, he luxuriated in it for a minute before he remembered it all—meeting the boyfriend, and the blackmailer, and prowling around under Raymond Hill.

Scrabbling for his phone on the bedside table, he checked the time. He needed to get moving—he had to deal with Hayk today.

Once he'd washed up he looked in the icebox. It shouldn't be a surprise that there was nothing more than the nothing that had been inside it yesterday, but he looked anyway. In the pantry cupboard he found a ripped-open box of granola bars and shook one out, with nuts and dark chocolate, and munched on it before he got dressed.

The unidentified device was still sitting on the counter, dirty blue plastic, one side of it crushed and cracked. The stray wire was cut cleanly at the end, he saw, with no connector, but the other end was soldered onto the circuit board inside. It was impossible even to date it, but he knew someone who could. He texted Svetlana:

Do you have time for me today?

In a kitchen drawer he found a paper bag, and stuffed the device into it, then went out to the hall, locking his door as he left. The drive to the office went fast, as traffic was light on Fridays in the summer, with school out and bureaucrats taking their long weekends. When he pulled into the lot across from his building, the attendant waved. They knew his car, and as long as he bought a pass every month, they never bothered to look at it. As he was crossing the street, his phone buzzed with a text from Svetlana:

I do nothing but work. You know where to find me.

Slater stepped through the handful of day laborers in the lobby and rode the elevator up to his floor. When he walked around to his office, there was a guy in front of it, standing there with his back to the closed door, his hands folded over his belt buckle the way police and military people did when they were standing guard without a weapon in hand. But this was no cop—a tight black tank top showed off gym musculature, and his unctuous black hair was slicked back. Colorful tats covered his arms and his chest.

"Step aside," Slater said as he approached.

"No one goes in there," he said, his accent perceptible when he pronounced the *r*.

"It's my office. I said step aside."

The guy planted a firm hand on his chest and shoved him backward.

"You shouldn't have done that," Slater said.

The guy had muscle, but gym rats and steroid pumpers always relied on it too much. The appearance of strength was enough to dissuade most people, but not Slater. Darting toward him, Slater punched him on the jaw, snapping his head. The guy got in a glancing right hook to Slater's upper arm, but before he had time to land another, Slater dick-punched him with a solid left.

The guy buckled around his crotch but lunged for him anyway, grabbing hold of Slater's boot as he hit the floor. He tried to pull him down, but Slater kicked him in the head with his other foot, and the guy let go, moaning and curling into a ball.

"Why do you make me do this to you?" Slater shouted, and kicked him in the ribs.

The guy writhed and yelped, and the office door flew open, revealing Max.

"What's going on?" Max demanded.

Slater forced himself to stop, forced himself to pull away, and took a step back. Max had on his dark-red suit. He usually wore it when he had bad news to deliver, or when he needed to collect on a bill.

"Who is this goon?" Slater said, breathing hard.

From behind Max, Hayk appeared, stepping past him into the hall. He was wearing a blue sport jacket over a plaid dress shirt, his gut hanging over his belt.

"Excuse me," he said to Max, and then eyed Slater, who was massaging his bicep. Looking to the guy on the floor, Hayk bent over him and shouted in whatever language the pair of them shared. The goon didn't shift from his fetal position, or even look up, but he waved a hand at Hayk, who lit into him with another stream of intense incomprehensible abuse.

Straightening up, Hayk eyed Slater, and spoke calmly. "I apologize for him. He's supposed to act like a professional."

"You go everywhere with the heavy?" Slater said, jutting his chin toward the guy on the ground.

Hayk shrugged. "Sometimes in business, one makes enemies."

"It happens in every business," Max said. "No way to avoid it. Let's sit down."

Nimble trumps bulk, Slater thought, stepping past the crumpled figure as he followed Max and Hayk into the office. This was why he didn't want to rat out Ram—if Hayk ever tracked him down, this goon would flatten him. Ram was soft enough that Hayk could even do it himself.

Stepping into his own office, Slater grabbed the paperwork from his desk drawer, then went into Max's office and pulled the extra chair to the side of the desk, so he was facing Hayk rather than sitting beside him.

"So what happened the other night?" Hayk said.

Slater handed him the sheet with the timeline. "As you suspected, she was meeting someone."

Hayk glanced at the paper but then eyed Slater. "A man?"

Wordlessly, Slater handed him the stack of eight-by-tens. Hayk studied the top one.

"Whose house is this?"

"It's a short-term rental in South Pasadena," Max said.

Hayk flipped to the next photo, and inhaled sharply. Looking closer, he muttered, "No."

It was a photo of Bella embracing Ram. Her eyes were closed, and Ram's head obscured their mouths, but what they were doing was unequivocal. Hayk flipped to the next photo.

"Oh, no," he cried, and looked at the next one. "My princess."

Hayk's face had turned red, and he screwed his eyes shut, stifling sobs, his shoulders heaving. After a moment, he inhaled sharply and got control of himself.

"Can I have some water," he said, "or maybe a coffee?"

"We don't have a sink in here, or a coffeemaker," Max said. "How about a belt of scotch?"

Hayk nodded and set the stack of photos on the desk, then rubbed his face with his big meaty hands.

He really was emotionally attached to that woman, Slater thought, watching him. It wasn't just that he was angry at the broken contract, or at being lied to. This kind of pain was raw, and ugly. Slater stifled a sigh. He hated window-shade jobs.

Max pulled a bottle from his bottom drawer, along with three glasses, and poured a shot for each of them. Max took a small sip of his, and Hayk took a mouthful, then downed it all. Slater slammed his too, enjoying the burn in his throat. This was the good stuff—it tasted woody and nutty and warm.

Hayk picked up the photos again and went through them. "Who is this asshole?"

"Slater wasn't able to identify him," Max said.

"You said it was a rental. So she didn't go to his house."

"Correct."

"I'll kill him," Hayk said.

"I don't think that's the appropriate response," Max said. "He might not even know she's married. You need to talk it through with Bella."

"There won't be any talking," Hayk said. "I'll let my lawyer do that."

"I'm sure it's hard to see it in this moment," Max said, "but keep in mind that everyone makes mistakes. It's part of being human."

"You're giving me New Age advice now?" Hayk said sharply. "You're going to sell me some crystals and a scented candle too? You don't get to defend her."

Max leaned back in his chair and swirled the amber contents of his tumbler. "You're right. I never even met her. I'm just saying you should sleep on it before you confront her with this. Talk to your lawyer."

Hayk looked at Slater. "Is that what you think too? That I'm supposed to forgive this?" He gestured to the stack of photos. "That I shouldn't dispose of the trash?"

"Lowlifes need to get tuned up sometimes, sure," Slater said. "Maybe this guy is a lowlife, or maybe he's just an idiot. Either way, he doesn't deserve the death penalty. No one is beyond redemption."

Hayk scoffed and waved dismissively, then scooped up the photos and the timeline and stuffed them into the manila envelope.

Looking to Max, he said, "What do I owe you?"

"Fifteen," Max said, and sat up.

Slater watched as Hayk pulled a fat bankroll from inside his jacket and peeled off fifteen C-notes. Max definitely knew how to make money at this. The extraction didn't perceivably reduce the girth of Hayk's roll. He tucked it away again and quickly riffled through the bills, then folded them lengthwise, set them on the desktop, and slid them toward Max.

Max dropped the cash in his top drawer, not bothering to count it, and by the time he'd closed the drawer again, Hayk was on his feet. He reached across the desk, waiting for Max to rise, and then shook hands with him. Turning to Slater, also on his feet now, Hayk held his gaze and gave him a firm handshake too. This meant they were done, Slater realized. It was Hayk's way of formally ending their dealings.

They followed Hayk as he stepped into the front office, clutching the envelope full of evidence.

"Don't kill anybody," Max said.

Hayk grunted and pulled open the door. The bodyguard was on his feet now, facing the office, his hands at his sides, balled into fists. He dropped his chin, and from beneath his heavy brow, locked eyes with Slater, murder in his gaze. Hayk said something to him that sounded abrupt and impatient. The guy didn't respond, but unclenched his hands and turned to follow Hayk toward the elevator.

"I hope he has that ape on a short leash," Max said, closing the door.

"I'm really glad he didn't ask for a follow-up to uncover the boyfriend's identity."

"Your friend Ram is lucky that we're not cut-throat enough to sell him out."

"At least he paid you," Slater said.

"That, he did. Do you want your cut?"

"Put it with the business cash."

Stepping into his office, Max said, "I'll make a note of it in the ledger."

Slater chuckled. "That'll make O'Dowd happy."

O'Dowd was their accountant, and she had been haranguing them to keep better books. Max would record the payment on the tattered envelope in the cash box in the safe, but Hayk had paid in cash—O'Dowd was never going to hear about it.

When it had been long enough for Hayk and his heavy to have cleared the building, Slater went down to the lobby, scanning the sidewalk and the parking lot for any sign of the guy in the black tank top, just in case he was hanging around in hope of a rematch. Climbing into the Thunderbird, he got the air blowing, then pulled into the street, headed for Glendale.

Parts of the suburban town had been tarted up in the last few decades, but Svetlana's workshop was on a backstreet that remained decidedly seedy. Pulling up in front of the run-down storefront, Slater eyed the heavy steel bars on the boarded-up windows and the onetime front entrance, wondering if that door even opened anymore.

Snatching up the paper bag with the broken electronic device in it, he walked around to the alley and the back door, pressing the bell and looking up into the camera lens aimed at him from high on the wall. The lock on the door snapped open. He stepped into the dark antechamber and stood with his arms at his sides. The scanner was silent—maybe it had no moving parts—but he could see some of the tech for it above his head, components and cables running across the ceiling. It was more fun in the old days, when Svetlana's morose lackey would come in and frisk him, groping his butt and his crotch as indifferently as if he were assessing overripe fruit at the supermarket.

Finally the inner door buzzed open, the scanner presumably having shown that he wasn't packing a heater. Inside Svetlana's gloomy workshop it smelled of machine oil and hot plastic. The workbench that ran around the walls was piled with a mess of tools and wire and electronic components. In the corner a dark-haired woman was hunched over a project.

She glanced up as Slater entered, then returned to her work without acknowledging him.

Svetlana was on the opposite side, her copious bulk perched on a stool. He didn't remember ever seeing her in a skirt before, but today, probably because of the heat, her legs were bare. The print dress she wore was a riot of bright yellow and orange with brown dots. Sunflowers, he realized, stepping closer.

"What have you brought me?" she said, swiveling toward him, her Russian accent flattening the vowels.

"So you saw it."

"On the scanner, yes." She gestured toward the computer screen on the bench in front of her. It showed a black-and-white rendering of a fuzzy human form—his form. At his waist was a bright rectangle highlighting the metal in his belt buckle, and nearby the jumble of his keys and his boxy phone, and off to one side a bright blob. The paper bag was invisible to the scanner, leaving the device seemingly floating just below his ghostly hand.

"How does my pancreas look?" Slater said, peering at the image.

Svetlana cackled. "I'd have to turn the power way up to see that."

"I don't actually know what this thing is," he said, handing her the bag. "That's my question for you."

Svetlana pulled out the broken plastic box and unspooled the dangling wire. "Time has not been kind to this machine."

"How old is it?"

"Let me look." She turned to her workbench and found a flat tool, then used it to deftly pop open the plastic housing, separating it into two halves. She studied the green circuit board under the desk lamp, then reached for a pair of eyeglasses with a jeweler's loupe attached to each lens, and put them on.

"Made in this country," she said, eyeing the board. "Circuits are fried. It will never function again." Finally she turned to look at him, dropping her chin to see over her glasses. "It's from the 1980s."

"So what is it?"

"I believe it's a movement sensor."

"To detect when a door is opened?"

"It's more complex than that." She waved him over. "Look at these."

Slater stepped closer and watched as she prodded the guts of the device with a mini screwdriver. Two short tracks each contained a ball bearing, and despite the damage to the case, they moved freely when she tapped them.

"It's also about tilt. The device would report on its angle. Watch the little ball." She held the case flat on her palm and tipped it slightly, and one of the bearings moved a hair. "It says, 'Now I'm at thirty degrees.'"

"Did it report that wirelessly?"

"It couldn't. There's no radio on the board. This wire sent the information. It was connected to a computer."

"Do you know what it was used for?"

Svetlana shrugged. "No idea. It would have many uses in industrial machinery. It's not something made for the home." She put the broken cover back on the device, then tucked it into the bag. He was glad that she didn't ask him where it had come from. But of course she wouldn't. She was far too professional to do that.

"I also need some tech," Slater said. "Like a radio beacon that I can put on a wall, and then find it from outside the building."

"This, I can do," she said. "Magnetic base, or glue?"

"It'll have to be glue."

Sliding off her stool, Svetlana stepped into the next room, closing the door behind her. While he waited, Slater looked around the dingy cluttered workroom and eyed the woman in the corner. She wielded a pointed tool over a mess of wire spotlighted under a desk lamp. Opening the paper bag, he looked at the broken sensor. It didn't feel like it had anything to do with Tato's secrets.

When Svetlana returned a minute later, a swirl of golden sunflowers, she had a beige plastic disk in hand. It looked like a smoke detector.

"Battery lasts about three days," she said. "This one is already charged. Here's the power switch." She pointed out the little slider on the side, then sat on her stool and turned to her computer. "I'll link it to your account."

"I can use my phone to find it?"

"You'll see it in my tracking app," she said. "It

uses Bluetooth frequencies. The software will tell you the strength of the signal as well as the direction. You have to be within about twenty meters."

"Excellent."

Svetlana picked up a pencil-shaped wand with a glowing red tip and flipped the device over. A label with a bar code was affixed to the plastic sheet protecting the sticky base, and when she waved the wand over it, her computer beeped. She typed for a moment and stared at the screen.

"It's connected," she said finally, and peeled the label with the bar code off the device, crumpling it as she handed him the disk.

"I wish consumer tech worked as well as your stuff does."

"If it did, it would cost as much as my machines cost."

"What do I owe you?"

"Three dollars," she said. "Includes regular customer discount."

Slater dug out his wad of cash and peeled off three C-notes, handing them to her.

"We can put a sticker on it from one of the alarm companies," she said, tucking the bills into her bra and then unself-consciously adjusting her ample bosoms. "It's less conspicuous that way."

"Let's leave it blank. I don't think anyone will notice it."

Svetlana pursed her lips and nodded. "Most people assume it's a smoke detector. There are so many of those around that they disappear into the background. Like doorknobs and electric sockets and light switches."

Slater asked her about some mutual acquaintances, and listened to her gossip about them for a minute, then said good-bye and waited for her to buzz him out through the doors. Walking around to his car, he checked the clock on his phone. He had time to go back to the office before he met Doris.

EIGHT

When Slater got in, Max was still at his desk, and he called out a greeting as he went to his own office and dropped into his chair. On his computer he pulled up satellite photos of Raymond Hill. It was densely built up, mostly with apartment buildings, some small, some massive. From these images it was impossible to guess where the top of those stairs was. He could only estimate how far he'd walked from Tato's shop, and nothing in the overhead view looked like it might conceal a hidden stairway.

There was a sharp knock at the door. Slater rose and stepped into the front office, where Max was already on his way to answer.

"You expecting someone?" Max said.

"Not me. Do you think it's Hayk's tattooed muscle-head back for round two?"

"He wouldn't have knocked."

Max flipped the deadbolt and pulled it open to reveal Doris, who flashed him a smile.

"You must be the other name on the door." She was dressed in a polo shirt and summery linen capris that emphasized her petite figure. Her dark hair, streaked with gray, was pulled back, and she had the straps of a thin olive-green backpack on her shoulders.

"You can call me Max," he said, and pulled it open wider.

"What are you doing here?" Slater demanded.

"I knew you had an office, but you never invited me to see it." She waved her arm. "The whole building is clothing factories. I thought I was in the wrong place."

"Come in," Max said, and closed the door.

Doris stepped past him and squeezed Slater's arm in greeting, then peered into Max's office, and went over to look into Slater's.

"It's compact, but it's cute."

"We like to think of it as functional," Max said.

"At least one of you has a window."

"That's my office." Max looked to Slater, furrowing his brow. "You never told me your sister was a model."

Slater scoffed and put his hands on his hips.

"Oh, I like this guy," Doris said, leaning toward Max and touching his arm. "I know it's a snow job, fella, but I'll take it anyway. The name is Doris. I'm his mother."

"I can't believe that," Max said. "You had him when you were six?"

Doris giggled and cocked her head. "I can tell you have a way with women."

Slater frowned. "Stop flirting with him."

"I'm not flirting," she said lightly, "but I also don't see a ring on that finger."

"Unfortunately, I do have a sweetheart," Max said, absently massaging a palm with his thumb.

"Then I know you have your hands full," she said, "what with a woman and working with my son."

"He's pretty easy to get along with. Although the vegan thing can get a little annoying around suppertime."

"Hey," Slater said sharply.

"I've had years to learn how to work around it," she said, waving a hand.

"When did it start?"

"He never told you?" she said, raising her eyebrows.

"Quit gossiping about me," Slater demanded. "I'm standing right here."

Max grinned and held up a hand. "I want to hear this."

"He was fifteen," Doris said. "I had to send him to a ranch in Wyoming. One of those places where the hands-on work is supposed to supplant the bad behavior."

"It was basically juvie," Slater said, "with hard labor."

Doris frowned. "It was a little slice of arcadia. Rustic, and cozy, and in the most beautiful setting you've ever seen."

"Why did a ranch turn him vegan?" Max said.

"I never got the full details." She leaned closer, as if sharing a confidence. "I think it was about the horses. He had to work with them every day."

"You got to ride horses?" Max said, frowning at him. "It sounds like summer camp."

Slater huffed impatiently. "It's not as much fun as you think. It's hard work to learn how to ride. My back and my legs ached all the time, and I always smelled like a horse."

"I never knew that about you."

He threw up his hands. "My dark past."

"I think it was good for you," Doris said, and to Max: "When he got back, he wouldn't touch any animal products."

"What are horses like?" Max said.

"They're a lot like people. They have their own personalities. There's lazy ones, and laid-back ones. Some are nervous, or upbeat, or extroverted." He eyed Doris and raised his eyebrows. "Some are pushy and nosy."

Doris waved dismissively. "Arrest me for taking an interest in your life."

"We're trying to run a business here, woman. Max has work to do. He can't be standing around gossiping like he's at a cocktail party."

Doris turned to Max. "That's me busted. It was nice to meet you, Max."

He made a little bow. "The pleasure was mine, and it was no imposition at all. I hope you'll drop by again when you're in the neighborhood."

Slater shot him a look, resisting the urge to slap that grin off his face.

"Lunch," he said, and waved Doris out the door.

They waited for the elevator with a wiry guy carrying a heavy garment bag on his shoulder. Slater instinctively positioned himself between him and Doris. It was unlikely that he'd try anything with her, but she was slight, and if he swung that bag around without looking, he could send her flying.

"Do you still want to go to that Italian place?" Slater said.

"Unless there's something closer. We can walk."

"It's too far. We'll drive. Where did you park?"

"I took the metro."

As the elevator door opened, Slater gestured for the porter to go in ahead of them, then stood between him and Doris as they rode down to the lobby. In the parking lot, Slater unlocked the Thunderbird's passenger door and held it open for her, then walked around to the driver's side.

"Max seems nice," Doris said, once he'd pulled into the traffic.

"He's a bruiser," Slater said, glancing in the mirror as he changed lanes. "But he's good at what he does, and I know I can trust him with my life."

A few blocks away, in the Historic Core, Slater found a meter near the restaurant, then waited for Doris to climb out before he locked the doors, and walked with her toward the entrance.

"Have you been here before?" he asked, following Doris inside and waiting with her at the host's desk.

"A girlfriend told me about it."

"Does she work at Fort Ronnie?"

"Now, how did you know that?" she said, eyeing him sidelong.

"It's right up the block." He gestured in the direction of the hulking state office building. "There must be a thousand bureaucrats in there."

The host stepped up and flashed a smile, then led them out into the courtyard, to a table near the back. It was smart to use the *Hedera* to shade the space from the street and the parking lot next door, Slater thought, assessing the leafy green walls. It would grow on anything, in this case a chain-link fence, and it kept the space cooler. Technically that stuff was an invasive in Cali, but in Downtown it wasn't going to cause any trouble or try to strangle anyone's trees, because there weren't any.

They flipped through the menu and ordered, and once the waiter had stepped away, Doris shifted in her chair and furrowed her brow. Slater knew that look. She was about to get into it.

"So why were you up in front of a judge?"

He sighed. "I got into a scuffle, and I punched the wrong guy." He gave her the abbreviated version, omitting the part about hiring Max's sleazy lawyer friend Margo to stand up with him, and having the woman prep him on how to act and sound contrite, and then wearing a suit.

"At least you're not locked up," Doris said, absorbing it all. "You know you're smarter than this."

"I know. I didn't expect to get caught."

"That's not what I mean."

"So why are you gossiping about me with Andy and Conrad?"

"Because you never tell me what's going on."

Slater folded his arms. "I'm a grown man. I don't need my mother supervising my legal problems."

"All that therapy, and you're still so angry," she said, and shook her head.

Slater closed his eyes for a second, willing himself to be calm. He couldn't fool her. Not like most people. He took a deep breath.

"I made a mistake," he said. "I'm paying for it with eight weeks of anger-management classes."

"Is there book work?"

"Some writing. It's organized more like a group therapy session."

"It sounds easier than what we used to do when I was teaching," she said, pausing as the waiter set glasses of ice water on the table. "We'd bore the aggression out of them."

"With me, you just made sure I never had a minute to myself. Shrinks and wrestling team and out-of-state equestrian penitentiary."

Doris chuckled. "It was a ranch, and it cost a fortune." She watched him for a moment. "I kept you out of trouble most of the time."

He nodded. "Most of the time."

Once they'd eaten, Doris insisted on paying, and afterward Slater rose as she tucked her credit card into her backpack.

"The next time you're in my neighborhood," she said, rising and slinging her bag onto her shoulder, "you should drop by. That tree out front has bugs on it."

"The ironwood?"

"It's the one in the front yard. The evergreen with the little white flowers."

"What kind of bugs?" he demanded.

"I don't know. Little ones."

"Why didn't you tell me?"

"You weren't taking my calls."

"I need to look at it," he said flatly. "Now."

"Great. You can drive me home."

They walked back to the Thunderbird, and he opened the door for her, and held it until she climbed in. Slater got on the 110 and headed for Mount Washington, forcing himself to drive as calmly as he could because Doris was in the car—changing lanes way early, not weaving around the sloths, braking gently. Doris gossiped about her family, and told him a story about an out-of-town cousin.

Pulling into the driveway at Doris's house, he was relieved to see that her stupid boyfriend Albert's stupid Boxster wasn't here.

As if she'd read his mind, Doris said, "Albert must still be at his practice."

"Is that old quack still alive?" Slater said, shifting into Park.

"He's my age."

"He's a chiseler."

Doris scoffed. "Albert has more money than I do."

They climbed out, and Slater strode over to the ironwood. Doris stood back and folded her arms as he looked it over.

"It's not a bad infestation," he said finally. "I'm

glad you noticed. We caught it in time."

"What's the fix?"

"It needs to be sprayed. I'll go get something now."

"Nothing too toxic, I hope."

"It's a plant extract that the bugs don't like. It won't hurt the tree, or you—or Albert, unfortunately."

Climbing into the Thunderbird while Doris went into the house, Slater drove to a garden store and bought a sprayer of neem oil. When he got back to Doris's place, he pulled out the garden hose and attached it to the container. This stuff was so innocuous he didn't even need to wear gloves.

He spent some time spraying the ironwood, soaking the bark and the leaves until the container was empty. When he put the hose away again, it was close to sundown, with long shadows stretching over the neighborhood. He went to the front door and stuck his head in.

"I'm leaving," he said.

"How's the tree?"

"I'm pretty sure it'll survive."

"That's very good news."

"It would be a shame to see it die," he said, glancing back at it. "It worked so hard to grow here. All it wants to do is live."

"My sensitive son," she said, and leaned in to draw him into a hug. When she pulled away again, he saw that there were tears in her eyes. "I can't lose you."

Slater waved a hand. "No pressure, though."

"Most people wouldn't consider it a monumental request. Don't get yourself thrown in jail, and don't get yourself killed. You're all I've got in the world."

"You've got plenty in your life. All I do is stir up tsuris." He gestured at the house. "This place is paid for, and you've got your pension, and your Buick is running."

"All that is meaningless without people."

"I'll never understand you, woman."

She squeezed his arm. "Thanks for saving the ironwood."

Slater leaned down to kiss her. "Love you."

Climbing into his car, he felt a lump in his throat. He shouldn't even deal with it, all her guilt and drama, her absurd unreasonable expectations. If she only knew half the things he did. She'd give up on him, and stop calling, and stop gossiping.

Starting the engine, he got the air blowing. It felt good on his damp jeans, and soon the car smelled of neem oil. On his phone he checked on Ram's location. His car was in South Pas—near that rental house. On the same damn block. Was he with Bella again? If that's what was happening, the guy was an idiot, and he was definitely putting his life at risk. Maybe he was ending it with her, Slater reasoned. Just seeing her one last time, acting civilized by doing it in person.

South Pas was really close to here, right across the Arroyo. Flicking on his headlights, Slater backed into the street and drove fast to that part of town, pulling up a few minutes later across from the house. "Idiot," he muttered under his breath, seeing Bella's Bentley in the driveway, just like it had been the other night. Ram's Ranger was nearby, on the street in front of the next house. Slater parked farther up the block, then reached into the backseat for his blue ball cap.

It was still twilight, but it was dark enough for him to walk unnoticed past Bella's car, up to the gate across the driveway. He heaved himself up and climbed over it, ignoring the motion-sensor floodlight when it came on, and strode back to the boxed podocarps along the fence.

He didn't even have to wait to see them. The bedroom shades were up, the glass slid fully open, the room lights blazing. From his vantage point the pair of them were visible, but only from the chest up. It didn't look like a breakup—both of them had their shirts off. Ram was ravishing her neck, and Bella was moaning with pleasure, tossing her hair around.

He watched them for a minute, then decided he'd seen enough, and went back down the driveway. Once he was behind the wheel of the Thunderbird, he ditched the ball cap in the backseat and then adjusted the mirrors so he could keep an eye on the house.

It took a while. The sky was completely dark by the time the pair of them appeared in the driveway. Slater slouched lower in his seat, watching as Ram put his hands on Bella's neck, kissing her tenderly before she pulled open the car door. She beamed at him, and flipped her hair as she climbed in. Obviously Hayk hadn't dropped the bomb on her yet. For now she was still driving that car, still carefree, still a princess.

Ram walked to his vehicle and climbed in, revving the engine before he popped it into gear and drove away, soon followed by Bella. Slater watched the taillights round the corner. The guy was a fool for flaunting it like that. He knew Hayk could come after him, and he knew Hayk was trouble.

Maybe there was another reason Ram was doing this. Sheer stupidity wasn't uncommon, but Ram definitely wasn't naive—he was running a business, and probably fleecing his clients, which required some awareness of how the world functioned. Maybe he was profiting from her—getting paid for his time, or even blackmailing her himself.

Slater started the engine, then pulled into the street and headed for Raymond Hill. It wasn't that late, but Tato's shipping store was dark, and all the shops in the row were closed. At the end of the block he turned onto the boulevard and parked, then killed the headlights and the engine. As he climbed out, he tucked Svetlana's beacon into the small of his back, under his belt.

The ghost key to Tato's fire door was still in his front pocket, and he let himself in, crossing the office in the semidarkness to the door into the shop, where he punched the code into the green-glowing keypad to deactivate the alarm and silence its insistent beeping.

Back in the office, he pulled the wire shelving unit away from the heavy rolling door, then slid it open and stepped inside, moved the shelves back into place, and rolled the door closed again. He turned on the flashlight on his phone, then tapped at the screen to find the timer, and started it running. Aiming the light into the void, he set off.

It was completely dark and silent, just as it had been last night, and the wan lamp illuminated just a few feet ahead of him. Eventually the staircase and the open elevator shaft came into view. As he reached the foot of the stairs, he stopped the timer. Almost two and a half minutes. Knowing how fast most people walked, he thumb-typed a quick calculation—the tunnel was about seven hundred feet long. He could look at a map again to estimate where the top of this shaft was, but using Svetlana's beacon would remove any uncertainty.

He started climbing the stairs, zigzagging from the concrete wall at one landing to the dark gaping elevator shaft beyond the rail at the next. By the time he reached the top landing, he was breathing hard. With the light of his phone he examined the door. The walls around it were plain concrete, so no matter where he put the beacon, it would stand out. He dusted off a patch of wall as high as he could reach above the door frame, then pulled the beacon out of his belt.

Juggling his phone for light, he found the power switch and clicked it on, then peeled off the plastic sheet protecting the sticky base. The glue looked brown and oily, and had a faint chemical odor, far gnarlier than a consumer product. Svetlana worked in the shadows, off the books—everything she did was illicit. For all he knew this was some toxic Soviet-era epoxy. Careful not to let it touch his skin, he reached up and attached the device to the wall, pressing on it for a minute to make sure it adhered. He stepped back and cast his light upward. The beige disk stood out in this little concrete box, but it was a few feet away from the lone overhead bulb, so hopefully it wouldn't be noticed for a while.

Once he'd trotted back down the stairs, he eyed the steamer trunk again, and saw there was more scrap lumber here, in a small pile along the wall a few feet from it, still under the stairwell. Long disused, it was covered in a layer of dust.

He got his bearings in the tunnel again and started to walk, then killed the light and tucked his phone away, correcting his course whenever he strayed too close to the side. Each time it was the wall on his right that he brushed against. Either the tunnel had a slight curve to the left, or his body naturally drifted to the right.

At the big rolling door he paused to listen before he slid it open, then repositioned the shelves, and went into the shop to arm the alarm. Locking the fire door behind him and tucking the key into his front pocket, he went out to the street, glancing around to make sure he hadn't been noticed.

Once he was in his car, he looked at the map on his phone. Seven hundred feet from Tato's shop put the top of the shaft right in the middle of the densely built hilltop. That doorway could be anywhere along a wide arc. Starting the engine, he drove up into the warren of postwar apartments and cruised the quiet streets. It was an old neighborhood, with mature trees that obscured the backyards. On the block where the map showed he was at the dead center of the hilltop, he pulled over and parked.

On his phone he launched Svetlana's tracking app. It took a minute to figure out how to look for the beacon, wading through the clunky interface, with its mishmash of Cyrillic and broken English, but eventually he found it. The screen that came up for the beacon was plain black, with "нет сигнала" plastered across it, whatever that meant. He held up the phone and rolled down his side window. Nothing happened for a moment, but then the screen flickered to blue and said -90 for a few seconds, then the English word WEAKNESS, and then the black screen with the Cyrillic words again.

This was great news—it was working, and the beacon was within range. He just needed to get closer. Climbing out of the car, he walked up the block, keeping one eye on his phone. The blue screen didn't appear again, so he crossed the street and walked back toward his car, and then past it. This time he got higher numbers: -82, then -76. At that point a red arrow appeared at the top of the screen, urging him forward. It shifted position, pointing left, but then the screen went black again, "нет сигнала."

Slater turned left and walked up the cross street, in the last direction the red arrow had indicated, holding his phone in front of him. The signal kept cutting in and out, with the blue screen visible for a few seconds at a time, but he never got the arrow again. The highest number that came up, for a brief moment, was −60, accompanied by a green screen and IMPROVEMENT. Like what a grade-school teacher would write on a report card. He should sit down with Svetlana sometime and give her a crash course in clear language for her interface.

Circling the block, and with a couple of fruitless excursions down other streets, he decided the beacon had to be in one of three buildings. But even walking close to them on the sidewalk, slowing to a casual stroll, the signal wasn't consistent, cutting in and out. Staring at the screen, he huffed in frustration. He'd expected this to be easier.

One of the structures he'd identified was a sprawling house, rather than an apartment building like the others on the block, although it looked like it dated to the same era. He stepped onto the front walk, looking over the place, half watching his phone. The tracking app was ambivalent, turning blue for a moment and then losing the signal.

From the front stoop of the building next door, a few yards away, a woman called to him: "Can I help you?"

He'd noticed her earlier, lounging in the shadows, her face intermittently illuminated by the blue glow of a phone screen, her natty hair bundled up with an orange ribbon. Few of these old apartments would have been retrofitted with air-conditioning, and it was a lot cooler outdoors at this hour. It also made sense that she'd wonder what he was up to, as he'd walked past her building several times.

"I lost my cat," Slater said.

"Where do you live?"

"Over there." He gestured vaguely. "In the next block."

"Cats never go farther than three hundred yards."

"Who knew?"

Slater looked at the house again. A light came on behind the curtains in one of the ground-floor rooms. Someone was home—he saw movement, a body passing between the lamp and the window.

He could feel the neighbor's eyes still on him, her interest in him palpable. It was too suspicious to be skulking around here in the dark, he decided. It would have to wait until daylight. Before he could turn to leave, the woman called to him again.

"What's your cat's name?"

"Harold," Slater said. "He's black with white feet. Green eyes."

"Give me your phone number. If I see Harold out here, I'll call you."

"He might be back at my apartment by now," Slater said. "I left the window open for him. If he's not, I'll put up some posters in the morning."

He walked back toward his car, glad that it was parked out of view of the woman's stoop, and climbed in. Firing up the engine, he drove down from Raymond Hill and got on the freeway, headed to his apartment.

NINE

Once he'd nosed the Thunderbird into his garage and waited for the door to roll down, Slater trotted up the stairs.

The fifth of bourbon sat on the kitchen counter, glowing and warm and inviting, more reliable than any man would ever be, waiting there patiently for him. But not yet. He pulled off his boots and stretched out in his recliner. Ram had sent a text, he saw:

> Can't get the thought of your weenie out of my head.
> I want to smoke you.

The guy was a sex maniac—Slater had seen him just a few hours ago with a woman. Some people really didn't care about gender, and went for whoever, but he'd also known people who needed the extremes, needed to get with men and women concurrently. That felt like what Ram was doing. Who he slept with didn't matter, but he was reckless, and Slater couldn't completely parse what he was up to, what his motivations were. No way was he going to sleep with him again.

Setting the phone face-down on his belly, he thought about Andy. He'd once said he thought Slater was a sex addict. Was that how Andy thought about him—the way he saw Ram right now? Reckless and out of control?

Slater scoffed at the memory. The very idea was absurd. He was judicious about who he slept with, and he wasn't obsessed, or all intense about it, like Ram was. He'd even forgone the applejack tonight because a hookup was part of the plan. But that was routine, not some pathology. It was Friday night, and it was early, and he'd been working—he deserved sex.

Lifting his phone, he opened the hookup app and scrolled through the dick pics and torsos and photos of other body parts. A message popped up from a guy with perfectly ripped abs and massive pecs:

Want to party? I gots the means.

The photo was tantalizing, but Slater swiped him away. The guy clearly hadn't read Slater's brief profile, which clearly stated "No drugs." The last thing he needed was to be managing some unpredictable tweaker.

He paused at the head shot of a guy with a sweet smile and a high forehead, not too vain to wear his glasses in his hookup photo. There were no photos of him below the shoulders, which meant he might be the type who'd want to chitchat and waste time and go on a coffee date first. But it was worth a shot. Slater messaged him:

Fuck me. My place only.

Setting the phone down and closing his eyes for a minute, he started when the phone buzzed with the guy's response:

You certainly don't waste any time. Where are you?

Slater thumb-typed his address, and added:

Take a ride-share. There's nowhere to park.

Pushing himself up out of the recliner, he went into his bedroom and changed into a tight white T-shirt that showed off his body, then spent a minute snatching up his laundry, and dumped it in the bottom of his closet.

A knock sounded at the door, and Slater went to pull it open. The guy looked exactly like his photo—the same eyeglasses, the wavy black hair, the clean-shaven jaw.

He flashed a smile. "You're really here. I almost didn't come up."

"I know it's a little grungy," Slater said, and beckoned him in.

"I couldn't really see the neighborhood in the dark," he said, and stepped inside, surveying the room. "Or did you mean your apartment? Good thing I'm here for you and not the decor."

"What's your name, son?" Slater said as he closed the door.

"It's Ira." He turned back to him, a wry grin on his face. "Did you just call me 'son'? I'm probably older than you are."

"And feisty, I'm thinking."

Ignoring that, Ira looked him over. "You have a great body."

"Let me show you more of it." Slater led him into the bedroom, then stood close to Ira and met his mouth, his hands on his shoulders. Ira sighed with pleasure as Slater mouthed his jaw and his neck.

Ira ran his hands over Slater's butt, then grabbed his belt and pressed into him.

"You're hard," he said, almost as if that were a surprise.

Slater pulled back and started to unbutton the guy's shirt, then pushed it off his shoulders. Even though he didn't look like a blue-collar type, he had tan lines at his neck and on his biceps. Slater sat on the edge of his futon and kissed Ira's soft belly paunch, then undid his belt buckle and his fly, taking him into his mouth.

Ira went with it, getting harder, and groaned, but then put a hand on Slater's head to stop him.

"Slow down, cowboy."

Slater sat back to pull off his T-shirt and his jeans, and watched as Ira set his eyeglasses on the bedside table, then climbed on the futon, gently pushing Slater back. He maneuvered himself on top of Slater, then leaned in to his mouth, exploring with his tongue. His skin felt warm and perfect as Slater ran his hands over it.

Ira leaned close to Slater's ear. "Do you want to fuck me?"

Slater chuckled and shifted to the side of the bed, where he grabbed a condom and unwrapped it.

"Let me," Ira said, and rolled it on for him, frowning in concentration, then kissed him again, squeezing his cock.

Slater moved closer, massaging his fingers between his legs, then inside him, eliciting a gasp. Grabbing his thighs, he pushed his way into him, gently at first, then thrusting deeper. Ira folded his hands behind his head and watched him, his gaze intent. Slater met his eye. The look on his face heightened the rush, and a moment later he came.

Pulling back, Slater stretched out beside him, wrapping one arm around Ira's neck, his other hand on his cock, and mouthed his ear, and his jaw, stroking him. When Ira came, he yelped, arching his back.

Spent, Slater rolled away and covered his eyes with his arm, his breath gradually slowing.

"I'm so content right now," Ira said.

His voice pulled Slater back to wakefulness, and he lifted his arm to look at his profile in the low light.

"Are you Israeli?" Slater said.

"How did you know that?"

"Your name. Plus you look like half my mother's Ashkenazi relatives."

"You're Jewish."

"You sound surprised," Slater said flatly.

"I guess I shouldn't be."

"What are you doing in this neighborhood?"

"Why wouldn't I be?"

"It's kind of rough. I usually see the Israelis around Fairfax."

"I'm staying downtown," Ira said. "I didn't really want to invite anyone into my hotel room."

"That's smart. There's a ton of homeless people around there. You'd have an overnight guest whether you wanted one or not." Slater put his arm over his eyes again.

"Have you been to Israel?"

"A long time ago. One of those discovery trips for young people."

Ira caressed his chest. Slater could almost hear the wheels turning. It usually happened with Jewish women, not the guys—somehow they figured out that aspect of his ethnicity, and then they tried to get with him.

"Did you like it there?" Ira said.

"I remember I liked that people were direct. No bullshit, no games."

"Interesting. Maybe you'll come back some day."

"Maybe," Slater said, and shifted onto his side, willing sleep to overcome him.

Sometime later, Ira woke him, his hand on Slater's arm. "I have to go."

"Just twist the deadbolt," Slater mumbled, his tongue thick.

"Can I get your phone number, or your email?"

Slater sat up and looked around for his jeans. He scooped them up and fished a business card out of the hip pocket. Ira was already dressed, he saw, as he handed it to him.

"You're in insurance," Ira said, scanning the card. "I thought it would be something less mundane."

"I'm not a desk jockey, if that's what you mean. I work in the field."

Ira chuckled and pocketed the card, then went to the front door, pausing for a perfunctory kiss before he left.

Once Slater had set the lock again, he found a tumbler and poured out his miserly ration of bourbon, then slammed it, coughing as it burned on the way down, and went back to bed.

TEN

It was early when Slater woke, and sweaty hot already, the sun streaming in the windows. He felt clear-headed, like he hadn't had much to drink. That was a relief.

Once he'd washed up, he found an ancient little four-pack of saltines in the pantry, munching on them as he went to get dressed. Despite the heat, he pulled on a white undershirt and then a heavy dark work shirt with long sleeves—it was the look he'd need today.

Trotting down to his garage, he lifted a leaf rake from the wall rack and put it in the trunk of the Thunderbird, along with a broad-brimmed hat made of woven palm straw, and from the armored cabinet, one of the cameras he'd bought from the Russians. Svetlana made a couple of different versions of her stealthy wireless camera, hidden in clocks and tchotchkes and lamps, and like the radio beacon, this one was disguised as a smoke detector.

He backed out of the garage and drove to Raymond Hill, where he parked half a block from the big house he'd stood in front of last night. Opening the trunk, he donned the straw hat and flipped the broad brim down to conceal his face, then grabbed the rake. There was a patch of grass beside that house, and if he looked like a gardener, he could get close to it without arousing suspicion.

Slater walked over to the lawn and stood there, close to the house, the rake handle resting in the crook of his arm, and pulled out his phone. Svetlana's app showed that the beacon was still broadcasting its signal, but it was weak, displaying the blue screen with –72, then the empty black screen with the abstruse Cyrillic message, then –64.

Lifting the rake, he walked around behind the house, and stood at the wooden fence separating it from the building next door. The signal seemed stronger for a moment, –60, but not strong enough for the directional arrow to appear. Walking slowly, he paralleled the fence, but the signal disappeared again.

It was frustrating. Turning back toward the house, he walked along the side of it, back to the patch of lawn out front, and stepped closer to the apartment building next door. The readout said –74. It seemed strongest near the house, but it still wasn't strong enough to directionalize. Was the top of that shaft right below his feet, connected to somebody's basement? Doubtful, he decided, watching the screen. Basements were rare in LA—lots of places had tar deposits not far down, so it was risky to dig very deep, and the mild weather meant water heaters could sit outside.

Focused on the changing numbers on the screen, and with his straw hat obscuring his peripheral vision, he didn't see the guy approach until he was almost on top of him. With Slater's dark Latin features, it was usually safe to assume that no one would question him or even look twice when he was dressed like a gardener. But this guy really was a gardener, judging from his heavy work clothes. Sweat beaded his sun-darkened forehead, and he carried a pair of gloves in one hand. As he marched up, he said something terse in Spanish.

"No comprendo." Slater shifted his hat up on his head and met his eye.

"Did Jim hire you?" he demanded, not missing a beat.

"I'm not actually working on the yard."

"So that's just for decoration?" he said, pointing to the rake.

"Kind of," Slater said, and glanced over his shoulder, then leaned closer and lowered his voice. "I'm doing surveillance."

His eyebrows shot up. "On this place?"

"I'm not sure. It might be that one, or the building behind it."

The guy's face softened, and he matched Slater's confidential tone. "Who are you looking for?"

"I followed a suspect to this block, but I didn't see which place he went into."

"Someone bad?"

Slater nodded and held his gaze. "Real bad."

"Like murder?"

"I can't really talk about it."

"Who are you, anyway? Police?"

"Not a cop." Slater dug in his pants pocket and palmed a twenty, making sure the guy got a glimpse of what it was, then held out his hand. "The name is Andrew Jackson."

The guy met his palm and took the concealed bill, not looking at it, and tucked it into his front pocket. "Do you need a hand? I'm going to be working on the grass for a while, and then there's the pruning. What does the guy look like?"

"Just act like I'm supposed to be here. And give me some space."

"Fine—I'll stay out of your way. I thought you were trying to poach my contract."

"Which yard are you working on?"

"These three," he said, pointing them out, "and two across the street."

"Nice work on those *Ceanothus*," Slater said. "People forget to water them when it gets this hot."

"They mostly take care of themselves, but they do a lot better with a little attention."

"Good man. You don't do this house?"

"It's not my contract. I work up to the property line."

Slater followed his arm as he pointed it out. There was no fence, and the lawn was contiguous to the apartment building next door, where the woman had been lounging last night and advising him about his nonexistent cat. But he could see where the boundary was, as the grass closer to the house had been mowed recently, and unlike this guy's territory, it hadn't been properly fertilized or reseeded in years.

"About that camellia," Slater said, nodding to the tree in front of the apartment building. "The roots need aerating. The soil under it is like concrete."

"Yeah, I've been meaning to get to that."

"Do you mind if I work on it while I'm here? I'll be able to blend in."

The guy laughed. "Free labor—why would I say no to that?"

"Have you got a spade?"

"Sure. Have you done this before? Camellias have shallow roots."

"I know what I'm doing."

He walked toward the street, where his truck was parked, and soon returned with the tool, handing it to Slater. "Use the hose, if you want," he said, gesturing to where it lay coiled in a pile beside the apartment building. "It's ready to go."

If Slater wasn't going to be able to pinpoint the location of the beacon, at least his best guess was that it was somewhere in or under that sprawling old house. He'd planned to mount the illicit camera in the lobby of the building where he found the beacon, but he couldn't very well walk into someone's house and do that. Instead he'd have to watch the place, see who lived there, and come up with another plan.

Strolling over to the camellia, he positioned

himself where he could keep an eye on the house while he dug around the roots, forcing the spade into the hard earth with his boot and breaking up the surface. As he used the blade to smash the displaced clods, a little blue square turned up in the dirt. He paused to pick it up, turning it over in his hand. It was a ceramic tile, glazed a shiny dark-blue on one side, unfinished on the other, and smaller than his palm. Tossing it back on the ground, he eyed the house and continued digging.

The front door of the house swung open, and a guy headed up the walk toward the street, not even glancing at him. Slater watched him from under the broad brim of his hat, absently scraping at the dirt with the spade. He was in his twenties and had a trim beard, his hair in a pomp. Crossing the street, he climbed into a red Prius and drove away.

Slater moved around the base of the camellia, breaking up the earth, and soon found another blue tile, identical to the first one. Remnants of the long-gone hotel that had once been here, maybe, brought to the surface by the expanding roots of the tree. It could be from a kitchen or a bathroom or a swimming pool.

Someone in the house opened the curtains on one of the ground-floor rooms. It was hard to see inside from here, but he could get closer. Before he made his move, a woman appeared, walking from the street up to the front door of the house. She was young too, her hair in dreads, and wore a billowy green dashiki. At the door she didn't bother to use a key, pulling it open to step inside. That struck him as odd. Why wouldn't they keep it locked?

Slater planted the spade in the soil and went to the side of the apartment building to get the hose. From this vantage point he could see through the window into the house—a big living room with a TV flickering on the wall. The sofa in front of it was blood red, and the chair at the side was lime green. That was a lot of saturated color. Whoever decorated that place was either schizophrenic or nine years old.

Hauling the hose over to the camellia, he soaked the ground he'd dug up, and broke apart some more of the hard lumps once they loosened up from getting wet. Before he dragged it back, Slater drank from the end, savoring the cool water.

Once the hose was back where he'd found it, he pulled the spade out of the ground and carried it over to the back side of the house, walking along the window. The curtains were open here too, and he peered inside as he passed. It was hard to see the dark interior from the sunlit yard, but he could make out blond wooden furniture, a beige sofa and a dining table, and another TV mounted on the wall. Why would they have two TV rooms?

Then it struck him. The building wasn't a house; it just looked like one on the outside. These were separate apartments. Maybe it had once been a house and got subdivided. Either way, he was a freaking idiot for not figuring that out.

Back in the front yard, he picked up his rake and walked over to the gardener's truck, where he deposited the spade. The guy was across the street now with a leaf blower, and Slater nodded to him as he headed toward the Thunderbird. He ditched the rake in his trunk, along with his straw hat, and took the smoke-detector camera, concealing it in the back of his belt, pulling out the tail of his heavy shirt to cover it.

Apartment buildings were different than houses. Even if they knew the other tenants, people who lived there didn't know who was and wasn't supposed to be around. Walking up to the front door, he saw that it wasn't even latched. Inside was a hallway, with a flight of stairs leading up. There were no security cameras, he saw, glancing around as he walked past the staircase and down the hall.

He pulled out his phone and checked the signal from Svetlana's beacon. It was stronger here, reading "–38," and the red arrow had reappeared, pointing to the left. There was only one door on this side of the hall, and two on the other, each with a letter, A, B, and C, which meant three units on this floor. No mail room, no storage space, no stairs leading down. The beacon had to be in one of the apartments.

There were only two floors, judging from the exterior, so there were likely three more units upstairs, but the shaft with the freight elevator wouldn't be connected to the upper apartments; it had to be here. He turned around to face the front entrance, and the red arrow on Svetlana's app shifted to the right side of the screen, still pointing to the same side of the building, to unit C. By his reckoning, he hadn't looked into this apartment from the yard—the one with the colorful furniture and the other one with the blond wood had been on the opposite side of the structure. The red-arrow indicator was persistent now and unwavering in the direction it pointed.

Finally. Slater tucked the phone in his pants and pulled out the smoke-detector camera, stepping over in front of the door to apartment C as he looked for the tiny recessed power switch. Once he'd clicked it on with a fingernail, he peeled the protective sheet off the sticky base, then reached as high as he could on the wall opposite the doorway to attach the device, and pressed it into the wall for a few seconds to make sure it had a firm grip.

It wasn't conspicuous, he decided, stepping back to assess it. Like Svetlana said, those things were everywhere, so they melted into the background.

As he walked out the front door, Slater took a deep breath. The surveillance would be a lot easier now, with a camera that would update him via the cell network, and motion-sensitive software to record clips only when someone came or went.

Andy had texted earlier, and on the way back to his car, he pulled out his phone to read it:

I need your brawn.

That made him grin. It might be a sexual come-on, or he might want some furniture moved. Either way, Slater didn't mind. He liked spending time with Andy. He texted back:

On my way.

It was well after lunchtime, but the freeway wasn't too congested, and Slater was soon pulling up to the surface lot behind Andy's building. A sandwich board labeled FULL blocked the driveway, so he cruised past and found a street space around the corner. Climbing out to feed the meter, he could hear loud music echoing off the neighborhood's high-rises. It must be a concert happening in the square.

Upstairs at Andy's door, he knocked and waited. When Andy pulled it open, he was wearing a T-shirt and boxer shorts, and flashed that sweet smile. Following him inside, Slater saw that one of his multipaned windows was propped open. It faced the square, and Slater went over to look out. There was a stage set up on the big lawn, with a crowd gathered in front of it. At center stage the vocalist wore a bright-red dress.

"I like this band," Slater said.

"Is it live?" Andy dropped onto his little electric scooter, sitting sideways, resting one arm on its handlebars.

"It's a concert. I couldn't get parking."

"It sounds like *ranchera* music. I didn't … know you were a fan."

"Their sound is based on *cumbia,* but they modernized it. And why aren't you a fan? This is the most LA band there is."

"I grew up in Orange … County."

"That's no excuse for having no taste," Slater said, glancing back to shoot him a look.

"I like that it's upbeat. It sounds kind of sad too."

"But good sad, right? It makes you want to dance."

Andy sighed. "I wish I could walk … over there and dance with you."

Slater turned and stepped over to the scooter, squatting in front of him and putting his hands on Andy's thighs.

"I'd rather listen from here," he said, holding his gaze. "The company is better." Leaning in, he nuzzled Andy's belly through his shirt, then shifted up and kissed his neck.

Andy leaned into it for a minute, his hand on Slater's arm, but then straightened up. "Hey—you've got work to do."

Slater chuckled and sat back on his heels. "Your text was cryptic. What am I supposed to do?"

"I got a smart switch for the room lights." He gestured to a box on the table. "You have to install it."

Slater rose and studied the package. "Have you got a screwdriver?"

"In the drawer by the … sink."

The electric panel was beside the front door, and Slater went to pull it open. Someone had clearly labeled all the breakers, and he popped the one marked LIGHTS, then spent a few minutes installing the switch. When he reset the circuit and went back to hit the switch, it worked normally, turning the lights on and off.

"The mechanical part is done," he called to Andy. "From here it's IT stuff."

Andy looked at his phone. "What's it doing?"

"There's a little light that's blinking."

Andy spent a few minutes engrossed in his screen, then looked up and said, "Turn on the lights."

Slater frowned, about to retort that he wasn't the damn butler, but then the lights came on. He'd been talking to the software.

"You did it," Andy said.

Slater went to the kitchen drawers to put the screwdriver back. "You never asked me for help before."

"I figured you're getting all that free … sex from me. This is a small bit of payback."

"So that's how it is," Slater said, and stood in front of him, hands on his hips.

"You're not my … boyfriend, so I might as well monetize it."

"I'd do your handyman stuff even if I was your boyfriend."

"That's very generous of you."

Slater eyed him. "Do you want me to be your boyfriend?"

Andy stifled a sigh. "Slater, you're like the eight-year-old who eats the frosting off the cupcake and throws the rest in the dirt."

He frowned. "What's that supposed to mean?"

"You only want the good parts. It wouldn't work in a relationship. I'd want love."

"You think I'm incapable of love?" Slater demanded. "Is it because I sleep with other people sometimes? You do that too—don't even try to lie about it. I know you do."

"And it pisses you off, right? That's what … I'm talking about. It's a package deal. If you don't want the hard parts, and the … pain, you don't get the love either."

"You're starting to sound like a shrink. I spent enough time with those nutjobs in my youth."

"Don't get me wrong," Andy said, waving his arm. "I'm happy with … what we're doing."

Eyeing him, Slater worked to suppress his ire. "Such as free hardware installation."

"And you get access to all this." Andy gestured to his body.

"I do enjoy all that," he said, and took a breath. "Speaking of crazy people, I talked to Doris. You don't need to deal with her anymore."

"I see—so I can delete her from my … contacts, and block her number, because … you finally talked to her."

"That's a great idea," Slater said. "Although I can tell you're not really going to do that."

"Don't tell me who I can talk to," he said sharply, "and I won't … make any demands of you."

Slater was breathing hard. "Why do you do this to me?"

Andy rose, looking unsteady on his feet, and stood to face him, close enough that Slater could feel the warmth of his skin. "What do I do to you?"

"Pull me in two directions."

Resting his hands on Slater's neck, he leaned in to kiss him. Slater went with it, and got lost in it.

After a minute Andy pulled him toward the bed, where he sat and reached for Slater's belt buckle, working to loosen it, determined to get it open despite his impaired fine motor skills. Slater watched patiently, his dick tightening in his jeans. Once Andy got his fly open, Slater undressed, and then pulled Andy's shirt off. As it came free of his head, Andy grabbed Slater's arm and pulled him down on top of him. He pushed Andy's shorts down, exposing his already hard cock, and straddled him, then lowered his weight onto his wiry frame. He knew Andy enjoyed the sensation, and they lay that way for a while, sweaty and connected, listening to the band outside, Slater mouthing his ear and his neck.

Rolling to the side of the bed, Slater found the bottle of lube and then grabbed Andy's cock. Moving closer, he stroked them together as he nuzzled his jaw. Andy came first, and Slater, pressing his nose into Andy's hair, inhaling his scent, soon followed.

With his arm under Andy's neck, he stretched out, breathing hard, listening to Andy catch his breath.

"I have to go," Slater said finally.

"Just stay until it gets dark."

"I have work."

"Get me a towel first."

Slater rose and found one in the bathroom, tossing it to him before he got dressed and let himself out.

ELEVEN

On the street outside, Slater headed toward the parking lot he always used, but then remembered he'd left the Thunderbird at a meter, and changed course.

Most of the garment factories at his building were closed this late in the day, and when he walked in, no one was hanging around the lobby. Upstairs the office was dark, and he flicked on the lights, eyeing the bony statue of Rey Pascual and briefly poking his head into Max's office to make sure it was empty.

At his own desk, he pulled up the web interface for Svetlana's gear, and clicked on CAMERAS. A bubble came up that said "движение!" Slater sighed. What the hell did that mean? Some of her customers had to be Russian-speaking, or maybe even in Russia. That's probably where her programmers were too, considering their degree of

English-language proficiency. When he clicked on the bubble, it went away, revealing a list of four files. This, at least, he could understand—the camera he'd put up in that apartment building had already made four motion-triggered recordings.

The first clip was of a frizzy blond head approaching the apartment door, unlocking it with a key, and disappearing inside. The camera was too high to see her face clearly, and the wide-angle view distorted things, but when he rewound the video, he had a glimpse of her profile as she approached. He knew her—the Eastern European clerk from Tato's shipping store.

The next clip was the same woman, now wearing a windbreaker, even though it was a hot afternoon. In front of her she maneuvered a wheelie bag through the apartment door and into the hallway, lifting it by the tall handle to get the wheels over the sill. She glanced toward the front entrance and greeted someone. From the look on her face, it was someone she knew. A moment later a man walked into the frame. Like her, he looked to be in his twenties, and was dressed for the weather in a short-sleeved shirt and chinos. Lithe, and with a roman nose, his shaggy brown hair fell over his ears.

"You're leaving," he said.

"It's my time."

"Where are you going?"

"First to New Orleans. After that, I'm not sure."

"It will be hot there."

"Maybe, but it will be cheaper than here," she said.

"From LAX?"

"There's an airport in Burbank. It's closer. I change planes in Houston."

"Well, have fun," he said. "Maybe I'll see you someday in Europe."

The woman pulled the suitcase toward the front entrance and stepped out of frame, and the guy went into the apartment, and closed the door, and the clip ended.

They hadn't exchanged keys, which meant they both belonged in apartment C. But there had been no intimacy, and they were acting formal with each other, less familiar than roommates would. Slater watched the clip again. The guy's accent was like hers, Slavic, with flattened vowels. "In *yu*-rope," he'd said. It was the way Svetlana and her brother sounded. But these two were using English as their lingua franca, which meant they didn't share a native tongue.

The next clip was time-stamped an hour later. Slater watched as the guy left the apartment, locking it behind him. The last recording came not long after that, a brief depiction of the guy returning with a white convenience-store shopping bag in hand and stepping inside. The video ended like the others, a still image of the empty hallway and the door marked c.

Slater refreshed the page, but there were no new recordings. His phone buzzed in his pants, and he set the keyboard aside to pull it out and check. It was a text from Ram—a raunchy photo of his fully engorged woody. As an anatomical feature it was actually pretty impressive. But Slater had ignored him last night—why hadn't the guy taken the hint that he wasn't going to sleep with him again?

Thinking about it, Ram had been weird in bed, acting like he was high even though he wasn't. Slater eyed the dick pic again. It would be so easy. He already knew the guy, and Downey wasn't that far. But the yapping, he remembered, and the way his hands moved, pawing him, so insistent. He tucked his phone away.

It was Saturday night, and he was on his own, and sober. The time was right to hook up. But he didn't really need to—he'd been with Andy earlier. For a second he toyed with the idea of going back to Andy's, but he knew he couldn't. Andy would get sick of him, and he didn't want him to get the wrong idea. Slater wasn't even sure what that was anymore. He'd made that crack about half-wasted cupcakes, but it didn't make any sense.

He thought about the smell of Andy's hair, the way his skin was always warm from his revved-up metabolism. His random twitches had been odd at first, but he knew how to lean into them now, how much resistance to present, when to be firm and when to acquiesce.

Not Ram, and not Andy. Pulling out his phone, he hesitated before he opened the hookup app. One little tap and it all began. No, he decided, as he stared at it. It didn't have to happen every single day.

A notification flickered on the screen: "близость." Waking the phone, he tapped on Svetlana's app. A bubble that said VEHICLE appeared.

Something about his vehicle trackers. He was only running one of those right now—on Ram's car.

Tapping through the screens, he soon found what the alert was about: Ram's car was really close to him. He brought up the map and watched as the green location circle shifted along the street, hopping and resizing itself as the tracker sniffed out new Wi-Fi signals. Ram was only a few blocks away, and getting closer, moving slowly on the streets of Downtown. The guy had texted him that dick pic just a few minutes ago. Was this moron stalking him?

Slater sat up and grabbed his keyboard, and pulled up the photo Ram had texted. It looked even raunchier on the larger screen. He opened the metadata and scanned the details. The photo had been created months ago. So he hadn't taken it in his car on his way downtown. It was just a stock image of himself that he used to flirt with people, like a brand logo, or the thumbnail head shot on an email account.

Glancing at his phone, Ram's car was still inching along the block. Slater jumped up, pausing long enough to bolt the door, and went downstairs. It was completely dark out now, and cooling off a little. Glancing at his phone, he crossed the street, then jogged through the parking lot, past the Thunderbird and into the next block. On the screen, Ram's car had stopped. It was right here—he had to be almost on top of it.

Looking ahead, he saw the familiar Ranger backing into a space at the curb, in front of a row of shuttered clothing shops. Slater stood in the shadow of the building and tucked his phone away, watching Ram maneuver his vehicle. Overheated from hustling, he pulled off his heavy work shirt and tied its arms around his waist, relieved to be free of it. The evening air felt good on his sweat-drenched undershirt.

Ram killed the engine and climbed out, then paused to stretch, as if he'd been behind the wheel for a while. His park lights flashed as he locked it, then he crossed the street, walking the opposite direction from Slater's office. He was moving like he had a purpose now. Slater followed, hanging well back on the quiet sidewalk. A block and a half farther, at the edge of the Fashion District, Ram stopped at a brightly lit doorway and punched a keypad. Even from this distance Slater could hear the lock click open. Ram pulled on the door, and stepped inside, and disappeared.

Slater knew this place—it was a sprawling office building that covered most of the block. Jogging again, he got to the door and looked through the glass. The main entrance was around the corner, he knew, so this had to be a side door for the service elevator. It had locked itself again, and the narrow utilitarian lobby space was empty, but Slater could see the glowing red readout above the elevator, and the numbers were ticking upward—Ram had to be on board. It stopped at 8.

Offices, not apartments, Slater thought, stepping away from the door. What was Ram doing in an office building on a Saturday night? Turning on his heel, he walked to the end of the building, where the alley led off the street. It wasn't well lit, and not wide enough to park in, but it was heavily used—just beyond the range of the streetlights, a row of tents huddled in the shadows. The whole block was a long linear homeless encampment.

The fire door to the office building was locked, he found when he pulled on it, but right above his head was an old-school fire escape zigzagging up the outside of the building. The lowest flight was cantilevered to fold up out of reach from below until weight was put on it. The bottom step was at least twelve feet up. There was no way to get to it.

Slater smelled the tang of homelessness before he heard the guy's heavy footsteps approaching from the direction of the tents.

"Are you trying to get up there?" the guy asked, as Slater turned to him. Even from this distance his ripe odor was powerful.

"It's too high. I can't do it."

"I could give you a boost. For ten bucks."

Slater looked him over. The guy was tall, and looked solidly built, although it was hard to tell under his ill-fitting quilted jacket. His hair was thick and matted, but he had a heavy jaw. He might actually be strong enough to lift him.

"I'd have to step on your shoulders," Slater said.

He glanced down at Slater's feet. "Those look like sturdy boots. Give me twenty."

"Are you sure you can handle this?"

"I'm strong, dude." He looked up and positioned himself under the end of the ladder. "Payment is in advance."

Slater dug out a couple of sawbucks and handed them over, then quickly retied the arms of his work shirt tighter around his waist. After he pocketed the cash, the guy interlaced his fingers and held them out.

"Here goes," Slater muttered, and stepped into his hands.

The guy lifted him up, but Slater lost his balance, and twisted sideways, hopping to the ground.

"Start from a crouch," the guy said. "It works better."

Slater tried that, stepping into his hands again with his center of gravity lower, amazed that the guy could lift his weight so easily. He had to concentrate not to lose his balance, and once he was high enough, he planted a boot on the guy's shoulder. With his arms extended to compensate for the unsteadiness, Slater stood taller and looked up. The end of the ladder was just out of reach.

"Can you stand up straighter?" Slater hissed.

The guy grabbed his ankles, and with a grunt, thrust him upward a few inches. Slater lost his balance and started to wobble, but he was high enough now, and grabbed for the bottom rung as he went down, and managed to get a grip.

"Got it," he said, and the guy let go of him and stepped away.

He only had to hang on for a few seconds as his weight pulled the ladder down, and soon his feet were on the ground, and he was at eye level with the big guy again.

"You ought to be in the circus," Slater said.

He laughed. "Go on up, before someone sees you."

Slater hustled up the narrow steps to the first landing, then up another flight. Leaning over, he looked down at the alley. The ladder had retracted again, and no one had followed him up.

Trotting up the stairs, he saw that the door on each landing had the floor number on it. When he got to 8, he found the fire door locked. At the end of the short landing was a window, and he stepped over to it. It was old, the paint on the worn wooden sill peeling. The room beyond was dark. Slater heaved on the sash, but it wouldn't budge. He straightened up and took a breath. It had been too long. Ram would be gone by now, inside whatever office he was headed to.

From below came the glint of a flashlight. Slater flattened himself against the wall, then sidestepped to the fire door. That had to be a security guard, or worse, a cop. No way was he going to get popped for trespassing. He already had enough trouble with the legal system.

Men's voices drifted up from below. They weren't going to climb up after him, but they could definitely outwait him. Slater stepped onto the stairs leading up, treading quietly, and after climbing a few flights, stepped onto the roof. He crossed to the fire door in the shed that housed the elevator machinery, the white gravel surface crunching beneath his boots. It was solidly bolted shut.

Sooner or later they'd come up here to check.

He stepped to the side of the roof and stood close to the low wall, leaning over to look down into the alley. There were no lights or voices below the fire escape now. But they were probably watching from the end of the alley. That was standard procedure, waiting at the corner, so that one person could cover two exits.

He stepped onto the fire escape and trotted down, as quietly as he could, and tried the door on each floor. All of them were locked, of course, but he remembered the window beside the landing on 4 had been open. It still was, he saw, taking a deep breath as he approached it. The office was brightly lit, and when he crouched to look inside, he saw a man with his back to him, sitting at a wide computer screen, staring at a spreadsheet.

Slater lifted the sash as high as it would go, then crouched and stepped inside, feet first, swinging his leg over the credenza that sat under the window. Once both feet were on the carpet, he straightened up. The guy had swiveled in his chair to face him, concern in his eyes. In his forties, he was blond, and had a red beard, and needed a haircut. He looked a little soft, but he was basically fuckable.

"What's going on?" the guy demanded.

"I have a meeting with Dorothy."

The guy gave him the once-over. "There's no one here named Dorothy. Why did you come in the window?"

"I might have gotten the office number wrong. Is this 541?"

"This is 409. You came in off the fire escape?"

"You know, you're in good shape," Slater said, looking him over. "Do you work out?"

The guy visibly recoiled. "Who *are* you?"

"I can see that you're busy. I'll show myself out."

Slater stepped quickly to the office door and pulled it open, finding himself in a wide hallway. As he closed it behind him, he heard the guy call, "Hey." But his tone was half-hearted, uncertain rather than angry, and that was a good sign—he might not follow him, or call the cops, or summon the guards from the front desk.

Rounding a corner, he found the main elevators, and ducked into the stairwell beside them, hustling down as fast as he could. When he got to the door marked LEVEL 1: LOBBY, he eased it open a crack, peering out. Not far away, at the front entrance, he could see a uniformed cop, watching the street outside, hands on her belt. No way was he going to walk past her. Still dressed in his gardener's clothes, he didn't look like an office worker—he looked like someone who'd climbed up the fire escape.

Just across the lobby from where he stood, a corridor led sideways past the elevators. That was his way out. Slater untied his heavy shirt from his waist and shrugged it on, then buttoned it up and tucked in the tails. Pulling the door wide, he walked across the space, treading softly. To his relief the cop didn't hear him, or turn to look, and in moments he was out of her view.

This hallway led to the back entrance of a convenience store, a shortcut for the office workers on their way in, so they could buy their morning coffee and snacks without walking back out to the street. It was still open. Slater pulled open the back door and stepped inside. The clerk, wearing a red-striped shirt and standing behind the counter, looked up when he came in. Slater greeted her with a casual "hey" and went to the drinks cooler. He stood for a minute, studying the selection of cans and bottles, not seeing them but rather trying to catch his breath without it being obvious.

Eventually he pulled out a bottle of lemonade. Before he could head to the register, a different cop stepped in the other door, the one that led to the street. He glanced at Slater, with that heavy suspicious gaze that cops had, then eyed the clerk when she spoke.

"What's going on out there?" she said. "I've seen two of you guys go past."

"Some homeless guy went up the fire escape in the alley," the cop said. "The woman who called it in said it looked like a high-wire act. You really don't want those people coming into your building. They'll set up their tents and burn the place to the ground."

Standing at the snack fridge, Slater grabbed a box of soba noodles and went to the register, setting it and the lemonade in front of the clerk. He glanced at the cop and jutted his chin in greeting. He knew he looked suspicious—knew he could easily pass for homeless. He could feel the cop's eyes on him. From his front pocket he pulled out his wad of cash, holding it in plain view and methodically digging through it, fanning the bills to make sure several C-notes were visible, then pulled one of them out.

"Nine eighty-five," the clerk said.

Slater tucked the C-note back into his wad and extracted a sawbuck, then handed it to the clerk, holding his cash as if he'd forgotten about it, watching her as she made change. Pocketing the coins, he picked up his purchases and turned toward the door. The cop avoided his eye, disinterested in him now. It had worked—a homeless guy wouldn't be flashing that kind of scratch. Stepping out to the street, Slater headed back toward his office. That had been close.

Once he'd gone a block or so, he stopped at a utility box and set the bottle of lemonade on top of it, then pulled the top off the soba noodles and broke apart the chopsticks. He ate on the sidewalk, leaning over the gutter as he shoveled noodles into his face. When he was finished he went a few steps to a trash can and ditched the empty box.

As he was about to walk away, he spotted Ram, across the street, strolling back in the direction of his car, oblivious to Slater's presence. Slater watched him for a minute, then hustled across the street and tailed him. Ram turned the corner and crossed the next street in the middle of the block. He was definitely going back to his vehicle.

As he got near it, striding along the row of shuttered shops, Slater walked faster, closing the distance between them. Ram was almost at the Ranger when he heard Slater's rapid footsteps behind him, and turned to look.

Ram furrowed his brow. "What are you doing here?"

Slater strode up to him and planted a hand on his chest, shoving him toward the adjacent shop. Ram struck its steel shutter with a loud *bang*, his arms flailing.

"Are you stalking me?" Slater demanded.

"You're the one following me," Ram shouted, regaining his balance and holding up his hands to ward him off.

"What were you doing in that office building?"

Ram's eyebrows shot up. "You *were* following me."

Slater stepped closer and slapped him hard, right and left, a solid kovac.

"Stop it," Ram shouted, pushing him away. "I was at a twelve-step meeting."

Breathing hard, Slater held back. "I'm supposed to believe you're a drunk, or a junkie?"

"There's other kinds of twelve-step. It's a group for sex addicts."

That almost rang true, Slater thought, studying his face. "You were only in there for a few minutes. Meetings last longer than that."

"Only two of us showed up. We shot the breeze for a while and then called it a night."

"I guess I believe you," Slater said. "I know you're a sexual person. You tried to hook up with me an hour ago."

Ram threw up his hands. "There you go. I can't help myself."

"You almost got me popped."

"I saw the police in the lobby. You're the one they were looking for?"

"I had to sneak in. I barely got out, no thanks to you."

"Whose fault is that?" Ram demanded. "I didn't tell you to follow me in there. How long have you been stalking me?"

"Nobody's stalking you. I saw you on the street when you were walking up to that building. You don't live around here, or work around here. I couldn't figure out why you were skulking around this neighborhood like a lowlife."

Ram scoffed. "I've heard you use that word before. You know how people who say 'no drama' are always the ones who bring the drama?"

"What are you talking about?"

"It's you." Ram leaned toward him and poked him hard in the chest. "You're the lowlife."

"Fuck you," Slater snapped, slapping his hand away.

"With pleasure," he said flatly, and then laughed.

Slater put his hands on his hips. "I wish I knew what was going on with you."

"It's pretty straightforward. I need program because I sleep around too much. Sometimes with risky people. Like Bella."

"Are you blackmailing her?"

He frowned. "Why would I do that? She'd hate me."

Studying his face, Slater decided he was being sincere. Maybe he really was that clueless.

"I hope she's worth the risk," he said finally.

Holding his gaze, Ram's expression softened. "So what are you doing right now?"

Slater sighed. "Work the steps, brother."

He gestured widely. "We're both right here. Carpe diem, no?"

Slater turned to walk away.

"You're killing me, man," Ram called after him.

TWELVE

꘎꘎꘎꘎꘎꘎꘎꘎꘎꘎

At the parking lot across from his office, Slater climbed into the Thunderbird and drove to his apartment, mulling over what Ram had told him. When he got upstairs he poured out his ration of bourbon, then took a satisfying sip and carried the tumbler to his recliner, setting it on the carpet as he stretched out.

On his phone he checked on Conrad's location. The moron was at his station. When had he started working nights? Slater dialed his number.

"What do you need?" Conrad said when he picked up.

"So I was driving by a building on Sixth tonight," he said. "There were cops swarming all over it."

"So what?"

"I wondered if they had a description of the guy."

"OK—so you know there was a guy, and you

know that he wasn't apprehended, based on just driving by."

"Correct," Slater said. "What does your cop computer say about it?"

"How do you know I'm at work?"

"I can hear office noise in the background. When you're at home it always sounds like video games. Plus the quiet desperation of a rapidly aging hot mess."

"If you're concerned about a hot mess, look in the mirror." Conrad lowered his voice. "What were you up to tonight?"

"Minding my own business," Slater said. "Driving in a conscientious manner, slightly below the speed limit, with both hands on the wheel."

He let out an audible sigh. "Give me a minute."

Slater heard the sound of a keyboard clacking before Conrad spoke again.

"What you saw from your car was correct. They didn't locate the guy. He climbed up a fire escape in the alley, and he wasn't sighted again."

"I bet he works in the building," Slater said. "Were there any witness descriptions?"

"The person who first reported it said the guy was Latin, and wearing jeans and a white T-shirt."

"That could be anybody. Did anyone else come forward?"

"No one reported an actual break-in, so no one was interviewed."

That was a relief—that two-tone blond on the fourth floor hadn't ratted him out.

Conrad spoke in a near whisper. "What were

you doing climbing up a fire escape?"

"It wasn't me. Like I said, I was just driving by. So I thought you were on the day shift—why are you working so late?"

"Because crime never sleeps."

"But we know you will. You should spread your jacket over your desktop first. That way your stationery won't leave lines on your face when you wake up."

"You're welcome, Slater, for all the information," Conrad said.

"Settle down."

He didn't reply to that, and Slater listened to the dead air, imagining him sitting there at his desk with his phone to his ear.

"I have to go," Conrad said finally.

"So quit bugging me," Slater said, and hung up. That guy could be such a dick-smack.

Taking a sip of his bourbon, Slater put on the radio. There was good house music on the weekend, and he turned it up a little, and let his mind sink into the rhythm. Another slurp and his tumbler was empty, just like that. It wasn't even that late. Is this what normal people did—not drink, not have sex, just go to bed like this, like an empty husk, with the city vibrating all around?

It was Saturday night, and he was sitting here alone, surrounded by the void. This was the densest part of the metropolis, with people everywhere, stacked on all sides of him. But it felt like a yawning crater. Like Tato's empty tunnel.

Fuck it, he decided, and got up. Hoisting the

bourbon bottle, he chugged from it, pausing to cough when it burned in his throat, grinning at the fire, at the heady intensity of it. Hoisting it again, he chugged until it was empty.

———•———

It was light out when he woke, and his head hurt. It could be worse, he knew, sitting up and wincing at the stab of pain. He'd had it worse before. Eventually he rose and went to pee, then shook a few ibuprofen tablets into his mouth from the bottle in the bathroom. In the kitchen he drank from the tap and splashed water on his face to quell the nausea. Back in his bedroom, he checked the time. It was still early, and he lay down again and slept another hour.

When he woke he felt a little better, and grabbed his phone. No outgoing calls during the night. That was a relief. There was no new activity from the camera at that apartment building on Raymond Hill. It still had some battery life, as it was online, listed as CONNECTION. But it seemed odd that the shaggy-haired guy hadn't gone out again since yesterday.

Forcing himself out of bed, Slater got dressed and grabbed his satchel as he headed down to the garage. From the armored cabinet he took the lock-reading probe, and the heavy binder full of keys, and loaded them into the bag. His head was wooly, and he hadn't exactly formulated a plan yet, but that guy had to leave apartment C again at some point, and Slater needed to get inside.

Climbing into the Thunderbird, he backed out of his garage and headed toward the freeway. The ramp was blocked by a cop car parked sideways across it, its light bar flickering blue and amber, so he went past. Craning to look down onto the road-way as he drove over it, all he could see was empty pavement. Streets were closed on Sunday morn-ing sometimes for events, but never the freeway. Construction, maybe, or just a routine overturned freight truck.

He cruised through Downtown and crossed the river into East LA, enjoying the light traffic, and suddenly realized he was driving right by the cemetery. It hadn't been a conscious choice to come this way, in his hangover-clouded state of mind, but here he was.

Turning into the lot, he parked and then walked across the hard-packed dirt and dead grass, scan-ning the headstones for the one marked IBANEZ. Even though it was Sunday morning, there was almost no one here, save for a trio of adults and a kid standing in the distance, one of them hold-ing a bundle of sunflowers. It was an old cemetery, and most of its residents had been buried decades ago—no one who cared was left.

When he found the headstone, he sat down on the dry grass, cross-legged, facing it. He had only vague memories of the day they'd planted the wooden box here, but he remembered that Doris had been a wreck. He wondered idly if she ever came here. But this wasn't about her.

"So there's this guy," Slater began, speaking

quietly, leaning toward the headstone. He talked about Andy, and how they'd met, and how the guy never told him what to do. It was frustrating, he explained, that Andy was way too familiar with Doris, and then he related the cupcake metaphor. "What the hell does that even mean?" he said. "What am I supposed to do with that?"

Of course there was no answer. He stared at the name, his own name, chiseled in stone. "If you were around, you'd tell me what to do." But he knew there was no point in being resentful about that. Or in talking to a dead man.

Eventually he got up, and swatted the dust off his butt, and walked back toward his car. There was a lump in his throat, for some reason, and he worked to swallow it. That was a stupid reaction, getting all sticky about a man who'd died ages ago. Or was it about Andy? That didn't make any sense either. His defenses were down from being hung over, he decided. "Snap out of it," he muttered under his breath.

A few minutes later he was up on Raymond Hill. He nosed the Thunderbird onto a different street than where he'd left it yesterday and parked in the shade of a big mulberry, down the block from the apartment building, then killed the engine and pulled out his phone. Svetlana's app showed no new recordings at apartment C. He set the software to alert him when the camera picked up motion, then set his phone aside and cracked the window so he wouldn't overheat.

It wasn't the heat that was making him feel

weak and nauseous, he knew; it was the booze. Reaching over to the glove box, he dug around and found a granola bar. It was soft and gooey but still edible, and he ate it slowly, absently watching the quiet street. Afterward he started to doze, and woke when his phone buzzed with an alert.

It was the smoke-detector camera, he saw, and tapped on the recording. The guy with the shaggy hair stepped out the apartment door, wearing sunglasses and a day pack over his shoulders, and locked it with a key before he walked out of the frame.

Reaching into the backseat, Slater grabbed his ball cap and pulled it on, then slung his satchel over one shoulder as he climbed out, pausing to take a few breaths and steady himself before he set off.

There was no sign of the guy as he strode toward the apartment building. He would have gone the opposite direction, down the hill toward the shopping street and the metro. Slater found the front door still unlatched. It probably hadn't closed properly for years, he saw—it didn't even fit into the frame anymore.

No one was in the hallway or on the stairs when he stepped inside, and he was happy to see that the lock on the door to apartment C was a standard model, the type landlords loved because they were cheap and easy to swap out. He pulled the lock-reading probe out of his satchel and connected it to his phone. The screen went black and said "готов." Standing close to the door, he slid the probe into the lock.

The screen went red and displayed "ошибка." He didn't know what the word meant, but that color meant the probe wasn't getting a reading. Slater slipped it out and in again, repositioning it slightly. Finally it turned green and came up with a number: 275.

Kneeling in the hallway, he pulled the binder full of keys out of his satchel and found the one with that number on it, sliding it out of its sleeve and then tucking the binder away. On his feet again, slinging the heavy satchel onto his back, he tried the key in the lock, and it turned freely, retracting the bolt with an audible *thunk*.

Slater stepped inside and closed the door behind him, then flipped the deadbolt. He was standing in a small kitchen. It had been renovated but still had an antique vibe, with a high coved ceiling and a narrow ironing-board cupboard. Over by the window, two chairs sat under a kitchen table, and on top was a half-full mug of coffee and a laptop, sitting open, its screen dark.

Walking into the short hallway, he found the bathroom off one side, and the bedroom opposite. It looked like a kid's room, with a set of bunk beds. The bottom one was wider, and unmade, and beside it on the floor was a black suitcase, zipped open to reveal a jumbled mess of clothes.

There was no lounge space, he realized. Even a hasty postwar construction job would have included a living room. Back in the kitchen, opposite the hallway, there was a closed door, and he stepped over to it and tried the knob. It wasn't locked.

When he pulled it open, he found a shallow space, not even two feet deep, like a small closet—but in the back wall was another door. Twisting the knob, he pushed it open.

This is what would have been the living room, he realized, stepping inside and glancing around, then closing both doors behind him. It had a completely different vibe than the rest of the apartment—painted bright white, it was light and airy, with tall windows that looked onto a small backyard with a *Syzygium* hedge along the fence.

Slater had walked along the other side of that fence yesterday, but he hadn't made it into this little yard. He couldn't have seen into this room anyway—the lower half of the glass was frosted and opaque. There were security bars on the windows, but unusually, they were on the inside, and painted white. He hadn't noticed those on the other side of the building, when he'd glanced into the other apartments.

No longer a living room, this space was set up as an art studio. In the middle of the room were two easels, one mostly covered by a heavy sheet of canvas, the other with a painting on it. It was in Renaissance style, of a photorealistic winged angel clad in a brick-red tunic, pointing skyward and rolling her eyes. Or maybe it was his eyes—the gender was ambiguous. It was still a work in progress, he saw, leaning close to it—the paint looked wet.

A drop cloth covered the floor beneath the painting, and there was a stool and a worktable at one side, with an array of paint-stained foil tubes and a trio of coffee cans with dozens of brushes standing in them. Why would anyone need that many brushes? Against the wall was a pile of canvases mounted on wooden stretchers. They were in several different sizes, and the one facing outward was blank.

Standing in the middle of the room, he looked around, taking it all in. The walls had an odd texture, and he stepped closer to examine it. It was a layer of wire mesh, he realized, painted white to blend in and held up with staples every few feet. It went all the way up the walls, and stretched across the ceiling as well. Even the window glass beyond the security bars was covered in a fine spiderweb of wire. It covered the back of the door he'd come through, and at the base of the walls it curled onto the wooden floor a few inches. Here it was unpainted, and he could see that it was made of metal.

The most interesting thing in the room, however, was the other door. It was painted white too, but without the mesh on it, and it looked heavy. In place of a handle it had a wheel, like a bank vault. He knew how those worked—it had bolts that went into the frame at three or four different points. The mechanism looked old, and oddly, for such a secure door, there was no lock or keyhole, just the wheel.

Stepping over to it, Slater grabbed the wheel with both hands and pulled, but it didn't budge. Twisting it took some effort, but it didn't stick, and he could hear the rumble of the bolts retracting. When it stopped turning, he pulled on it again, and the door swung open noiselessly, revealing a narrow space flanked by a concrete wall. It smelled of earth, and when he stepped in, he saw the top of the stairs, and on the opposite side, the low gate for the freight elevator. Slater had to smile, to take a moment to savor the success. This is what he'd been looking for—he'd stood right here on Friday night.

His beacon was still there, above the door, and he reached up to peel it off the concrete. Pulling his satchel around, he tucked the beacon into it, then shifted the heavy bag onto his back again.

He'd seen enough, he decided, and stepped back into the studio. A quick look at the second easel, the one with the sheet of canvas draped over it, and he'd be done. Before he could push the heavy door closed, however, there was a noise from the kitchen. Slater froze. It was the front door. He'd thought the guy would be gone for a while, since he was wearing that backpack.

"Stefan?" a man's voice called. It was muffled, but he recognized the reedy timbre—Tato.

There was nowhere to hide in the studio, he saw, quickly glancing around. Slater hustled back into the shaft, pulling the big door closed. It couldn't be bolted, as there was no access to the mechanism on this side, only the pull handle. But Tato wouldn't be able to tell it was open unless he tried it.

Good thing he hadn't left his heavy satchel in the kitchen, as he'd been tempted to do, and good thing he'd closed both of the weird serial doors into the studio. It was a habit he'd got into in the course of doing this kind of work: always leave things the way you found them.

It was completely dark in here with the heavy door closed, but he knew where the stairwell was, and he stepped over to it, feeling for the top step with his boot. Once he found it, he trotted down the first flight, then another, and paused to listen. There was no sound at all, until suddenly the heavy door above swung open, casting diffuse light from the studio into the elevator shaft.

"Dummy," Tato muttered to himself.

He must think Stefan had left the door open. Was he just testing it? If Tato decided to bolt that door, Slater might be here for a while—at least until the shipping store closed. As he listened intently, the light in the shaft faded to black, and he heard the door close. Suddenly brilliant light flooded the stairwell. Slater winced and turned away from the naked bulb on this landing, mounted in a wire cage at the edge of the elevator shaft.

Flattening himself against the wall farthest from the light fixture, Slater could feel his heart pounding. If Tato came down the stairs, his options were to flee downward and outrun him, or stand his ground and punch the guy in the face, then leave the way he came. If he took the tunnel, whoever was working at the shipping store would see him, and be able to identify him. It would be easier to coldcock the guy—he could take him with one hand, even with a hangover—but he'd need to surprise him and strike fast, before Tato had time to register who it was.

Slater quietly shifted the weight of the satchel to the middle of his back and balled his fists, ready to act. A creak of movement came from above, and then the sound of wood striking wood, and then the whirr of an electric motor, and the rumble of machinery. The elevator—Tato was taking the elevator down.

Slater stood motionless, but there wasn't enough shadow to conceal his presence. The whole stairwell was lit up, with fixtures on every landing. If Tato happened to look as he went by, of course he'd see him. Slater held his breath as the platform slowly dropped into view. Tato was facing the other way, wearing baggy shorts and another loud Hawaiian shirt. His hand was on the control box, holding the DOWN button as the elevator descended. It must be a switch that wouldn't work unless it was depressed.

As the platform sank out of view, followed by Tato, Slater took a breath. Eventually the rumble of movement stopped, and a moment later the lights winked out. He heard footfalls on the gritty concrete floor of the tunnel far below. Gradually they faded to silence.

Slater waited a little longer, then walked back up the stairs and pushed open the heavy door into the studio. Gingerly closing it again, he stood in the bright room and listened to make sure no one was in the kitchen. Hearing only silence, he went through the double doorway, closing both behind him. Stepping out into the hall, he paused to lock the front door with his ghost key, then walked out to the street.

A man was approaching the building as he stepped outside. Slater recognized him from yesterday: the guy who'd left in the red Prius. He eyed

Slater and murmured a perfunctory greeting as they passed. Not connected to apartment C, Slater decided. The stealthy camera aimed at the door had shown only the woman who'd left town and the guy with the Roman nose. Stefan. That's whose clothes were on the floor in the bedroom, and who Tato had been looking for—he'd called his name.

As he walked toward his car, Slater peered down the adjacent driveway toward the side of the building where apartment C was. It was hard to tell exactly where the shaft came up, but he could see the tops of the painting studio's windows, and the adjacent wall definitely had a stretch with no windows or doors in it. The top of the shaft didn't take up a lot of space, he reasoned. Anyone poking around that enclosed backyard would easily overlook the windowless section.

Slater heaved his bulky satchel into the trunk of the Thunderbird, glad to have its weight off his shoulder, then slammed the lid and got in behind the wheel.

THIRTEEN

At his office the lights were off. Slater sat at his desk and woke his computer.

There were three new notifications from the camera outside apartment C, but he didn't bother to watch the clips, as he knew what they were: Slater letting himself in, then Tato arriving, and then Slater leaving. Instead he pulled up an overhead view of the neighborhood and zoomed in on the building. There wasn't an obvious secondary structure in the small backyard. That meant the top of the shaft was integrated into the building, and accessible only from that studio room.

Next he did a web search for "wire mesh," and was peering at the screen to parse the results when he heard the front door open. Max's voice, along with a woman's—his girlfriend, Vanessa. Slater got up and went into the front office.

Max was wearing his gray suit with a yellow tie,

and Vanessa was in a somber plaid, with gold jewelry warm against her dark skin, her hair in myriad intricate little braids. Lots of black women spent big on their hair, but everything about Vanessa looked expensive and polished.

"You look like hell," Max said, giving him the once-over.

"Thanks, partner."

"Don't listen to him," Vanessa said, flashing a smile. "You look fine."

"And you always look like a million bucks," Slater said. "What are you doing with this goon?"

She laughed. "I was telling Max that I'd thought of a name for your agency. You could call it Rey Pascual." She gestured to the little statue on the front desk.

"I'd be worried that people would think we're bulletproof," Slater said. "In Guatemala he's venerated for that kind of protection."

"Using him as the face of the business would send the wrong message," Max said, eyeing the statue. "He may be the king, but he's also dead."

"I wanted to ask you something," Slater said to Vanessa. "You're a scientist, right?"

She nodded. "An astronomer, specifically."

"That's the one where they look through telescopes," Max said. "Not the one where they predict the future based on your birthday."

Vanessa shot him a look. "Thank you for clarifying that."

"Always happy to help," Max said, and chuckled as he stepped into his office.

"You have a science question?" she said, turning to Slater.

"Why would you cover the inside of a room with wire mesh? The windows, the ceiling, everything."

"What kind of mesh?"

"It's definitely made of metal. Not copper—it was the color of steel or aluminum."

"What gauge is the mesh?"

Slater held his finger and thumb slightly apart. "Like this."

"If it covers the whole room, it's probably a Faraday cage. It's to stop signals from getting in or out. We have them at my school to test sensitive equipment free of electromagnetic interference."

"Like radio waves? It blocks all of them?"

"You can see through the mesh, right, so light can get through, and light is electromagnetic waves. But it stops the frequencies we use for communication. TV and radio, the cell network, Wi-Fi, satellite signals. The gauge of the mesh might be fine-tuned to block specific technologies."

Slater nodded, absorbing it all. It explained why he'd had so much trouble picking up Svetlana's beacon—he'd mounted it on the wall of a radio-proof room.

"There's an office building by the airport that's covered in wire mesh," Vanessa went on. "You can see it from the freeway. It's a defense contractor."

"They don't want their secrets to leak out."

"Or outside signals to get in."

"Thanks for the info," Slater said, and went to the front door.

"Enjoy your Sunday," Vanessa called after him.

Slater had another contact who might have relevant information, and as he rode the elevator down to the street, he tried to remember her name. It didn't matter, he decided finally. He knew where to find her.

Climbing into the Thunderbird, he pulled into the traffic and drove to the Arts District. It was similar to the neighborhood around his office, with century-old industrial buildings, but here they had been converted into tony restaurants and upscale retail.

Pulling up to the place, he found the woman's name emblazoned on the sleek white facade in chic rusty metal letters: SAFFRON SWATI GALLERY. Slater parked at a meter and climbed out. Tall wooden boxes lined the sidewalk out front, positioned so that pedestrians could pass but not leaving enough room to pitch a tent. The boxes were planted with rosemary, or maybe a close relative. It wasn't a bad idea. That stuff was hardy, and perennial, and aromatic enough to improve the scent of the streetscape—no small task with so many homeless people around. The merchants managed to clean up the trash and paint over the graffiti, but lots of the neighborhood still smelled like a dive-bar latrine.

Slater paused to pluck a spiny leaf from one of the plants, then rolled it in his fingers and sniffed it. Definitely rosemary.

The gallery was a big open space with oil paintings positioned along broad white walls. A flight of blue metal stairs ran up to a set of offices. It had been a warehouse, maybe, and he could see why the makeover worked as an art gallery—the high windows provided lots of natural light.

Near the front door was a pot with some kind of *Aglaonema* in it. It looked anemic, even though it was getting the right kind of light in here. Next to it was a chic glass-topped desk with a woman parked behind it, the only person in the space. She was curvy, with long black hair, and wore a dressy blouse that showed a bit of cleavage.

"We don't have a public restroom," she said, looking up as he stepped in. *"No hay baños públicos."*

"I'm not homeless, toots," Slater snapped. "I'm looking for Saffron."

Her eyebrows shot up. "She's not here today. Can I help you?"

"I'm an insurance investigator." He dug a business card out of his hip pocket and handed it to her. "I interviewed Saffron on a case a while back. I wanted to ask her some art-world questions."

She studied the card and then looked up. "About a specific case?"

"I just need some general information."

"I'm in the art world. Try me." She took her own card from the tray on the desktop and handed it to him.

"Celeste," Slater said, glancing at the card before he pocketed it.

"Thank you for pronouncing it correctly."

Slater eyed her. She looked Latin, and had a Hispanic surname, so of course he'd said it the Spanish way, "Ce-les-*tay*." He looked around at the empty space. "It's pretty quiet in here."

"Most of our clients make appointments. We don't get a lot of walk-ins, even on Sunday."

"That means they're spending big, if they call first."

Celeste gestured to the chair in front of her desk. "Sit down, if you'd like."

She was watching him closely, Slater realized, as he dropped into the chair. He knew that look in her eye, that spark of interest.

"What kind of information are you after?"

"Why would someone set up an art studio inside a Faraday cage?"

"What's a Faraday cage?"

"Wire mesh that blocks radio waves. It isolates the whole room from cell signals and Wi-Fi."

Celeste looked thoughtful for a moment, then broke into a smile. "You're an insurance guy, right? I know exactly why."

"Spill it, sister." Slater glared at her and gestured impatiently.

"What's the information worth to you?"

"How much do you want?"

"It's not really a secret," she said, "so I can't ask you to pay me for it. How about dinner?"

"I only sleep with guys," Slater said flatly.

Celeste sighed heavily and looked tired. "Story of my life." She leaned toward him, folding her arms on the desk. "Some high-end art is fitted with an electronic tracking device. With paintings, I know the first iteration of the technology was a tracker hidden in the frame or in the stretchers. But that's not the valuable part, and it's easy to discard the frame. The newer version of the device is attached to the canvas itself."

"I get it. A Faraday cage would prevent it from being located." He folded his arms. "Why wouldn't a thief just pull off the tracker?"

"They're difficult to remove without damaging the canvas. Even an art thief would hesitate to do that, as it would destroy the value of the artwork." She raised her eyebrows. "The French government actually banned them for any art object older than fifty years. But here the individual owners make the rules."

"Is it a standard practice?"

"For expensive stuff. Personally I hate the idea of attaching anything to the artwork, but I'm an art lover, not an asset owner who wants to protect an investment."

"How does the technology work?"

"Once or twice a day it broadcasts its serial number via the cell network to a monitoring company. For paintings, if you roll it up, like when a painting gets stolen and removed from its frame, the device detects that and sends the signal more often. Personally I'd just put it inside an aluminum art tube. The effect would be the same as your Faraday cage." She paused, a smile playing on her lips. "But then, I'm not an art thief."

"What do these devices look like?"

"I can show you one."

Celeste rose and walked toward the blue staircase, her heels echoing on the concrete floor. She pushed open a door under the stairs, and Slater followed her in. When she flicked on the lights, he saw that it was a workroom with a big table in the middle, strewn with tools and cutting mats and lengths of wood. Against the back wall was a set of open shelves with more equipment.

It was unusual that she wasn't afraid to be alone with him, he thought, watching her dig through a stack of paintings that stood upright in a wheeled cart. But then, Celeste seemed like she had street smarts.

She extracted a canvas from the collection and brought it to the worktable, setting it face-down. With a pair of needle-nose pliers, she pulled out four staples along the sides of the frame, then lifted off the backing board. Attached to the inner side of the canvas was an industrial-gray disk, thin and just a few inches wide, with a matrix bar code printed on it.

"That's it," she said, and tapped on it.

"It must have a battery inside."

"There's a proprietary flexible battery. The whole thing bends with the canvas if you roll it up. They market it as lasting ten years. After that, the company can change it, but it has to go to their workshop. It's a bit of a pain."

"But worth the trouble, for a valuable artwork," Slater said. "How much is this one worth?"

"Half a mil," she said casually, and flipped it over.

It was an oil painting of a dark landscape, with shadowy bare trees standing dormant for the winter,

184

silhouetted against the red glow of dusk.

"If I saw that at a thrift store," Slater said, "I wouldn't look at it twice."

"It is a rather dreary image."

"Rather," he said, and leaned closer to inspect the brushwork. "There is way too much discretionary money in this world."

"I hear you, brother." She pulled a cell phone out of the pocket of her trousers. "You can actually read these tags with a smart phone. The software queries a database that keeps track of the item's provenance. You just need the manufacturer's app."

Celeste tapped at her phone, then waved it over the canvas. It chirped as it passed over the gray disk, and she held it out for him. The screen showed an image of the painting, and below that, a button labeled OWNERSHIP INFORMATION.

"Can anyone get that app?"

"Sure. It's called Herostrat."

Slater pulled out his own phone and made a note of the name as he followed Celeste back to her desk, asking her to spell it for him. He sat down across from her again.

"Another question." He pulled up the image of the ticket stub he'd found in the old trunk, then handed her his phone. "Do you recognize this?"

"'Los Angeles, California,'" she said, reading from it and swiping at the screen to zoom in. "Nice engraving. It's old."

"I know that much."

She frowned and handed his phone back. "I have no idea what it is, but I know someone who would. My friend Truman used to be a tour guide. He's really into local history."

"Can I call him?"

She recited a phone number from memory, and Slater thumb-typed it, then looked up at her.

"You said he used to be a tour guide. What does he do now?"

"He's a private detective."

"So he'll want to get paid," Slater said. "I'm going to call him now."

He listened to the guy's voice-mail greeting, then left a message with his name and number, adding, "I got your details from Celeste at Saffron Swati's gallery. I'm working an insurance case, and I need some historical information."

"I'll text him that you're legit," Celeste said, once he'd finished. "I'm sure he'll call you back."

Slater tucked his phone into his jeans as he stood up. "Your *Aglaonema* is root-bound."

Celeste frowned. "My what's what, now?"

"Your potted plant." He pointed to it. "You need to deal with it. It's suffering."

She glanced at it, and her eyes narrowed. "It's a plant. I don't think the concept of cruelty applies."

"Get it repotted," he said firmly, and walked out.

On the sidewalk it was brighter, and a lot warmer. As he strode toward his car, Slater passed a homeless guy, who eyed him and said, "Spare change?"

"No," he said flatly, and caught a whiff of him, that familiar tang of vinegar and ammonia, and started breathing through his mouth.

"Fuck you very much."

Slater turned back and balled his fists. "Pardon me?" he demanded, stepping toward him.

The guy turned to look at him, his eyes growing wide, and then broke into a trot and hurried away. Slater watched him go, resisting the urge to follow him, and spin him around, and punch him in the face.

Instead he turned and walked toward his car. There were more of those people every damn day. It was starting to look like the Middle Ages, with rich idiots who could drop half a million bucks on a painting of dead trees, and broken peasants shuffling along the street outside, begging for coins.

It wouldn't have mattered if he had punched the guy, as this neighborhood was quiet today, and no one would be watching. Still, he knew he needed to hold back, to suppress the red mist. If a cop happened to see him do something like that, what with his current legal problems, he'd wind up in the hoosegow.

Climbing into the Thunderbird, his phone rang, and he pulled it out to check. It was a 213 number—the one that he'd just called. He answered "Ibáñez."

"It's Truman," he said. "I got your message. What do you need?"

"Can you meet me at my office? It's in the Fashion District."

"Easy," he said. "Are you there now?"

"On my way," Slater said, and rattled off the address.

FOURTEEN

When Slater got to his building and went upstairs, Max and Vanessa were gone. He sat at his desk and did a search for the Herostrat app. "Art security for the twenty-first century," the company's splashy website said, but the descriptions of the system and the technology involved were breezy and vague, and didn't reveal anything about the frequencies used by the tracking device.

There was a knock at the door, and Slater locked his computer and got up to open it. Standing there was a twinkie-looking twenty-something guy with coiffed brown hair and rust-red pants, wearing a backpack over a T-shirt.

"What do you need, son?" Slater said.

His brow furrowed. "I'm Truman. I'm supposed to meet Slater Ibáñez. His name is on your door."

"Right. That's me." He pulled it wider and

waved him inside, then closed it and flipped the deadbolt.

"This whole building is garment workshops," Truman said, following Slater into his office. "I thought I had the wrong address."

"We like it that way."

"It's kind of brilliant. Like urban camouflage. So you're a PI?"

"I'm not. I investigate insurance claims." Slater sat behind his desk and grabbed his computer mouse.

"Celeste said you had a question about local history."

"I photographed a document that I want you to look at," Slater said, peering at the screen as he pulled up the ticket stub.

Truman set his backpack on the guest chair, then stepped around to stand beside him and look at the image. Leaning back in his chair, Slater took a moment to look him over. The guy was sweating. He must have come on foot.

Resting a hand on the desktop, Truman moved closer to the screen. "It's a ticket, right? From the design I'd say early twentieth century." He grabbed the mouse and zoomed in. "Tunnel 4, seat 6. I'm thinking 'tunnel' means it was in a stadium. Nowadays they say 'gate' instead. For most of the twentieth century, the only stadiums were the Coliseum and the Rose Bowl. It says 'Los Angeles,' so I'm thinking it was an event at the Coliseum."

It was a sharp deduction, Slater realized. He really was the guy to ask.

"The graphic looks like a ten-year-old holding a garland," Slater said. "What kind of event would that be?"

"It should be easy enough to figure out. It says Tuesday, August 9. How often does that date fall on a Tuesday? We can narrow it down to a few specific years."

Truman pulled out his phone and then casually sat on Slater's desk, tapping at the screen. The guy must walk a lot, Slater thought. He had great calves.

"Here we are," Truman said. "There's 1955, and 1949 ..." A smile spread across his face. "Got it. 1932." He met Slater's eye. "It wasn't an event for children. The boy with the garland is just a symbol."

"So what was it?" Slater demanded.

"You know what happened in 1932."

"I don't."

"Guess. You'll get it. Think summer."

"I'm not going to guess," Slater said. "But if you don't tell me, I will punch you in the face."

Truman's eyebrows shot up. "The Olympics," he said quickly. "Jesus, dude—chill. The first LA Olympics were in 1932." He gestured to the screen. "That was a ticket to one of the events at the Coliseum."

It fit, Slater decided. That trunk, and the fabric inside—it could all be that old.

"It doesn't say which sport," Truman said, punctuating his words by waving his arm, "but they only did a few back then. The traditional ones— foot races, and jumping, and decathlon. The 1932

Olympics really made LA a world city."

"Do you know anything about the Raymond Hotel?"

"Sure. It was on Raymond Hill. There were two versions. One burned down in 1895, and the second one was torn down in 1934. That's not long after your ticket stub would have been used. I doubt if there was any connection to the Olympics, though—the athletes were housed in Downtown and in South LA."

"How do you know all that?" Slater said. "You pulled those dates out of your head."

Truman grinned. "I read a lot. It's interesting stuff."

"Did either of the hotels have a tunnel system?"

"It wouldn't surprise me. Especially the nineteenth-century version. I know there was a train station for the hotel at the foot of the hill, where the metro line is today. Before there were trucks it was definitely easier to move things in tunnels. There are still miles of them downtown, under Broadway and Main and Fifth."

"They used horses back then?"

"In a tunnel you'd use manual labor," Truman said, waving his hand. "You wouldn't want your grubby servants crawling around the manicured hotel grounds, offending the sensibilities of the Eastern elites."

"Right," Slater said, watching him explain it, entertained by how earnest he was.

"LA is really effective at erasing its past. It's like a sandbox. You'd never know what was there before.

People live on top of old rail tunnels in Angeleno Heights and Echo Park and don't even know they're there. It wouldn't surprise me at all to learn that the Raymond Hotel had them." His brow furrowed. "Why do you think there were tunnels?"

"Just a hunch," Slater said. "Listen, I know you're a detective, and you need to get paid for this consult."

"It wasn't really any work. Just stuff I already knew. But," Truman said, and cleared his throat, "if you want to grab a coffee sometime …"

"I don't really do that," Slater said, swiveling his chair toward him. "The flirting and the chitchat. But I'll fuck you, if that's what you want."

Truman blushed. "I do want."

"Can you have guests? If you live with your mom, we can go to my place."

"Why would you think I live with my mother?" he demanded. "I'm not a teenager."

"No judgment," Slater said, raising his eyebrows.

"I live alone. It's eight minutes' walk from here."

"Great," Slater said. "Have you got any booze?"

Truman looked thoughtful. "I might have a hard cider in the fridge."

"We can stop for a snort on the way."

Slater rose and went to the front office, then into the corridor. He waited for Truman to step out, and then flicked off the lights and twisted his key to lock the deadbolt.

"Who's Maximillian?" Truman said, gesturing to the names inscribed on the office door.

"Wasn't he the king of Mexico?"

"The emperor. And that's with one *l*. This guy uses two. And I'm pretty sure the emperor of Mexico didn't have an Irish surname."

Slater chuckled. "You're a smart-ass, you know that?"

"Actually, I'm a detective."

"He's my business partner."

"How difficult was that?" Truman said, and threw up his hands.

Slater led the way around to the elevator. "Which way is your pad?"

"A couple blocks southwest."

"I know a bar on the way."

They were alone on the elevator, and as the door closed, Truman moved toward him, pressing him into the wall and meeting his mouth. It was a nervy move for a scrawny guy, Slater thought, but then Truman probably wasn't thinking about getting into a fistfight. Slater went with it, savoring his taut warm mouth, running a hand into his luxy hair. Truman pulled away when the doors rumbled open in the lobby, a smirk on his face.

They walked a few blocks to the place Slater knew. It was basically a dive bar, ancient and unadorned and cheap, and it was quiet now, as the daylight faded.

"I've never been in here," Truman said, following him inside.

Slater sat on a stool at the bar, and Truman perched on the adjacent one, still wearing his backpack. The bartender was a bony woman with a smoker's sallow complexion, her blond-gray hair tied behind her head. She stepped over and said, "Boys?"

"Do you do margaritas?" Truman asked her.

"No complicated drinks, honey. I can throw some tequila and lime juice over ice."

Truman looked to Slater. "What are you drinking?"

"Tequila sounds good."

"Let's do tequila shots," Truman said.

Slater nodded assent and chuckled.

The bartender set two shot glasses in front of them, then turned to grab the handle-size bottle from the well, and poured them to overfull. Slater dug in his pants for his wad of cash, setting a fifty on the bar. As she finished her pour, the bartender plucked the bill and stepped away.

"Thanks," Truman said. He leaned closer to the bar and carefully lifted his glass. "Together?"

Slater picked up his own shot and gestured with it. "*Salud.*"

They drank in unison, and Truman slammed his empty glass down, stifling a cough. "You speak Spanish?"

"Not really." The bartender returned with his change, and Slater said, "Another round."

She nodded and reached for the bottle.

"This has to be the last one for me," Truman said. "Otherwise I won't be able to enjoy the next thing."

Slater eyed him. "Let's not forget about the next thing."

Two was all he'd planned on anyway—it was

just enough to take the edge off his hangover. He could already feel the warmth spreading from his belly.

The bartender poured for them again, and took a bill from the bar top, and they slammed the second round.

"It burns," Truman growled.

"It'll put hair on your chest." Slater rose and gathered up his change, leaving a few singles for the bartender. "Ready to go?"

Truman followed him outside, his hands on the straps of his backpack, looking a little dazed. "You don't mess around."

"Which way?"

Truman gestured up the street, and they set off. Dusk was ending as darkness overtook the sky, and it finally felt cooler.

A few minutes later, walking up on an old red-brick industrial building, Truman said, "This is me." Inside, he hustled up to the second floor, taking the stairs two at a time. His apartment was a huge open loft with a high ceiling.

"You live alone here?" Slater said, looking around. The only new construction was the drywall around the bathroom. The rest was old brick, wooden rafters, and tall factory windows.

"It's not that expensive."

"It's a lot of space. It must cost a fortune to heat in the winter."

"I don't even try."

Truman stepped close and put his hands on Slater's waist, and kissed him, his mouth tasting faintly of the smoky tequila. Slater pulled him closer and ground his swelling woody into him.

"Oh, man," Truman said, pulling away. Flushed and grinning, he led Slater toward his bed. "So what are we going to do?"

"First, let's get your clothes off."

Slater grabbed Truman's T-shirt and pulled it over his head. He unbuttoned his own shirt, and untied his boots, and soon they were both undressed. Truman was already hard, he saw, and Slater pushed him down on the bed, and ran his hands over his body, exploring his warm skin, nibbling his neck and meeting his mouth.

"You're so hard," Slater said, squeezing his cock. "Do you want to fuck me?"

"I guess. If you want."

"Do you have a condom?"

Truman quickly sat up and dug in the bedside drawer. Slater had to grin. Despite his stated ambivalence, he was eager to do this.

After he'd rolled on the condom, Truman shifted closer, kissing his chest and massaging a lubed finger into him. Slater gasped at the intensity of it as he pushed his way in, and Truman built up a rhythm until he was pounding him, panting and wild-eyed. A minute later he came, with an electric spasm, grimacing, and then sank on top of Slater.

He shifted onto his side and grabbed Slater's cock, and met his mouth, and deftly stroked him. With a palm on Truman's chest, and his nose in his hair, smelling his sweat, Slater came, and grabbed his hand to stop him.

Afterward, Slater flopped on his back and folded his arm over his eyes. As he caught his breath he could feel the warmth of Truman's body next to him, and the rhythm of his breath. What a relief that he wasn't a talker.

———•———

Sometime later his phone buzzed, pulling him into wakefulness. It was on the floor, still in his jeans. Slater rolled to the side of the bed and reached down to grab it. There was an alert about activity outside apartment C. He tapped on the recorded video and watched as Stefan walked into the frame, still wearing his backpack, and used his key in the door. The clip ended when he went inside and closed it.

He tossed his phone back onto his jeans and stretched out again. Truman moved closer, sliding his arm under his neck. They lay that way for a while, tacitly enjoying the warmth, the physical proximity. He caressed Truman's smooth skin. The guy had great musculature, but he was slight. Working as a detective, his strength had to be his brains. No way would he be able to defend himself with his fists.

Eventually Slater sat up. "I have to go."

"You don't have to."

"I've got work."

"Your Olympic ticket stub."

"Thanks for not asking where that came from, by the way," Slater said, eyeing him.

"You're on a case, right? I know how it is. It's none of my business."

Once Slater was dressed, Truman got up and walked him to the door.

"Call me if you have any more history questions."

"I might just do that," Slater said, and trotted down the stairs to the street.

It was a short walk back to his office. Rather than going up, he went across the street to the parking lot and climbed into his car, then drove to his apartment.

No way was he going to overdo it again, he thought, eyeing the empty bourbon bottle on the counter. Dropping it in the trash, he looked in the pantry and saw that he was out of booze, with just the flask he kept for emergencies. That would be enough for tonight. He cracked the seal and poured his regular half-inch ration into a tumbler. A mere dribble, but this was definitely the limit.

After he pulled off his boots, and killed the lights, he stretched out in the recliner and sipped at the bourbon, then put on a podcast, *Sasquatch Search*. The team's explorations deep in the boreal woods were compelling, and often dramatic, but the narrator always spoke calmly as he described things, and as he listened, Slater sank into the even cadence of his voice.

Tonight as the team set up camp, one of them noticed an unexplained light in the distance, through the trees, and they set off toward it, trudging deeper into the forest, unsure of what they'd find. It felt like walking the tunnel under Raymond Hill, and as he drifted toward sleep, Slater found himself there, in the dark, gravel crunching under his boots, shifting course as his shoulder brushed the tunnel wall, or maybe it was conifer branches, moving closer to the answer, out there somewhere in the void.

FIFTEEN

His head was clear when he woke, and Slater was grateful for that, lounging for a minute in the bright daylight streaming in the dusty window before he pushed himself out of bed.

In the kitchen he filled a mug with tap water and put it in the microwave. While he waited for it, he pulled open the Frigidaire, but of course there was nothing edible inside. When the microwave beeped he shoveled some brown crystals into the steaming mug and swirled them around with the spoon, then sipped at the ersatz coffee.

Leaning on the counter, he checked for activity on Raymond Hill. There was one video recording, and below it a message time-stamped an hour ago that said "battery death." So this was the final clip. It showed Stefan returning to the apartment early this morning. Slater thought about it, absently sipping at his mug. The recording before this one showed Stefan coming in last night. Just to be sure, he watched it again. The guy had definitely come home twice without leaving in between. That meant he'd either climbed out a window, or more likely, had gone through that heavy door in the art studio, down the stairs to the tunnel, and out through Tato's shipping store.

Stepping into his bedroom, Slater dug through his closet and found a black dress shirt. Without an electronic eye on apartment C, he'd have to do a manual stakeout. He could drive to Glendale and get another smoke-detector camera from the Russians, and swap it for the dead one, but now that he knew who Stefan was, it would be just as easy to do it old-school.

After he dumped the tepid dregs of his pseudo-java in the kitchen sink, Slater trotted down to his garage and drove to Raymond Hill. Just up the street from Stefan's building, he parked the Thunderbird in a shady spot with a good view of the front door.

Stakeouts were inevitably boring, and usually time-consuming. He rolled the window down a few inches, and got comfortable, and let his mind wander. With one eye on the building, he did a web search for something Andy had talked about: "love without pain." The results that came up were mostly shrink talk, and his eyes glazed over just trying to parse the list. He scoffed and tucked his phone away.

Instead he put on the car radio, and turned the volume low. Just after the second round of hourly news headlines, he spotted Stefan walking out of the apartment building, wearing chinos and an olive-green shirt. Slater instinctively shifted down in his seat and clicked off the radio. Even from this far away, the guy was unmistakable, with that big nose and the hair.

Not even glancing at the Thunderbird, Stefan walked past on the opposite sidewalk. Slater watched in the rearview as he receded and then turned right at the end of the block. He was headed off the hill, into South Pas.

Starting the engine, Slater shifted into gear and pulled into the street. At the bottom of the hill, he spotted Stefan again, still ahead of him, on the other side of the boulevard already, moving fast. Slater pulled into the traffic and cruised past him, taking a gamble that he'd turn onto Mission, the first street where there were shops and eateries. Half a block up, he found a meter and pulled in.

His guess was right—Stefan's green shirt appeared in his side mirror, growing larger until he was parallel, and walked past him. Slater gave him time to get farther along the street, then climbed out and tailed him. A minute later, Stefan disappeared into a doorway. It was a coffeehouse, Slater saw, walking up on it, with big windows overlooking the boulevard.

As he stepped inside, Stefan was just sitting down at a table with a cup of foam-topped joe. The place was busy, with most of the tables occupied, but there was one open right next to the guy.

At the counter he ordered a soy latte, then carried it to the adjacent table and sat facing his quarry. Slater pulled out his phone and looked at the screen, not focusing on it but assessing the guy in his peripheral view. Sitting so close, he got a good look. Stefan was around thirty, and that nose was beautiful, and noble, like something you'd find on a Roman statue. There were little dabs of color on his dark shirt—paint. He had to be working on that partly finished painting in the studio.

Stefan propped his phone in front of him, against his coffee cup, and peered intently at it, then broke into a broad smile and waved at the screen.

"Stefan," a woman's voice cried, and he scrambled to turn down the volume. Even then, Slater could still overhear the call. There was a man's voice at the other end in addition to the woman's. The conversation was animated, and the three of them laughed, but the content was incomprehensible, as they were speaking another language.

After he ended the call, Stefan picked up the phone and sat back to tuck it in his front pocket, a contented smile on his face.

"What language were you speaking?" Slater said, eyeing him.

Stefan blushed, and met his gaze, his expression growing wary. "Serbian. I'm from Belgrade. I was talking to my parents. I apologize if it was too loud."

"You're an artist."

His eyes narrowed. "How do you know this?"

"There's paint on your shirt."

Stefan glanced down at it. "You're right. You could be a detective."

"I am a detective. I work for an insurance

company."

He flashed a crooked smile. "I should be more careful with my clothes. You'll learn everything about me."

"Not from looking at your shirt," Slater said, holding his gaze. "But I can see that you're smoking hot."

It was sheer bluster, and Slater knew it could easily backfire, but the guy had a vibe that transcended the cultural differences—it felt like he was a man's man.

Stefan's eyebrows shot up. "You mean I'm attractive?"

"That's exactly what I mean."

"People in this country are not shy."

"Maybe it's because of the American work ethic. Time is money. No time to waste."

"You look Latin American," Stefan said, his brow furrowing, "more than American."

It was a racist diss, and normally Slater would hurl an acerbic retort, but there was work to do—he had to let it go. "My father was," he said evenly. "I was born here."

"To return the compliment, you're also good-looking."

"Now we're getting somewhere," he said, gesturing broadly, and told him his name.

"I'm Stefan," he said, and grinned. "I'm surprised you even noticed me. I don't usually get that kind of attention."

"It was hard not to notice. You were shouting in Serbian."

He guffawed, throwing his head back, his voice rich and deep. That was it, Slater knew. He was in.

"Do you live around here?" Slater said.

Stefan hesitated. "I'm not supposed to have guests."

"Says who?"

"My host."

"I don't live near here, but maybe we could go eat lunch downtown."

"You mean in Los Angeles? I haven't been there yet."

"Seriously?" Slater said. "It's pretty hard to miss."

"I just arrived this weekend."

"So let me take you out."

"This afternoon I can't. I'm going to an English school to see if the classes would be appropriate for me."

"You don't need classes. You understand everything."

"You flatter me, Mr. Slater."

"It's just Slater. So maybe dinner?"

"I'd like to do that."

Slater pulled out his phone, and unlocked it, and handed it to him. "Put in your phone number."

Stefan spent a second thumb-typing, then handed it back.

"I'll text you from my number," Slater said, tapping at the screen, then eyed him. "Do you know the best way to learn a language?"

"Cultural immersion."

He shook his head. "Pillow talk."

"What does that mean?"

"Sleeping with a native speaker. Sexual immersion."

He laughed again, covering his mouth with his hand like a kid. "I'll call you this evening," he said, and got up, and was gone.

SIXTEEN

Slater stayed a few minutes to finish his latte before he left the coffeehouse. Walking back to where he'd parked, he saw that there was a tow truck stopped right in front of the Thunderbird. Its lights weren't flashing, but the driver's door hung open.

"Damn it," he muttered, and walked faster.

It wasn't about his car—parked in front of the Thunderbird was a blue Civic, twenty years old and thoroughly scraped and dented. The tow truck had it on the hook, its front wheels in the air. A woman stood at the driver's door, holding it open. She'd been crying—black streaks of eye makeup ran down her cheeks. Her bleached-blond hair was bundled up haphazardly, and she was dressed in black, despite the heat, in a long jacket and tight pants.

As he walked up, Slater saw that the tow driver, a burly guy with a beard and a red ball cap, was standing at the front end of the car. He jabbed a finger at the woman with the Civic.

"You're going to close that door, or I'll do it myself."

"You have to put it down," she cried. "It's not even three yet."

Slater stopped on the sidewalk and pulled out his phone. She was right—it was 2:58. Looking back up the street, he read the parking sign. It wasn't a tow-away zone until after three. This guy had definitely hooked the Civic before that. The Thunderbird was at risk too—he'd been so focused on keeping track of Stefan that he hadn't even checked the signs.

Scanning the street, he saw that there were no parking enforcement vehicles nearby, no cops. It was just this private operator, out here to capitalize on human carelessness, an opportunistic parasite.

"I'll drop it for four hundred," the driver said. "Cash only."

"I don't have that kind of money," the woman wailed, flapping her arm.

"It'll cost you more than that to get it from the impound." Sensing Slater's presence, the tow driver turned toward him. "The fuck are you looking at?"

"A bully, I'm thinking," Slater said.

The driver scoffed and stepped toward the woman in black. "I don't have all day. Step aside, sir."

"Don't you misgender me, you degenerate," she snapped. "Give me back my car."

Pushing between her and the Civic, the tow driver shoved her into the street as he slammed the car door. She was a wraith compared to this guy, and unable to resist him, she stumbled back a few steps, eliciting a honk from a passing car.

"Hey," she shouted. "You don't get to put your hands on me."

Marching toward him, she slapped him in the face. Slater had to chuckle at her nerve. The tow driver grabbed her by the lapels and shook her, but she fought back, and slapped at his head, then started pounding on him with her fists, knocking his ball cap off. The driver screwed his eyes shut to avoid her manicure, but he didn't let go.

Slater stepped over the tow hitch. This guy was too big to scrap with, but right now he was distracted. Stepping up behind him, Slater reached around his neck, and notched his windpipe into the crook of his arm, and started to squeeze.

The driver let go of the woman's jacket and grabbed at Slater's arm, gurgling, then pounded on it, and tried to punch him, heaving his fists behind his head. Slater held firm, and used his other arm as a lever to increase the pressure.

Through clenched teeth, Slater growled, "Why do you make me do this to you?"

The driver threw his fist down, pounding at Slater's crotch. A dick punch was the best way to get out of a choke hold, but the guy had thought of it too late, when his strength was waning, and he missed, instead striking his thigh. Slater twisted his hips sideways to avoid the subsequent blow.

"Yeah!" the woman in black cried, hopping up and down. "That'll teach you." She darted closer and pounded on the tow driver's chest with the heel of her fist, then hopped back.

In a few moments the big guy lost consciousness and went limp. His dead weight was more than Slater could support, but he maintained his grip as long as he could, then laid him out on the pavement, flat on his back.

"Nighty-night, motherfucker," the woman said, standing over him, and half-heartedly kicked his thigh with a mule-clad foot. "Is he dead?"

"He's fine." Slater stepped over to the tow truck's controls and lowered the Civic. "He won't be out for long, so you need to go."

"I can't—there's a car right behind me."

"That's mine," Slater said, stooping to make sure the tow mechanism was disconnected from the vehicle. "I'll back up, and then you back up. You'll have to give it some gas to get over this tow bar. You'll be fine."

The traffic was slowing for a light farther up the block, and a red sedan paused beside them, its side window rolled down.

"Is that guy all right?" the driver said, leaning toward them.

"He had a seizure," Slater called to him, standing up. "He's through it now. The ambulance is on its way."

"I hope he's OK," the guy said, then drove off when someone behind him honked.

Slater glanced at the tow driver. He looked a little blue in the face, a little too out of it. Crouching beside him for a second, he pressed two fingers on the guy's neck.

"He has a pulse," Slater said. And he was breathing. That was a relief.

"Fine by me if he's dead," the woman said. "You rescued me, mister. You just came out of nowhere in my time of distress."

"He shouldn't have assaulted you," Slater said, straightening up.

"Can I get your phone number?"

He frowned. "I only date guys. And you need to get out of here before the cops show up."

She cocked her head. "I wasn't born the fabulous femme fatale that I am today. I still have things that you'd be interested in."

Another vehicle slowed, and the passenger leaned out, her elbow on the door. "Is everything OK?"

"He had a seizure," the woman in black said. "We already called the ambulance."

"You've been crying."

"Keep moving, honey—you're blocking the traffic."

Slater watched the car as it pulled away, then eyed the woman.

"Don't run over this moron."

He walked past the Civic and climbed into his own car. There was no one behind the Thunderbird, so he revved the engine and backed up. The woman in black was already in the Civic, and Slater watched as the backup lights came on, and the car bounced as the front tires made it over the tow bar. She pulled into the street, steering around the body beside the truck, and roared away.

The tow driver was sitting up now, Slater saw, and glanced at his side mirror as he nosed into the traffic. The plate readers on that tow truck would have the Civic's tag number, of course, and Slater's, dutifully adding them to the repo database, but with luck the guy wouldn't remember Slater's face, or what had happened. Even if he did, the idiot had started the scuffle himself—he wasn't going to report it to the cops.

At the next corner Slater made a quick right, glancing in the rearview. No one seemed to be following him. The traffic on the street had been moving fast enough that no one would have had a good look at what had happened, but you never knew when some nosy passerby would try to follow and make trouble.

———◆———

If Stefan was visiting an English school, he'd be out of apartment C for a while. Slater drove back to Raymond Hill and parked, then strolled into the building. The ghost key was still in his front pocket, and he let himself in, and went to the studio. Sure enough, the outer door had a layer of the wire mesh attached to the inner surface. Now that he knew it was a Faraday cage, he closed it before he opened the inner door, preserving the bubble of radio isolation.

The painting of the angel was gone now, replaced by a mostly blank canvas that had just a few shapes outlined on it. He pulled the canvas off the second easel, revealing a finished oil painting.

It depicted a man holding a two-tined pitchfork, his back to the viewer, gazing across the fields at the trees in the distance. Although he had a decent butt, the painting wasn't especially interesting. But it looked old. Glancing at the nearly blank canvas, it was the same size, and the outlines sketched on it were in the same shapes—the man's figure, the fork, the curves of the landscape. Stefan was making a copy of it.

Slater lifted the original painting and flipped it over. It was clipped onto wooden stretchers, but the back was open, and the same kind of tracking device that Celeste had shown him was attached to the fabric. Pulling out his phone, he photographed the tracker, then flipped the painting over and took a photo of it, moving in close so that the studio wasn't visible in the background. Gathering up the sheet of canvas, he covered the easel again, arranging it the way he'd found it, and went out to the kitchen, and locked the front door as he left.

No one was in the hall, and he reached up the wall to peel off his camera. It took a layer of beige paint with it, leaving a white circle. Whatever was in the glue Svetlana had cooked up, it was powerful. He palmed the device and walked back to his car, ditching it in the trunk.

Before he got on the freeway, he stopped at a garden store to buy a bag of soil and a decent-size pot, choosing one made of black plastic, the same as the one next to Celeste's desk. The afternoon traffic was sluggish on the way to the Arts District, and he parked at a meter in front of the Saffron Swati

Gallery. When he stepped inside, the place looked abandoned, like it had yesterday, save for Celeste sitting at the front desk. As she looked up at him, a sly smile spread across her face.

"Your friend Truman told you what we did, I'm thinking," Slater said.

"In quite a lot of detail." She laughed.

Slater jabbed a finger at her. "You tell him that loose lips sink ships."

"It's just sex, Slater—not state secrets." Celeste waved dismissively. "Saffron's not in today."

"I want to talk to you."

Slater pulled out his phone and sat in front of her desk. Once he found the photo he'd taken of the painting in apartment C, he handed it across to her.

"Do you recognize this?" he said.

Celeste glanced at it, then met his gaze. "Did you see this painting?"

"I'm asking the questions here, sister."

"Such a hard-ass," she said, and then raised her eyebrows. "Except in bed, apparently."

Slater clenched his teeth and stifled a sigh as he took his phone back.

"Lighten up, *caballero*. I don't even have to look it up. I know that piece. It's called *Peasant with Hay Fork*."

"So it's famous."

"More like infamous. It was stolen last year. Someone pulled it off its stretchers at a museum in The Hague. Let me see if it was ever recovered." She turned to her computer.

Slater watched her clack at the keyboard. If the artwork in apartment C was the real thing, he already knew the answer.

"It's still missing," Celeste said, gazing at the screen. "This article doesn't say so, but I bet it has one of those tracking tags on the back."

"Does it say if there's a bounty for it?"

"Aren't you in insurance? I'm sure that's who owns it by now—some insurance company. If they paid out the full value, it cost them a couple million bucks."

"Seriously?" Slater demanded. "You can't even see the guy's face."

"Regardless, that's what it's worth," she said absently, absorbed in her screen.

"What is wrong with this world?"

Celeste turned to look at him. "I'll text this to you."

"Thanks for your help," Slater said, then pointed to the *Aglaonema*. "Can I repot that?"

"You want to take it with you?"

"I have soil and tools in my car."

"Are you sure you won't damage it?"

"I know what I'm doing," Slater said intently.

"That's what Truman said." She held his gaze for a moment and then laughed. "Sure, go for it— fix the plant."

"Do you have any outdoor space? I don't want to get potting soil all over your floor."

"You can work in the alley."

"I'll move my car around," he said, and walked out.

The alley was surprisingly clean, devoid of trash piles and tents and shopping carts, and Slater parked the Thunderbird next to the gallery's fire door, then stepped over and pounded on it with the heel of his fist. Celeste opened it a moment later, and he followed her inside, crouching to pick up the pot and carry it out.

There was late-afternoon shade against the wall, and Slater set the pot there so the delicate plant wouldn't get burned. From his trunk he took some hand tools and spent a few minutes gently loosening the mass of tangled roots, massaging them so they'd be able to expand into the new soil. It was only a few more inches of dirt than they had now, but it would make a difference.

Once it was in the new pot and he'd packed in the fresh soil, he tamped in a handful of fertilizer and then carried the pot back inside, depositing it next to Celeste's desk.

"It looks the same," she said.

"In the next few weeks it'll get healthier. It should grow some new leaves. It'll improve the vibe in here."

"More greenery will make the clients spend more green?"

Slater chuckled. "That might just happen. I'm going to take your pot in exchange for the one I brought with me."

"You can wash up in the restroom," she said. "It's under the stairs."

He went in to wash his hands, and when he looked up from the sink, Celeste was standing there, leaning on the door frame, arms folded.

"So you ask me about an art studio built to block radio signals," she said. "Then you ask me about a stolen painting. It's not hard to connect the dots."

"You're pretty clever," Slater said, shaking the water off his hands. "I'd advise you to stay out of my business."

"I'm not asking for details, or even if you found *Peasant with Hay Fork*. But hypothetically, say that you did. You'd ask for a reward, right? I want a cut."

Slater scoffed. "You gave me a few measly bits of information that I could have found online."

"Fair enough." She stood up straight and flashed her palms. "I've got nothing on you. But if you do collect, you should remember who helped you get there."

"Are you planning on telling anyone else about your wild speculations? Am I going to see posts online saying that I've got *Peasant with Hay Fork*, annotated with commentary about my sex life?"

"Why would I do that?" She frowned. "This is between you and me. Gossiping about it might interfere with you getting paid, and trust me, I want you to get paid."

"Maybe you really are clever," Slater said, and put his hands on his hips. "I'll tell you what—if I do happen to find any missing masterpieces, and you manage to keep your mouth shut, I might be able to help you out."

"That's all I'm asking." She turned and stepped away from the doorway.

As he walked out of the restroom, Slater looked

her over. It had been a mistake to come to her a second time.

"Loose lips," he said flatly.

"Dude—there's money involved. I'm not going to tell anyone."

Slater walked out the fire door, letting it slam behind him. Why had he given her so much information? He'd been distracted by that *Aglaonema*, and had let his guard down, like some idiot tyro. She could easily foul up any chance he had of cashing in. That meant he needed to work fast.

As he climbed into the Thunderbird, he thought it through. Of course he could walk into apartment C right now and recover that painting, but it was risky. Tato was too stupid to have stolen it himself, which meant he was involved with other lowlifes, most likely a syndicate. Those lowlifes would come after him. Plus that tracker would report its location as soon as it was carried out of that studio, which meant Slater could get popped for possession of stolen property. He needed to be smarter about this, and formulate a plan—and get Stefan on board.

He started the engine and checked the time. It was late in the day, but his handler at Cudahy Mutual, Della, would still be in the office. Shifting into gear, he headed toward the Financial District.

It wasn't a full-time gig, but Della regularly called him in to do research when the bean counters got nervous about paying out on a claim, or when they thought they were being played but didn't want to get their hands dirty. It wasn't always as profitable as what Max did, but it was easier than the window-shade jobs.

Cruising up to the skyscraper where Cudahy Mutual had its offices, Slater nosed the car down the ramp into the underground garage. The valet was already gone for the day, but there were plenty of open spaces. Striding over to the elevators, he rode up to the thirty-fourth floor.

To his relief the receptionist's desk was unoccupied when he walked in. He hated tangling with that icy blond, Crystal, who worked as Della's guard dog. On the surface she was all Swiss finishing school, but underneath she had the soul of a cage fighter. Walking through reception, he went up the hall to Della's office and rapped on her half-open door.

"Hey, handsome." Della looked up and smiled, then leaned back in her chair.

Pushing sixty, she had her hair styled in a cloud around her head, today wearing a summery print dress that flattered her figure.

"Have you got a minute?"

"For you, always."

"I'm going to email you something." Slater dropped into the chair in front of her desk, looking at his phone. He pulled up the article Celeste had sent to him, and forwarded it to Della.

"You're looking good," she said, watching him work.

Slater jutted his chin toward her computer. "It should be in your inbox."

She sighed and sat up to look at the screen,

then spent a minute reading. Slater gazed out the window behind her at the dramatic view, the hazy metropolis stretching across the basin.

"*Peasant with Hay Fork,*" she said finally. "That's ballsy, to pull a painting right out of its frame inside a museum."

"Museums are insured, right? I wondered what carrier owns this piece now."

"That's not really in my wheelhouse, but I'm sure I can find out."

"Specifically I want to know how much the reward is, or the bounty. What are they willing to pay to get it back?"

Della eyed him and affected a sweet smile. "Do you know where it is?"

"I know where it might be. I want to be sure it's worth my time before I get into it."

"Let me ask around," she said, and sat back. "So we should go out again sometime. I enjoyed that charity event."

"That was a one-time deal," Slater said. "I needed arm candy."

"What if I need arm candy sometime?"

He shook his head and stood up. "I'm bad for people, Della. I'd only embarrass you."

"Don't sell yourself short. I know you clean up nicely." She looked him up and down. "Although I like the way your jeans fit too."

Slater scoffed and stepped toward the door.

"I'm about ready to knock off," Della said, glancing at her wristwatch. "Do you want to grab a bite?"

"I have a dinner date."

"Is that a euphemism for some gay sex thing?"

He had to laugh. "It means I'm eating dinner with a guy. The sex comes later."

"That doesn't sound like you."

"He might know something about *Peasant with Hay Fork*."

"So it's work." Della waved a hand. "Off with you, then, you callous heartbreaker."

On the way down to the garage, he saw that Stefan had called. Not bothering to check the message, he dialed his number.

"Are you ready for our dinner?" Stefan said when he answered.

"Do you want me to pick you up?"

"I can take the metro. It stops near my apartment."

"Are you sure? You'll have to change trains."

"Slater, I'm European. I know how public transport works. What station should I meet you at?"

"Pershing Square," Slater said. "Take the Fifth Street exit."

SEVENTEEN

It was just a few blocks away. Slater drove, and left his car in a surface lot nearby, then positioned himself across the street from the station, where he could see the commuters coming up out of the earth. There was always a crowd of homeless people around that entrance, spare-changing and skanking the place up and picking fights, but over here he could wait in peace.

He leaned against the wall of the building, arms folded, and before long Stefan appeared among the crowd climbing out of the station, and Slater strode across the street. When Stefan caught sight of him, he stopped on the sidewalk.

"Aren't you afraid of getting struck?"

Slater frowned. "What?"

"You crossed the street in the middle of the block."

"There were no cars coming." He clapped him

on the shoulder. "Let's walk—it smells like a urinal around here."

"Where are we going to eat?" Stefan asked, walking abreast.

"That's up to you. What's your food thing?"

"What do you mean?"

"Everybody has a food thing. Like, you can't eat gluten, or you can't eat sugar, or you only eat raw food."

"I don't have any of these problems. What's the most typical Los Angeles thing to eat?"

"Tacos," Slater said flatly.

"Isn't that Latin American cuisine?"

"It is. Los Angeles is a Latin American city."

Slater led the way into the central market and to a *taquería*, where they joined the short line. When they got to the counter, Slater helped him order.

"How many?" The clerk asked.

Stefan said, "Just one."

"No, man, they're small," Slater said, and to the clerk, "Make him three."

At the other end, a staffer loaded everything onto a tray, and they found a table on the Hill Street side.

"My father would enjoy eating American style," Stefan said, eyeing the spread. "He appreciates gluttony."

"One taco is a snack," Slater said, gesturing to their plates. "Three tacos is a meal. Gluttony is five tacos."

Stefan grinned at him. "Is this a well-known rule?"

"It's just math."

After they'd eaten, Stefan sat back and watched the passersby. "I love this place. Why do they put wood shavings on the floor?"

"To absorb the spills, I suppose. It used to be a real Latin produce market. Now it's just an over-priced food hall."

"However you describe it, my belly is very happy right now."

Slater eyed him. "Does that mean it's time to hook up?"

"You mean romance?"

"I mean sex."

Stefan chuckled. "Do you live near here?"

They got up and walked out to the street, and down the block to the parking lot where Slater had left the Thunderbird. He opened the passenger door and then stepped around to the driver's side.

"It's old," Stefan said, looking over the car before he climbed in.

"I use the word 'classic.'"

"That makes it sound like something from antiquity. Socrates and Plato and Aristotle."

"You're in the New World now, toots," Slater said, starting the engine. "The Wild West. In this town, forty years ago is antiquity."

He pulled into the street and headed west, across the chasm of the 110 freeway.

"So many cars," Stefan said, gazing out the window. "So much traffic."

"It's actually not that busy right now," Slater said, glancing at him as he braked for a red light.

Once they were in his neighborhood, he pulled into a strip-mall parking lot. "I have to stop for a minute at the *tiendita*."

"What's that?"

"Like a corner store." Slater killed the engine and pulled out the key. "Do you need any snacks? There's no food at my place."

"We just had a meal," Stefan said, incredulous. "What is it with Americans and always the snacks?"

"I'll take that as a no," Slater said, and climbed out.

It was a liquor store as much as it was a *tiendita*, and he bought two fifths of bourbon, pulling out his cash and watching the clerk bag them.

Walking out, he carried them back to the car, where Stefan was waiting. He started the engine, and a minute later turned into his alley, and pulled into his garage. Slater got out and collected the shopping bag, waiting for the big door to roll down.

"This is a private garage?" Stefan said. "These tools belong to you?"

"It's all mine."

Slater led him into the building, locking the garage door behind them, and headed up the stairs. As he started up the second flight, he saw that Stefan was hanging back, standing on the landing below, concern in his eyes.

"I'm not going to hurt you," Slater said. "Unless you want me to."

"It's just … it's an old building."

"I know it's a dump. But there's no danger."

Stefan nodded, and took a deep breath, and started up after him.

When he'd unlocked his front door, Slater flicked on the lights and set his heavy bag of bourbon on the counter.

"Your car has more space than you do," Stefan said, looking around. "Why do you live here?"

"It's where I need to be."

"Why?" he said again, raising his voice.

"It has a private garage."

Slater stepped up behind him and slid his hands under his arms, caressing his belly and kissing the nape of his neck.

"Relax," he whispered.

Stefan turned and met his mouth. He was a tentative kisser, receptive but not very passionate. Pulling back, Slater unbuttoned Stefan's shirt, and kissed his chest, then pushed his shirt off and ran his hands over his smooth skin.

Stepping into his bedroom, Slater took off his own shirt, tossing it toward the closet, and sat on the bed to untie his boots, watching Stefan undress. He was wearing a pouch around his waist, he saw, under his pants, on an elastic strap. It must be where he kept his cash and his passport.

"Are you afraid of getting mugged?" Slater said, nodding to it as Stefan unbuckled it.

"Of course I am. You said it yourself—this is the Wild West."

Once Stefan had shed his trousers, Slater pulled him onto the bed, and explored that amazing nose up close, then kissed him, and mouthed his jaw and his neck, running his hands into his thick hair.

"What are you going to do to me?" Stefan said softly.

"What do you want me to do?"

He squeezed Slater's arm, and pursed his lips, but didn't reply.

"Do you want me to fuck you?"

Stefan nodded.

Slater was already hard, and he found a condom, and rolled it on, then maneuvered beside him. As he penetrated him, Stefan gasped, tilting his head back. Slater built up to pounding him, and pulled him closer, burying his nose in his hair. Before long he came, shuddering, then shifted onto his side.

When he grabbed Stefan's cock, he found that he'd already come.

"Well, that was easy," Slater said.

"I'm sorry—I couldn't help it. It was extremely erotic."

He chuckled. "You don't have to apologize for that."

Slater kissed him, and spent a minute focused on his mouth, running a hand in his hair. Eventually he pulled back, leaning on the pillows.

"I lied to you about something," Slater said. "I know you're working for Tato."

"How do you know about Tato?" Stefan's brow furrowed. "You said you're a detective. Are you investigating me?" His voice rose. "Are you working for the police?"

"It's nothing to do with the police. But I know Tato is a lowlife."

"Explain this word," he demanded. "Lowlife."

"A crook, or a gangster, or a thief. Someone who makes a habit of doing bad things."

"Tato said no one would find out. How did you find me?"

"I've been looking at Tato," Slater said. "I saw you in his shipping store, and then I saw you in the coffee place, so I said hello."

"I don't remember you coming into the shop."

It was just a guess—pure bluster—but he was right. Stefan obviously worked there too, like the frizzy blond who'd moved out of apartment C.

"Tell me what you're doing for him," Slater said.

"I can't do that. I'm a man of personal honor. I have an agreement with Tato."

"But you know Tato isn't an honorable man."

"Why are you researching him?"

"He's part of a larger investigation. Tell me about the blond woman who was working at the shipping store."

"You know a lot about Tato's business," Stefan said, and frowned.

"She's European too, but not Serbian, I'm thinking."

"From Macedonia. Her name is Elena."

"Was Elena doing the same work?" Slater said. "How long was she here?"

"She has a ninety day visa, the same as me."

"But she's not going to Macedonia now. She's on her way to New Orleans."

"Did you interview her?"

"I only saw her briefly in the store."

"Then how do you know what she's doing right now?"

"It's my job."

Stefan sighed. "Elena finished working for Tato, and has some time left on her visa. She's visiting this country using her earnings."

"What did Tato pay her?"

"The same as me. Two thousand dollars, plus a place to live."

"How long did she work for him?"

"About a month. She finished when I arrived."

Slater did the calculation in his head. Two grand net for a month's work—that wasn't even minimum wage. Tato was definitely exploiting these two.

"So you took over for Elena," Slater said.

"Are you going to give Tato to the police?"

"I have no reason to do that. His business doesn't concern me." Slater met his gaze. "You're the one breaking the law by working on a tourist visa. But that doesn't concern me either."

Stefan shifted uncomfortably. "Is your insurance company trying to recover something that Tato has stolen?"

"That's an interesting question." Slater eyed him. Despite his self-professed personal honor, Stefan was telling him a lot. That happened with civilians sometimes—the sense of guilt, the need to get it off their chest.

"Let me tell you what I know," Slater said. "I know that Tato is somehow involved with stolen artworks, and you just implied that you know that too. I know that you're an artist. I know you're staying in Tato's apartment. So my guess is that you're making a copy of a stolen painting."

"When you say it so frankly, it sounds diabolical." Stefan looked away. "But it's all true."

"Does Tato plan to sell the copy as if it were the original?"

"I don't know."

"You're right in the middle of it. How could you not know that?"

"Tato didn't explain it all." He gestured helplessly. "Maybe I don't want to admit to myself that I'm involved in something so illegal, and so immoral. But it's a logical conclusion: when a painting is considered stolen, collectors still want it, but they can't display it publicly. They keep it in their houses and admire it in secret. And they have to take the seller's word—no one who owns a famous stolen item can ask an expert to authenticate it. That means Tato can sell it several times over."

"You're making more than one copy?"

"The goal is three."

"What happens to the original?"

"I'm not sure," Stefan said. "Maybe he sells it too, or the next artist that he hires from Europe uses it to make more copies."

"What painting are you working on now?"

Stefan hesitated, and took Slater's hand, intertwining their fingers.

"I already know the rest of the story," Slater said. "It's just a detail."

"There are two. One is a Renaissance work called *The Righteous Seraph*. The other was taken from a museum in the Netherlands. It's called *Peasant with Hay Fork.*"

Slater had seen the painting of the seraph—the angel rolling her eyes and smugly pointing to the sky—when he'd first been in the studio. And he'd seen *Peasant with Hay Fork.* Stefan was telling him the truth about that, which made it more likely that the rest of his tale was legit.

"Tato is paying you two grand," Slater said. "If I paid you more, would you help me recover the paintings?"

"You just said Tato's business didn't concern you."

"It doesn't. But paintings are insured. I can't just ignore that."

Stefan shifted onto his side and propped his head on his hand. Slater could see the wheels turning.

"What would I have to do?" he said finally.

"I'm not sure yet. But I'll have to take the originals."

"Tato will think I've taken them."

"Working together, we can create doubt about that. Are your copies good enough to fool Tato?"

"He knows nothing about art. He's a business-man."

"He's a lowlife," Slater said. "Maybe we can leave him the copies. However it plays out, I'll come up with a plan so that he won't suspect you."

"Elena and I completed three copies of *The Righteous Seraph.* They're still in the studio. But I've only just started on *Peasant with Hay Fork.*"

"Maybe it won't matter."

"Even if Tato doesn't blame me, he won't give me my passport back."

"You gave him your passport?" Slater demanded.

"He insisted. And it's effective. My loyalty must remain with him."

Idiot. Slater sighed, and reached toward him, and ruffled his hair. "What if I can get you a passport? You can walk away from Tato and not look back."

"How much will you pay me?"

"Twenty-five hundred."

"Three thousand," Stefan said.

Slater furrowed his brow, affecting a thoughtful look. They'd quickly established the price tag on his personal honor. "OK—deal."

"For this much money, of course I will help you. How will you get the passport?"

"Let me worry about it. Do you use the back entrance to the studio?"

"The tunnel? How do you know about that?"

"Answer the question."

"A few times, yes, to go to the shop."

"Why does Tato need the tunnel?"

"He said it's not important. A historical artifact. But it's useful. If a painting is traced to his shop, he can just say that someone must have shipped it from there. It could be anyone."

That's why he had no security cameras, Slater realized. There'd be no footage to subpoena when they were looking for art thieves.

"The apartment is a safe place to work," Stefan

went on. "Away from the business, but still connected. The artwork and supplies can come and go without anyone in the neighborhood seeing suspicious activity."

Slater shifted position and put his arm under his neck, lost in thought. When Stefan spoke, it snapped his attention back.

"Do you love me?"

Slater met his gaze. "I don't," he said carefully. "This is just about having fun."

Stefan looked away. "I understand. I was hoping to have a romance while I was here."

Slater ran a hand into Stefan's lush hair. He couldn't stand the expression on his face, the longing. It made his stomach hurt.

"I'm not good for romance," Slater said. "I'm kind of broken."

"You've been nice to me."

To help earn the bounty on those paintings, he thought. To help muddy the water so that Tato didn't know when or how the originals had disappeared. But he didn't say that.

"I'm a wrong guy," Slater said. "But I can show you where the right guys are."

Stefan got up and went to the bathroom. When he came back, Slater was pulling on his jeans.

"We're going now?" Stefan said.

"Why not? Put on your shirt." Once he'd obliged, Slater said, "Stand against the wall."

His apartment was dingy, and painted a nauseating shade of beige, but the surface of the wall was even. Stefan dutifully positioned himself as Slater stood close and focused on him with the camera on his phone, framing him from the shoulders up.

"Look at the lens," he said, "but don't smile."

"Why do you need a photo of me?"

Slater hit the shutter button, then checked to make sure the image was clear. "To get you a passport. How old are you?"

"Twenty-seven. I thought you were going to get my passport from Tato."

"He might figure out what we're doing. It's easier to get a new one."

"How can you get a new passport? Do you mean a forged document? That's illegal."

"Just like art forgery," he said flatly.

Pocketing his phone, he pulled on a black T-shirt, then waited while Stefan finished dressing. As they walked out, he eyed the shopping bag with the bourbon bottles inside, still on the counter.

They got into the Thunderbird, and Slater waited for the door to roll up, then backed into the alley. Daylight was gone, so he flicked on his headlights, and once they'd cruised into Downtown, he pulled into the parking lot across from his building.

"There's a bar here?" Stefan asked, climbing out.

"This is my office. Come on."

Slater led him across the street and upstairs, unlocking the front door and flicking on the lights.

"What does this represent?" Stefan said, pointing to the statue of Rey Pascual.

"His name is Rey. He's good luck."

"Why is he wearing a crown?"

"Because he's the king of the graveyard. Wait here."

Slater stepped into his office and closed the door, then squatted in front of the safe. Once he got it open, he pulled out the cash box and counted out three grand, separating it into two bundles and pocketing half. On the tattered envelope inside the box, he wrote the date and how much he'd taken, then closed it up and locked it in the safe again, giving the dial a final spin to clear the tumblers.

When he stepped into the front office again, Stefan was holding Rey Pascual, studying him closely.

"This object is not art," he said. "It has been mass-produced."

"Fascinating." Slater handed him a sheaf of C-notes. "That's fifteen. You'll get the rest when I get the painting."

Stefan set Rey on the desktop and thumbed through the bills, his focus intent.

When he looked up, Slater held his gaze. "You're working for me now."

"Yes, sir." He grinned and unbuckled his belt, then pulled out his money pouch, zipping it open to tuck the cash inside.

Slater watched as he put it away again. The guy thought he was in the Third World.

"Nothing changes with Tato," Slater said. "You keep working on the paintings until I get your passport."

"I understand." Stefan tightened his belt and looked at him. "What now?"

Slater gestured to the front door. "Guys."

They went down to the car, and Slater drove to the Historic Core, and parked in a surface lot, where he paid the attendant the evening rate. The pub was up the block, on the second floor, with big open windows overlooking the street. Slater led the way inside, where it was loud but not too crowded yet. They sat at the bar, and Stefan twisted around on his stool to take stock of the other patrons.

When the bartender stepped over, Slater ordered beer from the tap. Stefan barely glanced at her and said, "The same." As she set down their glasses, Slater paid her and then twisted around, leaning back on the bar.

"People are friendly here," he said. "It's not a fashion show or a beauty contest."

Stefan tilted his head toward him, raising his voice to be heard over the music. "There's also a broad range of ethnicities. I'm not used to this."

"Diversity is what makes us strong."

"Do you think it's easy to talk with these men?"

"Sure it is."

"What should I talk about?"

"Just be yourself."

"I feel like a stranger here," Stefan said, and sipped his beer. "Do you think any of them are interested in art?"

"Maybe. If not, ask about baseball. Just say, 'Who won the game?'"

"Does this work?"

"This is a baseball town," Slater said, "and it's ball season. People love to talk about it."

"I can feel that this is a friendly place. Men are looking at me, even though I'm with you."

"See? Without me around, you'll bag yourself a summer boyfriend in a hot minute. You can even get here on the metro."

Stefan turned away, leaning toward the guy on the stool on the other side of him. Slater couldn't hear their conversation over the music. He surveyed the crowd and drank his beer. This place was relaxed—he had to remember to come here. It was lazy to use the hookup app all the time. Being in the same room was more visceral. He could smell a guy before he even hit on him, watch his body language, hear his voice. It allowed for a more authentic read than any photo.

Eventually Stefan turned back to him, his eyes bright. "You finished your beer. We can go, if you want."

"Who's your new friend?"

"Just someone to talk with."

"Did you get his number?"

"I didn't think to ask."

"You have to get on it, man," Slater said. "You snooze, you lose."

Stefan's eyes narrowed. "This sounds like an American form of wisdom."

"Well, that's where you are right now. Think of it as local knowledge."

Slater got up, and they walked down to the street, and headed toward his car. The parking lot had mostly cleared out, and the attendant was gone. Not far from the Thunderbird, a blond guy was climbing out of a dark Acura. In his mid-thirties, he was wearing a tight dress shirt that showed off his pecs. His car chirped, and he started to walk toward the street.

Stefan eyed him as they passed and said, "Hello."

"Beat it," the guy said.

Stefan stopped and turned back. "Pardon me?"

"Keep walking," he said, raising his voice.

"Why are you being angry? I only greeted you."

A few yards away, near his car, Slater stopped to watch.

The blond took a step toward Stefan. "What language do you speak?"

"Right now I'm speaking English."

"But you don't. Not really."

"I can't understand the aggression," Stefan said. "I'm no threat to you. Is it because this is such a big city? Everyone is a threat?"

"What I can't understand is why you people are overrunning my city. You need to go back where you came from."

"I plan to do that," Stefan said. "Eventually."

The blond eyed Slater. "And take your monkey with you."

He turned to walk toward the street. Slater strode after him and quickly caught up. The guy heard his footsteps and turned to look. By then Slater was on him, and grabbed his shoulder, and spun him around.

"Not your city," Slater said, and punched him in the face.

The guy's head snapped, and he lunged for

Slater, and managed to land a glancing blow to his ear. But Slater saw it coming, and countered with a gut punch.

"Why do you make me do this to you?" Slater shouted, his fist striking his jaw.

"Stop it," Stefan cried. "Stop!"

The guy stumbled a few paces a way, and bent over the asphalt, breathing hard. It took enormous effort not to go after him. Glaring at him instead, Slater took a breath and shook the rage out of his hands. When the guy looked at him again, there was fear in his eyes, and a satisfying dark streak of blood under his nose. Still partly hunched over, he jogged toward the street.

Slater walked back to the Thunderbird.

"Why are you so violent?" Stefan demanded.

"It was self-defense," he said, and shrugged. "It's unusual to meet someone like that. When they don't like immigrants, they usually move somewhere smaller and whiter."

"You looked like a wild animal."

Slater frowned. "I know what I'm doing. I didn't break any bones because I didn't intend to. I hardly used any force—just enough to sting a little."

"This country is crazy," Stefan shouted. "Guns everywhere, and you—you beat a stranger."

Slater put his hands on his hips. "Right—like nothing bad ever happened in Serbia."

Stefan recoiled. "I'm too young to remember the war."

"So the genocide thing is fading from memory. That's convenient. What about the one before that? Is it forgotten already? Just because you don't remember it doesn't mean it didn't happen."

Slater stepped over to the driver's door, but Stefan didn't move.

"Are you coming?" Slater said.

"I'm going to take the metro."

"Suit yourself." He gestured toward the street. "It's down that way."

"I know where it is," he shouted, and threw his arms in the air, and stalked away.

EIGHTEEN

Slater drove back to his office and parked in the empty lot. Upstairs he sat at his desk and woke his computer, then pulled up the photo of Stefan, and cropped it square, and upped the contrast. There was a bit of shadow behind his head, but it should work.

In his contacts he found the email address for the Scribe, and attached the photo, and typed a message:

> Check out my adorable nephew. He's traveling to Serbia, and possibly other Balkan states, on the 27th.

The Scribe was sharp—he'd either respond right away, or if he was asleep, first thing in the morning. But it wasn't that late. Slater sat back in his chair and waited. The reply came a moment later:

> He's a handsome kid. I haven't had hair like that since I was 5. Does he fly out of LAX?

The airport question was about what stamps the document needed, and the five meant he wanted five grand to make the passport. It was steep, and with what he was paying Stefan, he'd have to clear eight grand just to cover his expenses. But it was worth it—the Scribe was talented. Slater wrote back:

From LA. I should drop by sometime.

His reply came soon after:

It would be good to see you. I have a break after 3.

Three meant Wednesday. The day after tomorrow. That was fast. He also hadn't asked for the money up front, which was a little surprising, but then they'd worked together before. The Scribe knew where to track him down if he didn't show.

Slater typed a terse reply:

See you then.

He'd killed the browser and was about to lock his computer when there was a knock at the door. It was almost eleven, he saw, glancing at the screen. Nobody even knew he was here. The knock came again, louder this time. Slater got up and went to the front door, opening it a few inches, keeping his boot firmly against the inner side of it in case someone tried to push their way in.

Standing in the hall was a guy wearing trendy pants and a collared shirt, still in his twenties, by the look of him, his dark hair in an expensive pomp. Slater pulled the door wider, and noticed the guy's eyes briefly drop to his chest, and his crotch.

"What do you need, chief?" Slater said.

"You're Ibáñez?"

"Might be. Who's asking?"

"Can I talk to you for a minute?"

"We're talking now."

"Can I talk to you not standing in the hallway?"

Slater looked him over. His expression was intent, but not aggressive, and he didn't look like a knucklehead.

"Are you strapped?"

"What?"

"Armed. Are you armed?"

His eyes grew wide. "You mean with a gun? No."

Pulling the door open, Slater waited for him to step inside, then flipped the deadbolt.

"This is quite the place."

Slater knew what he meant. The office was tiny, and utilitarian, and a little grubby. Judging by his haircut and his shoes, this guy was from a different world—one where there was a lot more money.

He eyed Rey Pascual. "Is that the narco saint?"

"No," Slater said flatly.

He stepped into his office and dropped into his chair.

"Have a seat," he said, when the guy followed him in. "Can I get you an espresso, or a soda water with a lemon wedge? Maybe some gluten-free biscotti?"

His eyes narrowed as he sat down. "No thanks."

"How can I be of service this evening?"

The guy sat up straighter and squared his shoulders. He'd been rehearsing this; Slater could tell.

"What are your intentions with Andy?"

Slater threw his head back to guffaw.

"What's funny?"

"Well, first off, that you think that's anyone's business but mine. What's your name, sweetheart?"

"Kyle. And don't condescend to me. I came here to have a conversation."

"You're trying to scare me away from Andy, is that it? I could flatten you with my eyes closed."

He frowned. "I don't want to argue with you."

"Well, what else have you got? Unless you're packing a heater, that's all there is—words."

Kyle huffed in frustration. "Andy has a right to be happy."

"Are you sleeping with him, Kyle?"

"I'm not going to talk about that. I know you hang around his loft, and take up a lot of his time. But there's no emotional investment."

"But you want to invest," Slater said, "and for me to step aside. Is that it?"

"I want Andy to do what he wants."

"You think he wants me."

"I think he wants things that you're not capable of."

"Like what?" Slater demanded, raising his voice.

"Commitment."

"Did Andy tell you all this?"

"I kind of put it together myself."

"How did you find me?"

Kyle shrugged. "I saw you with Andy at the

central market one night. I asked him your name later. Your business is listed as a detective agency."

Slater studied his face. He wished the guy was lying, or had an attitude, or was a little older. That way he'd feel justified punching him in the face and frog-marching him out the door. But this earnest nonjudgmental stuff was like talking to a nine-year-old. It was hard to take it personally.

He sat forward, folding his arms on his desk. "Here's the deal, Kyle. What I'm doing doesn't concern you. Andy can do what he wants—just like you said. If you're into him, you should ask him to move in, or pop the question, or whatever it is that you people do."

Kyle raised his eyebrows. "You people?"

"Civilians. Normies. I don't even know what you call yourselves." He waved a hand. "If you're going to be exclusive with him, get him to tell me that."

"So you're not in love with Andy."

"I love fucking him," Slater said, "but I don't think that's what you're talking about."

Kyle sighed, and slumped back, and looked away.

Slater watched him for a moment. "You've got it bad for him."

"Yeah."

"You should be talking to him about this, not me."

Kyle got up. "You're not what I expected."

"What, did Andy tell you I was a booze hag? I know he thinks I'm an addict."

"I thought you might try to slug me, or give me the bum's rush."

"Then you're a brave man, to show up here alone, and unarmed, in the middle of the night."

Kyle scoffed and walked out.

Once he'd heard the elevator doors rumble open, Slater got up and killed the lights, then locked up and went down to his car.

On the drive to his apartment, he thought about Kyle. It wasn't every day he met someone so guileless. He didn't mind twinks, and he would have hit on him, if that wouldn't have made things more complicated with Andy.

Was he really wasting Andy's time, preventing him from having a real relationship? Why wasn't Slater capable of that himself—drinking wine with dinner, shopping for furniture, staying at a bed-and-breakfast in Ojai, whatever it was that people did in relationships? Maybe he was root-bound, like that camellia on Raymond Hill, or Celeste's potted *Aglaonema*. Caught in the muck, the cesspool of grifters and chiselers and lowlifes, not able to grow any farther.

Up in his apartment he pulled one of the new bottles of bourbon out of the bag on the counter, and cracked it open. He poured out his ration and slammed it, grimacing at the heady intensity. Tonight he'd formulated a plan to make some money, and committed himself to spending eight grand, and even managed to have a civil conversation with an entitled twink. That deserved a reward. He poured himself another few fingers, then killed the lights and went to stretch out in the recliner.

There was house music on the radio, and he slurped from his tumbler and let it wash over him. He was more tired than he'd thought, and as the warmth in his belly suffused his mind, and intertwined with the music, he quickly drifted toward unconsciousness.

NINETEEN

His phone was ringing when he woke. Alone, Slater was in his own bed, but he didn't remember getting here. Scrabbling for the phone, he picked up the call and mumbled "Ibáñez."

"You were right," Della said, sounding chirpy and fully awake. "An insurance company in Zurich owns *Peasant with Hay Fork*. The reward is denominated in francs, but it works out to about ten grand."

Slater cleared his throat. "So it's not worth my while. That's, like, half of one percent of what they paid out on the claim."

"It does seem a little low. But speaking as an industry professional, not your employer, and not your ad hoc arm candy—if you know anything about this, you have to come forward. Even if the reward is zero."

"For two hundred grand I'll come forward,

although I'd still be resentful, because a fair bounty would be three hundred grand."

"They're never going to give you that much."

"So they're never going to see that painting again. But thanks for checking, Della—I owe you one. Call me when you've got some work for me."

Slater ended the call and lay there, relishing the sunlight and the heat it brought. He knew she'd try again. Della wasn't the type to just drop it.

It was early, so he slept some more. When he finally got up, he looked at himself in the mirror, and considered shaving. Too much work, he decided. In the pantry he found a granola bar, and munched on it, then texted Andy:

Can I drop by?

In his bedroom he dug through his clothes and found a short-sleeved plaid shirt. It was something Doris had bought for him, and it carried the heavy weight of a lifetime of her expectations of what he should look like and who he should be, but it definitely suited a hot day.

On the way down the stairs to his garage, Andy's reply came:

I'm home.

Stepping past the nose of the Thunderbird, he opened his armored storage cabinet and found a solid pair of handcuffs, made of thick steel so they wouldn't chafe. The little key was attached with a length of wire, and he pulled it off and twisted the key onto his keyring, then folded the cuffs and tucked them into the back of his belt.

After he parked in the lot next to Andy's building, and paid the exorbitant weekday rate, he went upstairs and knocked on his door. When he pulled it open, Andy was wearing his usual boxers and tank top.

"I've never seen that shirt before," he said, walking back inside.

"Doris bought it."

"So what do you need?"

"Can't I just come over to see you?" Slater said, following him into the loft.

"Usually you want me to do some deep research, or you want to ride my dick."

"I wanted to sit with you for a minute."

Andy smiled. He knew what that meant. "That's good too."

Slater sat on one of the easy chairs under the windows, and Andy climbed on his lap, and wrapped his arms around his neck. Slater steadied him, his hands on his lower back, absorbing his random muscle movements. Leaning closer, Slater smelled his chest, and his armpit, breathing in the heady clean scent of his sweat, enjoying the vivid warmth of his body.

"So I was thinking about the things you said."

"It's true that each of my words … should be considered a precious pearl," Andy said, "but you'll have to be more specific."

Slater gently swatted his butt. "Love without pain. You were saying I didn't let myself be vulnerable. I want to try that."

"Really." Andy pulled back to study his face.

"You could handcuff me, and tie my ankles to your bed, and then do whatever you want."

"OK, I'm not doing that."

Slater shifted and reached into the back of his belt, producing the cuffs. "I brought these. I'll help you figure out how they work. Then you can come at me."

Andy took the cuffs from him, and looked them over. "They're so heavy."

"You're used to seeing those cop ones. They're easy to carry on a utility belt, but they're not very comfortable. These are."

"I wasn't talking about … that kind of vulnerability. But I'm glad you're … thinking about it." He leaned in to kiss him, and Slater got lost in his warm taut mouth. Andy pulled back, and nuzzled his ear.

"I've been burned," Slater said softly.

"I know that."

Andy met his mouth again, and after a while shifted away.

"So you just had a pair of handcuffs lying around."

"Tools of the trade," Slater said.

"It would take me a year to put these on you, or to take them off. The key must be the size of a toenail clipping."

"I can help."

Andy scoffed, and handed them back. "I do know something that would make you feel vulnerable."

Slater raised his eyebrows. "Spill it."

"You could meet my mother."

"The woman who wants to control your life."

"The one and … only."

"Affluent coastal Orange County. I don't know if I'd feel vulnerable, or more like I'd dislocated my shoulder."

"Think about it, at least. You're one of the few … people I know who could handle her. Besides, I met your mama."

"That was a miscalculation on my part. I may have been in a fugue state."

His phone buzzed in his pants, and Andy reacted with a whole-body spasm, like he'd been shocked.

"Sorry about that." Steadying him with one palm, Slater shifted to pull out his phone, and saw that it was Della. "I have to take this," he said, and picked up.

"I made some calls," Della said. "The insurer will go up to a hundred thousand. That's a lot closer to what you asked for."

"They're still lowballing me, but it's enough to make it worth my while. I'll bring the item to your office. Can you get the money up front?"

"They're Swiss, not Nigerian," Della said. "They're not going to screw with you."

Slater scoffed. "Tell that to my ancestors whose teeth wound up in the Swiss gold supply."

"Ouch," she said, and sighed. "Are you sure you can get the painting?"

"Positive."

"You'll need to make a statement for law enforcement."

"You and I both know the insurers couldn't care less about punishing the perpetrators," Slater said. "They just want the asset."

"Still, I'm sure there's an open police investigation. Europol or Interpol or somebody like that."

"I'll write down what I know. Let me know when you get the money."

He ended the call, and focused on Andy again, caressing his back.

"Sounds like somebody's making bank," Andy said.

"Listen, I'm getting turned on—do you want to fuck me, or should I just leave?"

"I'll fuck you, punk, if that's … what you want, and you'll … stay fucked."

Slater chuckled. "I think it's more like laundry. It doesn't matter how much you do it, you still have to do it again."

"So let's go. Pants off."

"I have to make a business call first."

"Then I'm going to drain the snake." Andy climbed off his lap and walked toward the bathroom. "And no handcuffs."

Slater dialed Stefan, but he didn't pick up. Maybe he was inside his Faraday-cage studio, where the phone would be offline. Or maybe he was avoiding him because of his self-righteous shock at Slater's American barbarism.

"Meet me at that coffee place," Slater told the machine. "You seemed upset last night, but you need to get over yourself. You're on my payroll now. If I don't see you there, I'm coming for you."

Andy came back, walking across the floor in his characteristic uneven gait. "What did I say about … the pants?"

Slater grinned at that and stood up, and unbuckled his belt, then slowly unbuttoned his fly, holding Andy's gaze. He could see the wood swelling in his boxer shorts.

Andy talked a big game, but sex with him took a lot of cooperation. He dropped onto the bed, and Slater carefully straddled him, leaning in to meet his mouth.

When he broke away, Andy said, "Do you want to blow me?"

Slater shifted downward, and pulled off Andy's boxers, and took him into his mouth. Andy groaned and arched his back as Slater worked him, his hand snarled in Slater's hair. The tension built until he came, groaning, his whole body vibrating.

Shifting up beside him, Slater mouthed his neck and his jaw, and massaged his chest, and kissed him. Andy grabbed his cock and stroked it. Even though he didn't have fine motor coordination, his muscle tone was like iron. With his mouth on Andy's, Slater soon came, and had to grab his arm to get him to let go.

Once he'd caught his breath, Slater shifted onto his back. Andy slipped his arm under Slater's and held his hand.

"Truth time," Slater said.

"Oh, god—do I need a lawyer?"

"I meant about me. About vulnerability. I might be able to do that someday. But even if it's possible, I don't think I can give you what you need."

"How do you know what I need?"

"I'm just saying, keep your options open. Don't count on me to change, or wise up, or make anything happen. I'm no damn good. You know that."

Glancing at him, he saw that Andy was breathing hard. Maybe it was still from the sex. He was grinding his thumb into Slater's palm.

"You think I'm fragile," Andy said. "I'm not. That's how … my mother thinks."

"Do not compare me to her."

"Then don't tell me what … to do about my love life."

"I just want things to be clear."

"The facts," Andy said.

"Just the facts."

Andy shifted, and nuzzled his armpit, and they lay that way for a while, connected and warm.

Eventually Slater sat up. "I have to go."

Once he was dressed, he went down to his car and nosed into the late-afternoon traffic, navigating to his office. The place was quiet, with no sign of Max. He sat behind his desk and woke his computer, then did a search for *The Righteous Seraph*. At the top of the list were a string of news items—it had been stolen from a church in Spain a couple of years ago.

A real-estate site showed that Tato's name was on the title of the building where his shop was. That meant the neighboring storefronts were his tenants. It had to be a lucrative business—why was he nickel-and-diming Bella? Slater sat back to think about it. It didn't make sense, unless he was doing it just for the power he felt in knowing someone else's secrets. Being a landlord and even art forgery were prosaic by comparison. Maybe he needed the thrill of prowling around in backyards, the rush of chiseling someone in person.

The building with the art studio was a six-unit condo, he found, digging around on the real-estate site, and Tato's name was on the records, but only as the owner of apartment C. Tato had taken title on the same date for both properties, and the previous owner for both was listed as the same entity, some revocable trust. It made sense that both ends of the tunnel were owned by the same person; otherwise it would have no practical use.

Slater knew now how it had to go down—what he had to do to maximize his payout and protect Stefan from getting burned. Pulling his keyboard closer, he typed "Statement" at the top of a new page, then wrote a few sentences about what Tato was doing with *Peasant with Hay Fork*, and how he hired the copy artists in Eastern Europe. Slater didn't add his own speculation as to why he looked for them over there, but the attraction was obvious—they were classically trained, and worked cheap, and had a visa expiry date when Tato could end his relationship with them. Slater added:

No details were obtained regarding the individual artists. No information on the perpetrators of the original thefts was discovered in this investigation.

Leaving the tunnel and the studio out of his account might also help protect the artists. He looked up the street address of the shipping store, and included that as the place where the artwork was discovered, along with Tato's full name. Below that he typed his own name, and then printed the page. Scrabbling in his top drawer, he found a blue ballpoint and signed it, adding the date. Finally he folded it into four, then tucked it into his back pocket. Pulling out his phone, he dialed Max.

When he picked up, Slater said, "Have you got a minute?"

"I've got thirty of them until my target is due to exit yoga class."

"You're on that other window-shade job?"

"I'm still running stakeouts."

"So what does it cost you when you get that guy to reset the IMEI on a cell phone?"

"One fifty," Max said. "If you need a clean phone, there's one in the safe. I just had him wipe it and change its identity. It's got a clean SIM card too."

"That would be helpful."

"It's in a thick red envelope. When you're done with it, just put it in airplane mode and then power it down, and we'll get him to do it again."

Slater ended the call and swiveled around to the safe. The red envelope was so thick, he saw, because it was lined with metal foil. It must be a security measure implemented by Max's phone hacker. Like the Faraday cage around Tato's studio, it would prevent any inadvertent communication.

He slipped the phone out and left the envelope in the safe. No way was he going to turn it on here, and link its location to their office. The point of wiping it and resetting the hardware ID each time was so that it couldn't be traced back to him or to Max. It would be a pain to lug two phones around, but at least this one was compact. Tucking it into his pocket, he headed down to the street, pausing to kill the office lights and lock the door.

Even with the evening traffic, he got to the coffee place in South Pas a little earlier than when he'd told Stefan to show up. He bought a soy latte and positioned himself at a table with a view of the entrance.

Stefan came in right on time. When he caught sight of Slater, he flashed a smile and walked over, dropping into the opposite chair. He was panting, and sweat beaded his brow, and dabs of paint dotted his shirt.

"Did you run?" Slater said.

"I didn't want to be late, after hearing your vague threat."

"In this city, up to twenty minutes isn't late. You just have to say 'traffic.'"

Stefan nodded. "More local knowledge."

He wasn't steamed anymore, Slater decided, watching him talk. He never knew what to expect when people got upset with him. Sometimes they stayed upset forever, and sometimes it evaporated by the next day, like this.

"I'm sorry I became angry last night," Stefan said. "You got angry because the blond man was angry, and then I got angry with you. It's like a contagious disease."

"It's good that you spoke your mind with me. It's better to get that stuff out in the open."

"I was trying to connect with this man. It's like when I meet someone homophobic. Usually if I can talk to people, their biases will soften."

"That sounds time-consuming," Slater said. "The shortcut is just to punch them in the face."

Stefan slumped back, and threw up a hand. "You have no remorse, I see. Why are you like this?"

"I don't have to explain myself to you. I will buy you a coffee, however." Slater stood up. "What do you want?"

"Thank you—a ristretto."

"I don't know what that is."

"The barista will know."

Slater stepped over to the counter, and when the woman approached, he said, "A ristretto."

She frowned. "I don't think we have that."

Slater called to Stefan: "She doesn't know what that is."

Stefan got up and approached the counter, his face reddening. "It means a very short espresso," he said quietly, eyeing the barista. "Half as much water."

"I can't really do that," she said, and shrugged. "The machines are automated."

"Then I will have a regular espresso."

She nodded and tapped at the keypad on the register. Slater paid her, and watched Stefan as he went back to their table, and sat, arms folded, jaw set.

Slater carried the espresso over and set it in front of him, then sat down. "You're still feeling culture shock."

"Culture indeed," Stefan said, avoiding his gaze. "An Italian coffee shop that doesn't know how to make Italian coffee."

"I'm getting your passport tomorrow, but we can get things rolling tonight," Slater began, and leaned on the table. He lowered his voice and outlined the plan. Once he'd finished talking, Stefan drained his cup.

"I understand," he said, and rose. "I will await your arrival."

Surprised at his terse response, Slater watched him walk out. No dubious questions, no suggested revisions, no pushback. He really was a follower—a foot soldier. Once he knew who the boss was, Stefan just took orders.

TWENTY

Slater later rose and left the coffee place, and walked down the block to where he'd parked. The sky was pink at the horizon as the daylight faded. Once he'd climbed into the Thunderbird, he checked his phone for art stores, and found one nearby. It had a parking lot in back, and he pulled in, then walked inside.

The only person in the cluttered interior was the woman behind the counter. She greeted him as he stepped toward her.

"Can you sell me a metal poster tube?" he said.

"We have an aluminum art tube."

"Show me."

She stepped into the back room and returned a moment later, handing him a silvery cylinder with a dangling black strap. It was long enough to fit the canvas once it was rolled up, he decided. Slater took it from her and fondled the strap.

"Is this leather?" he demanded, then glared at her. "What is wrong with you people?"

She frowned. "Excuse me?"

"Can you sell me one without the taxidermy?"

Wordlessly she went into the back and returned with a different model. The strap on this one was made of nylon. Setting it on the counter, she unscrewed the end.

"These are plastic." She handed him the cap. "Only the body is aluminum, but it's crush-resistant."

"This'll work," Slater said, examining the end cap and then feeling the thickness of the metal.

After he'd paid her, he slung the tube over his shoulder and walked out to his car, where he tossed it on the floor in the back. Pulling into the street, he drove a few blocks and turned into a supermarket parking lot, striding inside to the aisle with the picnic plates and the plastic containers for leftovers. He found the heavy aluminum foil that you could use for barbecuing, and grabbed a roll of it.

He hated these places, but it wasn't very busy, so he scooped up a basket and hunted for the booze aisle, where he pulled down a couple of fifths, and then a bag of granola, and some almond butter, and a box of the incidentally vegan Pop-Tarts. It didn't take long to get frustrated with the place. How did people do this every day? And what was he doing here, wandering around like a damn hausfrau? He carried the basket to the checkout.

Once he was outside, he put the shopping bags in the trunk of the Thunderbird, and pulled out the aluminum foil, and found a roll of duct tape in his duffel bag of road tools. Climbing in behind the wheel, he pulled open the aluminum tube, and wrapped several layers of the foil around the end caps, then duct-taped over it. One of the caps he taped to the tube, and for the other he made a flange of several layers of foil to overlap the aluminum body. No way would this leak a signal from a low-power device like the art tracker. Assessing his work, he decided it could pass for a repair job rather than something hinky, like a bale of smuggled drugs, or a homeless person's improvised storage system, or a pipe bomb.

Dropping the tube on the floor, he started the engine and drove to Raymond Hill, and left the Thunderbird down the block from the apartment building. He grabbed a pair of black latex gloves from the box in the backseat and tucked them into his hip pocket. With the aluminum tube in hand, he strode toward apartment C.

Slater rapped sharply on the door, and Stefan pulled it open a moment later, nervously eyeing the empty hallway, and beckoned him inside.

"The artworks are in here," Stefan said, opening the outer door to the studio. "We have to enter one at a time. Close the first door completely before you open the second door. It's like an air lock."

Slater waited for him to get into the studio, then followed the procedure, standing briefly in the narrow space before he opened the inner door.

"This is Tato's production studio," Stefan said.

Slater eyed the easel in the middle of the room. "And that's *Peasant with Hay Fork.*"

"I've started work on the copies." He gestured to the canvas on the other easel. It was more developed than when Slater had last seen it, just yesterday, now with thin flat color filling in parts of the landscape, and the sky, and the man's pants.

"Where's *The Righteous Seraph*?"

Stefan stepped over to a pile of canvas on the floor in the corner and lifted the top sheet. Slater had barely noticed them before, assuming they were either discards or raw material. A few layers down, Stefan carefully extracted the painting of the angel in the brick-red tunic, her finger pointing skyward. There were three more below it that looked identical, none of them on stretchers. Stefan spread each of them on the floor.

"Which one is the original?"

Stefan flipped over the top one, revealing a gray disk attached to the back of the fabric—the tracker. As he gently turned it over again, Slater stepped closer, and squatted to compare it to one of the copies.

"You're an amazing artist," Slater said. "I can't tell the difference."

"Some of this was Elena. I added finishing elements. The other ones are the work of Elena alone."

"Where did Tato find you?"

"There are many art schools in Europe. In the formerly communist countries, fine art is still highly valued. He came to a student show that had some of my work. I guess he thought my technique was appropriate for his business, and he hired me with the promise of sunshine and palm trees." Stefan gazed at the angel. "I wonder if Tato is the one who stole the original painting."

"He's not smart enough," Slater said, straightening up. "He's a bottom-feeder in a larger operation. Or maybe he's a subcontractor. That's why we have to be careful about taking these from him—there are other people involved." Digging in his hip pocket, he pulled out the wad of C-notes. "This is for you."

Stefan took the cash and quickly riffled through it, then reached for his money belt. As he tucked it away, Slater pulled on the black latex gloves.

Stefan frowned. "What are you doing?"

"I don't want to leave fingerprints on any of the art."

"Mine are all over these works."

"You can't do much about that now. I wouldn't worry about it—the insurance company just wants it back. They're not going to be looking for you."

Stefan squatted and arranged the four versions of the painting in a stack, draping a piece of blank canvas between each layer, then rolled them up and tied the bundle with a strip of white fabric.

"The original painting is the second layer, so the signal from the tracker won't be restricted," he said, and set the bundle on the table with the tubes of paint and the brushes. "How long will it take to alert the police?"

"I don't think it'll happen fast," Slater said. "There are too many steps. Once the monitoring company gets the signal, they'll tell the painting's owners, and they'll have to go to the cops in Europe.

They'll have to ask the local cops here, and then the locals will have to get around to looking for it." He gestured to the easel with the original *Peasant with Hay Fork*. "Can we put this in the tube?"

"I don't want you to take it," Stefan said. "Not until I have my passport."

Slater put his hands on his hips. "You don't trust me."

"Of course not. You're a brute."

Slater's eyes narrowed. He could sucker-punch this guy right now, and walk out with whatever he wanted. But it wasn't personal—Stefan was in over his head, working as a cog in a shadowy enterprise that neither of them could see, adrift in murky unfamiliar waters. He didn't know how to navigate the cesspool.

"You're smart to stick up for yourself," Slater said. "I'll get the passport in the morning, and bring it here, and we'll make the exchange."

Stefan nodded, and his expression softened. "After that, it's the end of my American adventure."

"This is a big country," Slater said, and set the aluminum tube on the table. "Go to Seattle, or the Northeast. Spend your money there. Just get away from Tato's orbit. You want to be far from here when they come for *The Righteous Seraph*."

Slater stepped over to the heavy door into the shaft and cranked the wheel until the bolts were free, then heaved it open. Turning back to the table, he picked up the rolled bundle of canvas. It was heavier than it looked.

"Be careful not to compress them," Stefan said.

"You're holding centuries of art history in your hands. It's worth millions of dollars."

"Lock the door behind me. I'll leave through Tato's shop."

"I don't think it's possible. The alarm will sound if you open the door."

"Don't worry about that. Listen, do you want to hook up later? It's a bad idea for me to come back here tonight, but you've been to my place. It's near Westlake Station."

"Is that an order from my employer?"

"You think I'm a molester?" Slater demanded.

"Calm down," Stefan said, and frowned. "You'll damage the art."

Slater stepped through the doorway into the shaft, then turned on his phone's flashlight and dropped it into his shirt pocket. It cast a feeble beam onto the concrete walls. He waited until Stefan had closed the door, and he heard the bolts roll into place, then went to the stairs and started down, zigzagging toward the bottom, holding the canvas on his shoulder the way he would a shovel or a maul.

As he trod the length of the tunnel, he stopped part of the way and set the bundle down. This was the last time he'd be in here. He turned off the light on his phone, and thought about all the earth over his head. Fifty feet of dirt and city. It seemed like a useless feature now, this tunnel, but Truman's explanation made sense, that it would have been used to hide a tony institution's ugly work: laborers hauling luggage and laundry and garbage.

In the years since the hotel was torn down, he could imagine this place as a Cold War fallout shelter, and more recently as a place to hunker down and survive the Mayan apocalypse. Maybe that's why Tato used 2012 as his alarm code.

Standing here in the insulated silence, he could hear his own heartbeat. He took a deep breath and heaved up the roll of canvas, then started walking again, not bothering to turn his light back on. Soon, predictably, his right arm brushed against the tunnel wall, and he adjusted his course.

When he got to the door into Tato's shop, he pushed it out slightly and listened. The lights were off, and there was no sound, so he rolled it open and reached in to unlock the wheels on the shelves, then pushed them outward.

Setting the canvas bundle on Tato's desk, he pulled the big rolling door closed and repositioned the shelves, then returned to the desk and sat down. Aiming the lamp at the drawers, he clicked it on and spent a few minutes digging through them. He'd already been through the file folders, so he dug deeper, into the loose paperwork. There was no sign of Stefan's passport.

Once he'd turned the light off and repositioned it the way he'd found it, he swiveled around and surveyed the storage shelves. There were several plastic tubs that might contain records, and he went over and opened a couple, using the flashlight on his phone to look inside them. One was full of blank white envelopes, and another had rolls of packing tape. There was no sign of any business paperwork. He hadn't really expected to find it—if he were Tato, running all these scams, he'd keep it off-site too.

One of the desks had a side chair without wheels, and Slater carried it over to the wire shelving unit and stepped up to look at the top shelf. There was a stack of flat boxes, and next to it a plastic tub, but behind them was just enough room for the roll of canvas.

Stepping down again, he pulled Max's ghost cell phone from his pocket and turned it on. Once it had booted up, he installed the app Celeste had told him about, Herostrat, then stepped over to Tato's desk and waved the phone along the roll of canvas. Nothing happened. He lifted the bundle and scanned the other side. This time the phone beeped, and he lifted it to look at the screen. It displayed an image of *The Righteous Seraph*, and below that, a red box labeled MISSING. He waited a few seconds, long enough for the app to report to its creators, then shut it down and uninstalled it. As Max had requested, he put the phone in airplane mode and then powered it down.

Carrying the bundle of canvas over to the shelves, he stepped on the chair and lifted it behind the boxes and clutter, then got down and assessed the shelving unit from Tato's desk, and then from the doorway into the shop. The roll was completely hidden from view.

Satisfied, he moved the chair back to where he'd found it, then went into the shop and reset the alarm. Nothing was going to happen right away with *The Righteous Seraph,* but now that the wheels were in motion, he felt compelled to work fast.

Stepping out the fire door, he locked it, then walked out to the street. A gold Continental was parked in front of the shop next to Tato's, and a guy was standing at the open driver's door. He had gray hair and baggy trousers, and wore a sleeveless argyle sweater. On the hood of the car were three shallow boxes—cigars. The smoke shop next door. It was shuttered now. This guy had to be the owner.

Slater nodded to him and turned toward the boulevard. The guy called after him: "Who are you, then, sneaking out the back door?"

Slater turned back, and stepped closer, and met his eye.

"I'm not sneaking," Slater said, affecting earnest nonchalance. "I work for Tato. He had a bunch of packing to do. With the bubble wrap and all that."

He frowned. "I thought he had that long-haired kid working for him now. I've never seen you before."

"You mean Stefan? He's new in town, so he's out exploring this evening. Tato calls me in when things get busy."

Slater glanced at the cigar boxes on the hood of the car. He had no interest in them, but he knew that brand, recognized the bright yellow and red logo. He'd hooked up with a guy who had been very proud of owning a box of those. They were from Cuba, and they were totally illegal.

"You sell those in your smoke shop?" Slater said, gesturing to the boxes.

"I guess you're OK, if you have the key to Tato's office," the guy said. "But I saw you in the shop with the lights off. I was ready to call the police, but then I realized you were setting the alarm. Why didn't you turn the lights on?"

"It's not that dark in there, and the panel has its own light," Slater said, and gestured broadly. "Mystery solved."

"So why are you wearing gloves?"

Slater looked at his hands. He'd forgotten about those. "All that cardboard dries out my skin." He peeled them off and tucked them into his hip pocket.

"You still haven't told me your name."

"If it matters, it's John Slade," Slater said.

"You don't look like a John. More like a Juan."

"Just like you don't look like a racist, but there it is anyway, spewing out of your mouth."

He frowned. "I'm not racist. We have a homeless problem around here. I can't believe Tato would hire a bum to work alone in there at night."

"I'm not homeless," Slater snapped.

"I guess you can't judge a book by its cover."

"Even though you just did. Twice."

The guy jutted his chin. "You know, you don't have a very good attitude for a manual laborer. Are you sure you're not homeless?"

Slater couldn't resist. He stepped closer and slapped the guy, right and then left, a firm kovac.

He flattened himself against his car, his face contorting into a sneer. "I'm calling the cops," he spat, "and then I'm calling Tato."

"Be my guest," Slater said, stepping back, hands on his hips. "While you're doing that, I'll call your Uncle Sam. He'll be interested to hear you're selling contraband Cuban cigars." He gestured to the shuttered storefront. "It'll be easy for Customs to drop in on your little business. They won't even need a ram—they can just smash the glass."

"Who are you?" the guy demanded.

"We've been through all that, smuggler." Slater jabbed a finger at him. "You stay out of my business, and I'll stay out of yours."

Turning his back, Slater walked toward the boulevard. As he rounded the corner, he saw the Continental backing out of its parking spot. Before he turned onto the street that led up Raymond Hill, he looked back toward the corner. The Continental must have gone the other way—no one was around, and no one was watching him.

Walking up the hill toward his car, he thought it through. He shouldn't have slapped the guy, should have played nice, should have let him just sling his insults. It could blow up in his face if Tato figured out he'd been in his shop and then discovered the rolled-up *Righteous Seraph* before anyone came looking for it. Tato would never call the police, what with the racket he was running, but he'd ship the art away and clean out the studio to protect himself—and he'd go after Stefan.

TWENTY-ONE

The drive to his apartment went fast in the late traffic. Slater settled into his recliner and checked the time on his phone. Stefan wasn't going to call him, he knew, and he'd already been with Andy today, but thinking about Stefan got him thinking about sex. He opened the hookup app and looked at nearby options, scrolling through the dick pics and torsos and head shots. In some way it all seemed inane. Maybe doing this was the definition of what a sex addict was.

Someone messaged him, a short line in Spanish that he couldn't understand. Clicking on the profile, the main photo was of a Latin guy wearing a cowboy hat. He was a little pudgy, still in his thirties, maybe, and based on one of the other photos, depicting him on horseback, he really was a vaquero—the hat wasn't just a fashion accessory.

Sometimes these guys were so new that they

had little or no English, which made it more work than it was worth. But if this one was willing to go online, and look outside the vaquero bar scene, it might work out.

Slater messaged him back in English:

I want to fuck you. No drugs. My place.

His reply came soon after:

¿Dónde?

That made him smile. The guy either assumed he could understand Spanish, or he thought Slater really should be speaking the language. More significant was that he wasn't going to waste time with chitchat. Slater sent him his address, then went into the bedroom to put on a clean shirt.

Not long after, a knock came at the door, and he pulled it open to the guy from the app, sans cowboy hat and blushing. Clad in a sharp black *guayabera*, he smiled in recognition when he saw Slater.

As he stepped inside, the scent of floral cologne struck Slater's nose. The guy said something in Spanish.

"I only speak the other language," Slater said.

"Forgive me—I made an assumption."

From the way he spoke, he'd been here a while. As he surveyed the apartment, Slater looked him over. He was built thick, and had a nice little paunch over his belt.

Turning back to Slater, he smiled again when he met his eye. The fact that he wasn't alarmed at how grungy it was meant that he'd seen places like this, or lived in one himself.

"What's your name?" Slater said, stepping closer.

Pronouncing it the English way, he said, "Daniel."

Slater leaned in and kissed him, and got lost in it. Daniel ran his hands along his belt, pulling him closer. At that moment there was a sharp rap at the door, and Slater pulled away.

"Are you double-booked?" Daniel said.

"Give me a second."

Slater looked through the peephole to find Stefan, standing there with an expectant grin on his face.

"Damn it," he muttered, and pulled the door open a few inches.

"I found you," Stefan said, and beamed at him.

"I thought you'd call if you were coming over."

"Are you going to ask me in?"

"This is awkward," Slater said, and opened the door wider.

"So you found someone else that quickly," Stefan said, eyeing Daniel, his face clouding. He snapped his fingers. "Just like that."

"You turned me down, remember?"

"He's welcome to join us," Daniel offered.

Slater looked to Stefan. "Fine with me."

Stefan's eyes narrowed. "That's extremely decadent."

"Not to me."

He hesitated for a moment, then stepped inside. "Speak of this to no one."

Stefan stood in the kitchen and eyed Daniel, who took a tentative step toward him. Eyeing them as he closed the door, Slater sighed. It's not like they didn't know what to do. He stepped over and stood between them, putting a hand on the back of each of their necks. He kissed Stefan, then turned and kissed Daniel. That was all they needed—Daniel stepped closer and kissed Stefan, running his hands into his hair.

Slater led them to his futon and pulled his shirt off. Daniel sat on the bed and reached for Slater's belt, intently unbuckling it and pulling open his jeans. Stefan got undressed, and climbed up behind Daniel, reaching around to unzip his shirt and pull it off. Soon the three of them were naked and sprawled on the bed. Caressing the two of them, kissing them in turns, Slater got rock hard.

When Daniel was between him and Stefan, he asked, "Can I fuck you?"

"Yeah," he said, and then turned to Stefan, and grabbed his cock.

Slater rolled on a condom and worked his way into Daniel, one arm around his shoulder, watching him as he kissed Stefan and stroked him. It was a turn-on, but it made him a little jealous that the two of them were so into each other. Maybe that's why he never did this.

Stefan was thrusting the way Slater was, into Daniel's hand. Slater pounded harder, making Daniel yelp. He buried his nose in his dark pomaded hair and then came.

Rolling onto his back, he threw the condom

on the carpet, then watched the two of them bring each other to climax. Stefan came first, and then Daniel, and afterward they lay there, panting, limbs entwined.

Stefan got up and went to the bathroom, and Daniel turned to Slater and stretched an arm across his belly. He heard Stefan return, and then the two of them talking softly as he drifted into sleep.

When he woke again, Daniel and Stefan were both getting dressed.

"I had fun," Daniel said.

Stefan stooped to tie his shoes. "I'm leaving too. Do we need a key to get out?"

"Just flip the deadbolt," Slater said.

They left together, and when he heard the door close, Slater got up and locked it behind them. Maybe Stefan was going to get his vacation romance after all.

Slater poured his ration of bourbon, then went to the window to look down at the empty street as he sipped it. He smiled at the memory of Stefan, shocked at the decadence, but not enough to stop him from wanting in on it.

Slamming the last of the bourbon, he went back to the bedroom and grabbed his phone. When he thought about that word, *decadent*, he didn't know exactly what it meant, even though he kind of knew how people used it. He'd assumed it was something about the corruption of wealth. When he looked it up, it had nothing to do with money—the definition was "marked by decay."

That goddamn little ingrate. Trust a European

to hurl a slur like that. It meant that for Stefan, there was a better, more perfect state of affairs than Slater's sleazy sex life. For Slater it wasn't decay, as he'd never aimed for anything loftier. What did that higher level mean for Stefan, he wondered. It was probably something to do with fine art, like the stuff he was counterfeiting, and classical music, and street cafés. Certainly not the mass graves dotting the Bosnian countryside, or the death camps fifty years earlier.

Fuck all that. The warm feeling of his ration was suffusing his belly, but he poured another half tumbler anyway, and stretched out in his recliner to sip it. Why was Stefan able to get his back up with a single word? He should be thinking about him like he'd thought about Kyle—in no way a threat. More like a nine-year-old shouting at the wind.

———·———

In bed, when he woke, Slater could smell flowers. The vaquero, he remembered. It was remnants of his gnarly cologne. Pushing himself out of bed, he went to the kitchen and put a mug of water in the microwave, and unloaded the grocery bags on the counter, and made a mug of powdered java.

He tore open the bag of granola, but there was nothing to pour on it. Using tap water was just too gross. After he ate a handful of it dry, he threw the bag in the pantry and sipped at his simulated coffee.

Cash for the Scribe, he remembered. He'd have to raid his reserve stash. He kept nothing of value in his apartment except that bag of cash, and it was unlikely that any strung-out junky thief who was desperate enough to break in here would find it.

In the bathroom, he sat on the floor in front of the sink and opened the cabinet doors, then reached up underneath, feeling around at the back of the bowl for the dusty freezer bag. Pulling it out, he counted out five grand. The stack was getting thin—he'd need to replenish it soon.

Zipping it closed, he stuffed it away again, then rose and washed up. After he pulled on his jeans and a dark shirt, he went down to the garage. The traffic wasn't bad on the 110, and he headed south, exiting onto Slauson. As he cruised along the boulevard, he thought about the Scribe. The nickname implied he was a writer or a record-keeper, but the guy's business was creating forged documents. It sounded distinguished, but it fit, as he delivered flawless product.

Hyde Park was an old neighborhood, still rife with tired commercial buildings, not yet frothing with the flippers and their gentrification projects. As he pulled up in front of the row of shops, he realized he'd never been here in daylight.

The low retail building was old enough to have decorative cartouches inscribed along the top, and the facade was studded with dozens of small bolted plates, a sign that it had been retrofitted for earthquakes. The shop with CARNICERÍA above the entrance looked like it had been closed for a while, and next to it was one marked AUTO SHOP. It had no garage bay, no space for cars in front, and the windows and the door were covered in heavy bars.

Slater parked in front and walked around to the alley, to the back door of the auto shop, and banged on it with the heel of his fist. Looking up, he saw the security camera pointed down at him, and he held up a palm in greeting.

Eventually the Scribe opened the door. The man was pasty, with wiry gray hair and blue eyes, and that mottled skin that Anglos got from a lifetime of exposure to the sun. He was wearing a dark work shirt that was open a few buttons, revealing tufts of gray hair on his sweaty chest.

"Ibáñez," he said, and waved him inside. "It's been a while."

It was warmer inside, and looking around, Slater realized that the space was the width of the auto shop and the *carnicería* combined. One side of the room was an organized hoard, with cardboard boxes and tubs stacked on shelves to the ceiling. A couple of computer screens and electronic equipment lined a workbench, and there was a wide table with cutting mats and art brushes and tools. Dim daylight filtered through the bars on the front windows, but mostly the space was lit by old-school incandescents overhead.

"I have something for you," Slater said, and produced the five grand from his hip pocket. The scribe flashed a smile and took the wad, then stepped over to the table and went through it quickly, counting the bills onto a cutting mat. Satisfied, he scooped them up and tucked them into his faded jeans.

"Normally I don't trust anyone," he said, "and I

always get the cash up front. But there's something about your face that I like."

"That makes two of you," Slater said. "You and my mother."

He chuckled and walked over to his workbench. Scrabbling among the array of paper, he returned a moment later and handed Slater a burgundy-bound booklet with a big gold crest on its cover.

Slater flipped it open. The binding wasn't stiff, but it wasn't old and worn out either. The photo page bore the image he'd taken of Stefan. The Scribe had edited out the shadow behind his head, replacing it with a blue-gray background. It had someone else's name beside it. Thumbing through the other pages, there was an entry stamp from DFW, dated a few days ago, and then a full-page U.S. visa sticker with a black-and-white rendition of Stefan's portrait.

"This is intense," Slater said, studying the colorful intricate engraving.

"I had to charge you a little more because of that. It'll pass any electronic checks on it when he's leaving the country."

"It looks totally legit to me," Slater said.

"The bones are from a real passport, so I don't think anyone could tell, except maybe the people in the shop where they manufacture them. But they're never going to see it."

"This will get him into Serbia?"

"And any country where Serbs are welcome."

Slater tucked it into his hip pocket. "You're the maestro."

He grinned. "Always a pleasure, Ibáñez."

The Scribe walked him to the door and let him out into the alley, and Slater went around to the Thunderbird. As he climbed in behind the wheel, he saw that Della had texted:

Funds have been transferred.

That was great news—he wouldn't have to hold the painting for long. Once he was back on the freeway, he cruised through Downtown in the stop-and-go traffic and headed for Raymond Hill. He parked around the corner from the apartment building, then walked to it and knocked on the door to apartment C. Stefan opened it a few inches, peering out, then pulled it wide for him to step in.

"I'm surprised you're home already," Slater said. "You left with that vaquero. I thought you might still be with him. Although that would be highly decadent."

"Daniel has a car, so he drove me home." He looked away, as if he were embarrassed. "Thank you for inviting me. I had a lovely evening."

"Me too." Slater looked him over. He was wearing chinos and a sharp blue dress shirt. "Are you dressed for work?"

"I have a shift at Tato's shop soon."

"Excellent. That means everything is running normally—until you leave." He handed him the passport.

Stefan quickly opened it and studied the photo page, his eyes growing wide. "Durko Durkovija? What kind of name is that?"

"It sounds Serbian to me. It's a Serbian passport,

and your photo is in it. That's all that matters."

"But it's not me. That's not my birth date. It's so illegal."

"It will convince anyone who looks at it. Even Serbian border guards. When you get home, burn it and get a real one."

"But I will know it's illegal."

"If you had your own passport, what would you do? Exactly the same thing—travel around the United States, then go back to your family."

"I guess that's true."

"So this document doesn't change that. It's a detail. You're not doing anything illegal."

Stefan looked unconvinced, but said, "OK."

"Don't forget that you're Durko when you buy your air tickets. Use your new birthday too."

His eyes grew wide. "I won't be able to use my return ticket."

Slater stifled a sigh. "So Durko will buy a new one." He took his wad of cash from his jeans and pulled out all the C-notes he had—eleven of them—and handed them over. "Will that cover it?"

"You're very generous," he said, and took the cash.

"Only because I plan to get paid for returning *Peasant with Hay Fork*."

"*The Righteous Seraph* is more valuable. Perhaps the reward will be higher."

"That ship has sailed. We'll stick to the plan."

Stefan nodded and unbuckled his pants, then tucked the passport and the cash into his money belt.

When he was finished, Slater said, "I need to take *Peasant with Hay Fork.*"

Stefan led the way into the studio, and he followed, opening the doors one at a time. Slater went over to the easel. The painting was clipped to wooden stretchers, and he flipped it over to make sure the tracking device was attached to the back.

"Can I just roll this up?" Slater said.

"No," Stefan said flatly, and took it from him. He removed the clips and then got a piece of blank canvas, and carefully rolled them together, folding the ends to protect the artwork before he slid the bundle into the aluminum tube. Slater found the printout of the statement he'd written, still in his back pocket, and tucked it into the tube, then screwed the cap on and made sure the foil flange was tight.

"I should go to work," Stefan said.

Slinging the tube over his shoulder, Slater went out to the kitchen, and waited for him to follow.

"After today, when are you supposed to work for Tato again?" Slater said.

"I have tomorrow off. Friday I'm supposed to be painting."

"You should leave town soon."

His expression clouded. "I know this."

"I'll go first. Wait a couple minutes before you head out."

Slater went out the front door and walked to his car, where he put the aluminum tube on the floor of the passenger's side, then drove downtown, and parked under the office tower that housed Cudahy Mutual.

When he got upstairs, Crystal was on the front desk, her peroxide updo carefully coiffed, wearing a pink sweater set even though it was the middle of summer. The diamond pendant on the little gold chain around her neck sparkled as cold as her icy eye. She looked up as he walked in and scowled at the sight of him.

"Tell her I'm here," Slater said.

Crystal held his gaze and raised her eyebrows. "And you are?"

"Fuck you, you bougie desk jockey," he said, and walked through to Della's office.

When he stepped in, Della sat up. "Is that what I think it is?"

Slater closed her office door and dropped into a chair. "That depends. Is there some money for me?"

"It's in an escrow account, but it's here. The bean counters downstairs are in control of it."

"I guess that's good enough." He set the aluminum tube on her desk.

"Can I see it?"

"I really don't want to open it. The painting has a tracker attached. Letting it broadcast its whereabouts will just complicate things."

"I can understand that," Della said, and picked up the tube, feeling its heft. "Cudahy Mutual has an RF-secure room downstairs where we can open it."

"Then you'll give it to your Swiss friends?"

"Once their representative has confirmed that it's authentic, they'll let me know, and I'll have the money transferred to your bank account."

"I'd rather get it in cash. It's a lot less trouble."

"You want a hundred grand in cash," she said, incredulous. "That's never going to happen."

"As long as I get it in some form. Otherwise I'm going to Zurich to knock some heads together."

"Relax—they've already transferred the funds." Della grinned at him. "They thought you were being greedy. The rep said, 'I guess your agent has middle-class aspirations.'"

"It sounds like she hasn't been paying attention. There's no middle anymore. It's haves and have-nots. Seraphim and peasants."

"Well, it looks like you're going to have a little more in a few days."

"I guess that's it, then," he said, eyeing the tube as he got up.

"Do you have time for lunch?"

Checking his phone, he said, "I have to get to my class."

Della frowned. "You're taking a class?"

"I don't really have a choice. It's court-ordered anger management."

"Seriously?"

"It's absurd, right? I made a dumb mistake."

"These things happen," she said, and leaned back. "Do your time, and it'll go away."

Slater watched her for a moment. Della looked all Westside and polished, roses and pearls and tailored clothes, but she knew how the world worked.

"I'll be looking for that money," he said finally, and walked out, ignoring Crystal's murderous glare as he went through the front office.

TWENTY-TWO

A couple of hours later, as he walked out of anger-management class, relieved to be done with it for another week, he saw that someone had called twice, from an unknown number in the 626 area code. It buzzed in his hand as he set off toward his car, again with a call from the same number.

"Ibáñez," he said, picking up.

"It's Stefan," he said. "You finally answered."

"What's going on?"

"I went to the shop, and I was working at the counter. It was crazy. I'm still trembling."

"Slow down," Slater said. From his tone, it sounded like Stefan was wound up. If the guy were standing in front of him, he could slap some sense into him, and give him a good shake, but on the phone all he could do was wait for him to focus. "What happened?"

"I heard Tato answer a telephone call in his office. He was shouting, and then he left. He just said 'Mind the store' to me, and then he was gone."

"He took his vehicle?"

"The big yellow car, yes. Soon after that, the police came. They showed me a paper, and made me stand outside the shop so they could search it."

"A warrant? They had a search warrant?"

"That's what they said. I had to talk to an officer. She asked me so many questions—was anyone else in the office, what was my job, how long had I worked there. She asked me if I'd seen *The Righteous Seraph*."

"What did you tell her?" Slater demanded.

"That I'd never seen it, of course. That I'd never even heard of it."

"Good man." He was at the lot where the Thunderbird was parked, and climbed in behind the wheel, cradling the phone to his ear with his shoulder, then started the engine to get the air blowing.

"She wanted to see my papers, but I told her Tato had taken possession of my passport, and I have no other identity documents. She said it's illegal to work on a tourist visa. I told her Tato said it was fine because my salary was below the legal minimum wage."

"Is that true? He told you that?"

"Of course not. But the officer was interested in this story, and wrote down many notes. Eventually she let me leave."

"She didn't know what to do with you," Slater said. "Did you give her your name?"

"I'm not stupid. I told her the name of my third-grade teacher."

"You need to stay away from the studio. They might find it."

"I went to the apartment when I left the shop. They didn't follow me—I checked. I quickly cleared out my things."

"Did they find *The Righteous Seraph*?"

"I don't know. I'm sure they will—there were so many police. Not all of them were in uniform. Some had denim pants with guns strapped to their legs. They were going through the office very methodically. It was terrifying. You said it wouldn't happen so quickly."

"Clearly I was wrong," Slater said. "Someone took the alert from the tracker more seriously than I thought they would. So where are you now?"

"Union Station."

"Do you want me to come over there? We could talk, and get dinner."

"I can't, Slater. I've had enough of crazy Los Angeles, and police, and art crimes. I'm going to New Mexico tonight. On the train."

"That's a great idea. It's beautiful there, and a lot calmer." He took a breath, then said, "I guess I'm not going to see you again."

"Maybe if you come to Europe one day."

"If Tato contacts you, don't talk to him again, no matter what he says."

"I've already thrown away my SIM card. This is a new number. He won't be able to find me."

"He'll have other things to worry about," Slater

said. "It sounds like he's headed for jail. So—call me if you get bored in the desert."

"Good-bye, Slater," he said, and ended the call.

Looking out the rear window, he backed out of the stall and drove the few blocks to his office. He hadn't anticipated that kind of felony response to the alert from the tracker. He and Stefan were both extremely lucky that the raid hadn't happened earlier in the day, before he'd transported *Peasant with Hay Fork.* When he got upstairs, the lights were on, and he stuck his head into Max's office.

"You look wiped out," Max said, looking him over.

"I had my anger-management class. I feel like I've been assaulted."

Max chuckled at that, and Slater went to his own desk. As he sat down, a text buzzed his phone. It was from Celeste:

This just hit the art news sites.

Her second message was a link, and when Slater clicked on it, an item came up with the headline, "Herostrat Technology Recovers Missing Artwork." Below that was an image of *The Righteous Seraph.*

How had this story broken so quickly? The cops wouldn't have made any announcements yet. But the name in the headline was the clue—the tech company would have been the first to get the alert that the painting had been located, and they were proud of the product. Herostrat was using the incident as PR, getting out ahead of the news to tout its wares.

Reclining in his chair, he wondered if they'd picked up Tato yet. Celeste would be hearing about *Peasant with Hay Fork* soon enough too. He didn't have to cut her in, but he knew he should—she was smart, and she'd helped him a lot. Once his payout landed, five percent for her would be five grand. He could get away with that, but if he gave her ten, he'd have a loyal informant for life. He'd already spent nine grand and change to extract that ingrate Stefan from all this. The guy had barely made it out of there with his wheelie bag, but at least he was able to sweet-talk the cops, and smart enough not to look back.

It was the cost of doing business, he told himself. The rest of that hundred grand was going to make life easy for a while.

There was a loud rap at the door. Slater got up and went into the front office.

"Are you expecting anyone?" Max called to him.

"I'm not."

When Slater pulled open the door, he found Tato, as before wearing a loud Hawaiian shirt and white socks under his huaraches. There was rage in his eyes, and his black mustache was quivering.

"Hey, blackmailer," Slater said cheerfully.

"Don't you call me that, you cheap window-peeper," he shouted.

"Don't insult me, or I'll break your nose."

"You just had to do it," Tato said. "You just had to ruin everything."

"Calm down. What are you talking about?"

Slater studied his face. Coming here was

irrational—if Tato knew about the cops raiding his business, he ought to be in the wind.

"Bella cut me off," Tato said, "and it's your fault."

"That's what you're angry about?"

"Of course I'm angry. Why did you have to poke your nose into my business? I told you we could work something out."

"It's not like it's a huge dent in your income," Slater said, and put his hands on his hips. "You weren't into her for that much."

"But it was regular income, and now it's gone."

"It wasn't a wise long-term investment. Didn't you think it was inevitable that her husband would find out eventually? He's a no-nonsense kind of guy. You're safer now."

"When you came to my office, you called me trash," Tato said. "But it's you." He raised his voice. "You—you're the trash. Stay out of my business."

Slater held up his palms. "I won't bother you anymore."

Tato scoffed and stalked away, around toward the elevator. Slater closed the door.

"What was that all about?" Max was standing outside his office doorway. His suit jacket was open, and he'd unsnapped his holster, ready for action.

"That was Tato," Slater said. "The guy who was chiseling Bella. I guess she stopped paying."

"I can't believe you let him yell at you like that, and didn't give him a tune-up."

"Yeah, well, I can be level-headed sometimes."

Max's eyes narrowed. "No, you can't."

"Maybe anger management is sinking in."

"That also sounds far-fetched."

Slater chuckled. "It's hard to get mad at the guy. I know for a fact he's got a lot worse coming to him."

Also from Dagmar Miura

That First Heady Burn

The first book in the Slater Ibáñez series sees Slater running surveillance on an injured tech worker and tangling with blackmailers, party girls, late-night hookups with a gamut of guys, and a lot of bourbon.

slater.dagmarmiura.com

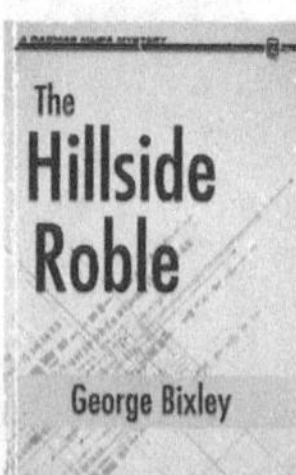

The Hillside Roble

Investigating a million-dollar heist at a gallery in the Arts District, Slater can't get a face-to-face with the owner, Eli, until he applies a little pressure. Eli turns out to be a minor celebrity, physically flawless but obsessed with his own image, and flaky in that uniquely LA way.

slater.dagmarmiura.com

The Mason Braithwaite Paranormal Mystery Series

No one is ever quite sure whether psychic investigator Mason gets results with actual psychic power or his more mundane flatfooting, but the disheveled redhead manages to resolve some intractable mysteries.

mason.dagmarmiura.com

Penstock Canyon

While helping out a friend suffering from late-night visitations, psychic investigator Mason is confronted with aliens on the roof and other liminal beings that have him questioning the very nature of reality.

mason.dagmarmiura.com

Truman and Celeste

Sometimes all a woman needs is a decent man—even if she's not sleeping with him. Join Truman and Celeste as they troll the gritty underbelly of Los Angeles, never hesitating to slam that cocktail, hit on guys, or ask the next relevant question.

truman.dagmarmiura.com

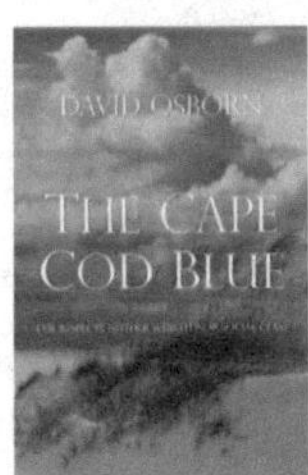

The Cape Cod Blue

The glittering, exalted world of art auctioning hides love, hate, and parricidal murder in a wealthy and socially prominent family when forgery of an anonymous Cape Cod painting is used to steal a world-famous portrait that's worth a fortune.

capecod.dagmarmiura.com

The Bone Bridge

Yarrott Benz, the 2016 Ippy Award winner for memoir, is forced to deal with extraordinary self-sacrifice in this harrowing account of teenage brothers, as different as night and day, trapped together in a dramatic medical dilemma.

bonebridge.dagmarmiura.com

The Psychic Vegan Cookbook

It has never been easier to cook vegan, and you don't even need to be psychic to do it. Whether your motivation is eating healthier or the welfare of other sentient creatures, Henrietta Flores guides you through plant-based versions of familiar dishes.

cookbook.dagmarmiura.com